Praise for the novels of Jennifer Armintrout

"Every character is drawn in vivid detail,
driving the action from point to point
in a way that never lets up."
—*The Eternal Night* on *The Turning*

"[Armintrout's] use of description
varies between chilling, beautiful,
and disturbing...[a] unique take on vampires."
—*The Romance Readers Connection*

"Armintrout continues her Blood Ties series
with style and verve, taking the reader
to a completely convincing but alien world where
anything can—and does—happen."
—*RT Book Reviews* on *Possession*

"The relationships between the characters
are complicated and layered in ways that
many authors don't bother with."
—*Vampire Genre* on *Possession*

"[This book] will stun readers....
Not to be missed."
—*The Romance Readers Connection*
on *Ashes to Ashes*

"Entertaining and often steamy romances
run parallel to the supernatural action
without dominating the pages."
—*Darque Reviews* on *All Soul's Night*

"Armintrout pu
a blood
—*RT Book Revie*

Books by Jennifer Armintrout

Blood Ties

BOOK ONE: THE TURNING
BOOK TWO: POSSESSION
BOOK THREE: ASHES TO ASHES
BOOK FOUR: ALL SOULS' NIGHT

The Lightworld/Darkworld novels

QUEENE OF LIGHT
CHILD OF DARKNESS
VEIL OF SHADOWS

JENNIFER ARMINTROUT

VEIL OF SHADOWS

A LIGHTWORLD/DARKWORLD NOVEL

MIRA

ISBN-13: 978-0-7783-2678-6

VEIL OF SHADOWS

Copyright © 2009 by Jennifer Armintrout.

**This book is dedicated to
all the family members who were angry
that I dedicated the last book to someone
who won the dedication in a Twitter contest.**

MIRA

Prologue

When the first of them appeared, there were skeptics. Some simply did not believe that these "creatures" calling themselves Faeries or Angels or Vampires or whatever were not part of some elaborate hoax. Perhaps a conspiracy, their own country's governments, or a shadowy world government, working to manipulate them. Into doing what, they did not know, but still they doubted what had come to pass.

There were others, though, who did not believe the event to be false. And though they were right, they were ridiculed. Their near-instant belief that their salvation had come—or, as some believe, their damnation, and they were, perhaps, closer to the truth—obscured how very serious and dangerous the situation was.

The initial shock of their appearance, whether it inspired pleasure or suspicion, did not last. For not all the creatures were kind, and some…some had to feed.

So, it was with fear and trepidation that the Humans began to move underground. Into shelters constructed for an imagined future war, into spaces that were undesirable before the creatures came.

And since they fled of their own accord, the visitors assumed the surface of the Earth with gratitude.

Years went by. Ten, twenty, a hundred. And in the vast cities that had formed beneath the surface, a rumbling of what had happened generations before twisted, became something sinister. The creatures had come, *forced* the Humans belowground, ruled them with hatred and cruelty. And though no immortal creature could remember this being so, it could not stop the rage of the Humans. It could not prevent the war.

Despite their numbers, their experience and their sheer power, the immortals lost the fight. Driven underground themselves, they eventually forgot their hatred of the Humans who had cast them out. One by one, they gave up striking back at the Humans, and began striking out at one another.

The wars that raged beneath the surface formed the Lightworld and the Darkworld, as they came to be known. Two separate factions with a common enemy, but different goals. And they hated each other.

The Lightworld longed for the Earth to be restored to the Fae races, as they had ruled parts of it long before Humans learned to interfere with the land. The Darkworld, those who did not believe in their right to rule over the Humans above, who only wished to return to the way they once were, found themselves outcasts, forced to the worst parts of the Underground.

In the cities of the Upworld, the Humans continued on, always aware of what lay beneath their feet, but never really knowing what the murky fear was doing. It was better for them, that way, for what you never know cannot truly hurt you.

One

─━∽⟨◉⟩∽━─

"**Y**ou were lucky beneath Boston," the old ferry captain, Edward, said. "You know what happened to them down in New York? Flooded 'em out. Drowned 'em. Them creatures that didn't drown, them were hunted by the Enforcers and killed."

Cerridwen opened her eyes, reluctant to leave the sleep that had been her refuge from the terrible sickness she'd felt while awake. The vessel they had departed on that morning, a ramshackle boat the man had kept calling a *ferry*—not, Cedric had assured her, in mean-spirited jest toward their kind—still churned and tossed. How the Human could stand, so straight and balanced, as the craft pitched from the crest of one wave to another, Cerridwen did not know. But the motion made her stomach seize, her head go dizzy.

Cedric and the rest of the Fae they traveled with seemed unaffected by the motion, as well. Cedric, particularly, seemed to revel in their time on the sea, standing at the prow, listening to the bearded old man call out stories against the wind and the spray. Though the blinding sun had set, Cedric still stood in the place he'd inhabited when she'd fallen asleep. Face turned toward the horizon, an expression of serene pleasure—or as much of one as Cerridwen had ever seen on the ancient Court Advisor. Calmness gilding his features the way the morning sun had, it seemed as though he had completely forgotten the precarious position of their future, and the violence they had left behind.

Cedric had been alive long before the rending of the Veil had spilled all the creatures of the Astral onto Earth. To him, the sun, the wind, the water were all old friends. They greeted him with familiarity and Cerridwen realized how much he must have longed to escape the cramped and dank Underworld. To her, born after the Fall and in the cavernous Underground, the elements showed only hostility.

Cedric nodded, but did not face the old man. "I did not know there were other cities… I thought that most had died in the battles, and that whoever remained of us were underground in the same area. That it was just too large—"

"If you'd kept going, you'd hit the end." Edward spoke with such authority, it was as though he'd been there.

It was not impossible to believe. Cerridwen had always wondered that the boundary between the Lightworld and the Darkworld was so well defined, and yet no one seemed to know if there were other boundaries, and if there were, where they lay.

"Everyplace where they didn't just get rid of you. New York, that was one of them. Boston, well…you saw what that's become. No one wanted to stay, once your kind were underground. Up and left. Most of the cities went that way. Decided it was easier to give up and leave than try to live with knowing what existed just beneath them." The old captain seemed to be amused by this.

It was not amusing. The Humans had forced them underground, then abandoned the very spaces they'd coveted for themselves. Cerridwen wondered if she'd ever understand these strange beings.

She sat up, her stomach lurching. But before she could speak, Cedric turned, the serenity bleeding from his expression. "You are awake."

She wished he would not look at her with such concern. Concern she did not merit. "As you can see."

"You should rest. The mortal healing has only restored your body. The sickness you have felt—"

"Seasickness, the Human says." She closed her eyes. It only made the sensation worse. "Is this because I am part Human? The element does not affect you."

"It is not because of your Humanity. It is because you have never been outside the Underground." He held out his hand for her, and when she did not move to take it, he stooped and lifted her, blanket and all.

"Put me down!" She had enough strength, despite her sickness, despite the wound in her ankle, to be outraged.

He did not listen, and she had not expected him to. He set her down gently in the place where he'd been standing before, let her lean on him for support. "Look out there, at the horizon. The place where the sky meets the water."

"I know what a horizon is," she snapped, pushing down the finger he used to point the way.

"That won't help," Edward called to them cheerfully. "Not a fixed object."

"It will help," Cedric reassured her. "We see things differently than they do."

She squinted against the sun. Its light did not assault her the way it had when they'd first emerged from the Underground, but she had to blink against it to make out the difference between the dark of the water and the blinding curtain of sky.

"You are resisting the elements, because you are unfamiliar with them. You fight against them," Cedric told her, and again he pointed out to the horizon. "They do not fight against each other. See how when the waves rise, the sky relents? You must learn to do the same."

It did make her feel a bit better. Though the craft still rocked against the waves, she did not struggle against the movement in an attempt to keep herself upright. Instead, she let the motion rock her, and she did not stumble or fall.

"Getting your sea legs," the old Human said. "You'll need 'em—you got a long way to go still."

"I thought we would meet up with Bauchan by nightfall." Cerridwen did not look away from the waves, or lean away from the comforting presence of Cedric standing behind her.

"We will," Cedric began. "But we will meet up with the ship that the rest of the Court is already on, and then we will sail across the sea. The False Queene's Court is on an island, what you might think of as the Land of the Gods, if your mother taught you about it." His tone suggested that he did not believe Ayla had instructed her daughter correctly in this matter, and he continued. "It was less difficult for us to travel when we lived on the Astral Plane. We merely spoke the words, or imagined the scene, and we could be anywhere."

"Not so much anymore, huh?" Edward called down. "Don't you worry, though. The captain of the *Holyrood* will get you where you're going, if not as quick as you're used to."

Cerridwen grew annoyed at the weathered Human's constant interruptions, and limped back to her pallet in the shade. She crouched and flared her wings for balance, resting her weight on the front of her feet. Something about this posture made Cedric look away, but she did not know what could bother him so. Probably, he still hated her for her stupidity. It was his right. She had foolishly betrayed her mother, her entire race, and gotten so many killed in the process. Both her parents, though she had not known it at the time, and countless guards and Guild members. If Cedric wished to hate her for all time, well, she would not argue with him.

But he had saved her, had he not? Not just from

the Elves, but from the Waterhorses in the Dark-world, and again in Sanctuary. When she'd been willing to stay and die beside her mother, he'd dragged her into the Upworld. When she'd been too weak to continue, still he'd carried her, despite his own fatigue. Perhaps he did not hate her. He was angry with her, that much was certain. He had made a promise to protect her, but if he truly hated her, would he keep that promise?

She was too weary to think of this now. There would be a confrontation with Bauchan when they reached the ship called the *Holyrood*, that was certain. At the very least, he'd question her right to kill her mother's treacherous Councilmember, Flidais, who had been working with him. In the end, no matter her reasoning, he would be upset over Flidais's death and would not accept her as Queene, being eager to steal away her inherited Court for his own False Queene.

A thought struck her, one she did not like. "Cedric, if there are others…other Undergrounds, like ours, could there not be other Queenes and Kings? Who believed that they deserve to rule over all the Fae?"

"I had thought of that." Cedric sat down, his legs folded beneath him. His wings, papery thin and colored like those of a moth, shivered on his back, sending motes of blue powder through the beams of sunlight that reached beneath the ferry's upper deck. "It is heartening to think that there are more of us. That might prove useful, especially if we can garner their sympathy in our plight. But there is no guarantee that we will be able to contact them, or that they will look kindly on rejoining Mabb's Court."

Cerridwen eased her weight onto her uninjured foot. "Mabb was the Queene. The true and rightful Queene of the Fae from before our fall to Earth. All other Fae fought behind her in the war against the Humans, did they not?"

"She was. They did." There was sadness in his eyes as he talked about her. Cerridwen, born after Mabb's death, had never seen the Faery Queene who'd preceded her mother. The rumors of Cedric's involvement with Mabb had persisted, though, and Cerridwen wondered if lost love was what made him seem so very troubled now.

"Mabb was not a popular ruler. Not once the Veil was torn asunder. Some blamed her, for allowing Humans to glimpse us as we were trooping, or for not punishing those in her Court who intentionally sought out the company of Humans." He fell silent, looked out toward the water. "Ah, well. It is not the past that will help us now. You will meet Lord Bauchan tonight. Are you ready?"

She snorted. "You make it sound as though I am going to war."

"You are, in a way." Though he shrugged, his expression held a seriousness that Cerridwen did not like. "You are fighting for control of your Kingdom."

Another derisive sound crawled up her throat, and she swallowed it. "Some Kingdom. My inherited subjects ran and left my mother when she needed them most. If they cared so little for her, why should they care about me?"

"By your same thinking, why should they care about Queene Danae enough to bend their knees to her?" He was right, and infuriatingly reasonable. Cerridwen said nothing. "Your mother would not have wanted you to give up. She did not wish to see her Kingdom in the hands of this False Queene. Perhaps…" he continued, then stopped himself.

She had seen him do this very same thing with her mother. Though he might have an idea, he would withhold it until invited, and would not speak out above his station to the Queene. Whether he did it out of habit or he held Cerridwen in the same respect that he'd had toward Ayla, she did not know. But it pleased her, nonetheless, to be treated as though she were worthy of deference. "Perhaps what?"

"Perhaps, when we see Lord Bauchan, I should speak on your behalf."

That destroyed the illusion. He thought she was incapable of speaking for herself without some disastrous outcome. A part of her agreed with him, was thankful, even, that she would not have to pretend at courtly manners and political thinking. She had no head for either of them, and even if she had, her hatred of Ambassador Bauchan, the fiend who had come to the Lightworld with the intent of causing civil war, would have broken her concentration.

"Yes, fine." She nodded, a bit too enthusiastically. "It would help keep up the pretense that you are the Royal Consort."

He nodded. "Yes, that is something that needs to be established early with Bauchan. I would not think that seducing the Royal Heir would be below him, if it would give him what he needed to succeed at his own Court."

"No longer the Heir—the *Queene*," she corrected, though even in her insistence the title was too new to be comfortable for her. "Perhaps we should do with Bauchan as we did with Flidais. After all, is he not guilty of the same offenses she is?"

"He is not," Cedric stated firmly. "Bauchan came to your mother's Court with no deception that we could not see, and in spite of the fact that your inheritance comes from Mabb's succession, he was not considered your subject when he arrived, and this Queene Danae is unlikely to accept your killing him. Flidais hid her plans, and turned traitor to her own Queene, in contrast. Besides, we need Bauchan. He is our only guide to finding Danae's Court and some measure of safety."

Silence fell between them again, the only sound the mechanical chug of the ferry's engine and the soft slap of the waves against the tiny craft. The sound had lulled her to sleep that morning, and, in hearing it again, woke the vestiges of those things she'd seen in her fitful slumber. Without knowing why she did so, she suddenly blurted, "I had a dream, earlier. While I slept from my sickness."

Cedric made a noise of uncommitted interest. "Do you believe it means something?"

Did she? It was such a simple dream, and she had

never truly believed in such nocturnal signs. "I do not know," she answered honestly. "If it does mean anything at all, I would not know how to interpret it. And I have never given much credit to dreams."

"If you tell me what it was about, I might be able to help you." He looked out to the water again. "Or, if you prefer to keep it secret, I will understand."

"There is no secret to keep. It was not disturbing, or terribly important." That was not entirely true. When she thought of the images, a feeling of grave urgency taunted her. "I saw a forest, as though I were standing in it, and I was alone. I came upon a clearing to see a white bull." She closed her eyes, and in her mind saw the shaggy, matted coat of the animal as it stood, almost ghostly white, in the darkness. "In the sky above the treetops, the stars made out the form of three triangles, locked together in such a way as to make one large copy of themselves." She stopped herself. "Can they do that? Stars, I mean? Do they show pictures?"

"They show forms that Humans can navigate by, forms that tell a story. But they cannot twist themselves into something they have not shown before." He seemed troubled, but in a flash that troubled expression was gone. "Ah, well. It was probably just a dream. Nothing worth worrying over."

And though she might have agreed with him before, the vision had crept back into her mind, insisting upon a place there. It would not have done that, if it did not have something to tell them. She did not know how she was so certain of this, but she was, and his studied disinterest irritated her.

"I am going to go watch the sea," Cedric announced, as though it were not a dismissal. "You could come, if you wished. The ferryman is good company."

"Human company," she said, waving a hand. "If that is your idea of good company, then you may indulge all you please."

His smile was tight, pasted on. "Yes, it will do you good to rest before we meet with Bauchan."

Only after he strode from beneath the deck, his tread heavier on the floor than any immortal creature's should be, did she realize how very much she'd sounded like her old self, the immature child who'd hastened her parents' deaths through impatience and petulance.

The ferry arrived at the place where Bauchan's ship was harbored just after nightfall, almost to the exact minute, that the ferryman had promised. At least, that was what he told them, and Cedric had no reason to doubt the Human.

Though Cedric had been sad to see the sun set—having no idea when he would get another opportunity to view its radiance and after all the years spent underground having become greedy for it—he recognized that it was for the best that they make this meeting under cover of darkness.

The ship was not moored at the docks but anchored at the mouth of the harbor—the farther away from Humans, the better, in Cedric's opinion—and the ferryman blew his horn as they approached. Lights appeared at the rail of the ship's deck, high, impossibly high above them, and as the little boat drifted sideways to meet the wall of red-painted steel, the ferryman silenced the engines and called out a friendly "Halloo!" to figures that Cedric could not see from his vantage point.

"What if they will not let us board?" Cerridwen fretted beside him. She stood, a blanket clutched tight around her shoulders as if ready to run, though there was no place to go.

The six guards who had accompanied them from the Palace, and who had been the last witnesses to the carnage wrought in the Underground, stood in their regal finery, toting the bundles that held all the wealth they were able to recover from the sacked Faery Palace. Cedric looked them over with some dismay. Though their clothes were that of courtiers, they held themselves in the stiff manner of soldiers still. Cedric only hoped that Bauchan would be dazzled by the velvet and silk, and not give a thought to the way the men seemed ready to throw themselves over the Royal Heir at the slightest sign of, well, anything, soldiers being more loyal than courtiers.

Cedric looked at Cerridwen now. She was, for all intents, the Queene. But she was hardly fit for the post, and hardly looked it. No matter how she'd carefully bathed and dressed, she could not hide the hollow look that sorrow had imprinted on her, nor the fatigue from her injury. He should say something to her now, to reassure her, but he could not. He did not know what would happen to them, should Bauchan refuse to bring them to Queene Danae's Court. He did not expect such a refusal, but for the past two days its possibility had been much on his mind.

Instead of comforting her, he concentrated harder on making out the conversation between the ferryman and the Humans on the ship. For their part, he could hear very little, but every word that Edward spoke was exactly as Cedric had coached, but cushioned in the gentle, rolling tones the Human preferred, as though no word should be hurried from his lips, and nothing of import should pass that way, either.

"Just another load of special cargo," he called out to the Humans high above their heads. "You'll be wanting to drop the gangplank, so I can unload it."

There was a pause, mumbling that was not clear.

"Oh, he's expecting this delivery, all right," Edward said easily. "Brought special by his importer, you know."

More of a pause, more mumbling. Cedric's antennae buzzed against his forehead, and he smoothed them back against his hair, willed himself to be calm.

Whatever they had asked him, Edward managed to sound very put off by it. "Well, go on and check with him, if you gotta. But I know what I gotta do, and that's get back to the missus before sunup, or she'll have my hide and I don't want to think what else…. Get goin', then, and give me a rope to tie up by."

The Human's words were met with a loud slap against the deck, the rope falling, if Cedric guessed correctly. Then, nothing. Silence, broken by the sound of the water trapped between the two vessels as it knocked from one hull to the next. Edward did not come down from his little wheelhouse, nor did he call out any encouragement to them.

"What is happening?" Cerridwen hissed, as if afraid to interrupt the gentle sounds of the night sea.

Cedric did not raise his voice much above a whisper, either. "He will not call down to us now. Sounds carry across open water, and if any Enforcers patrol the harbor, you would not want them to overhear exactly what cargo is being traded, would you?"

She shivered, sank farther into her blanket.

Something screeched, and Edward appeared below the deck, waved to them to come to the back of the boat. He doused the lights on the craft, all but the small green and red ones that shone over their heads to indicate their presence.

"He wants to 'inspect the cargo,'" Edward said, rubbing a hand across his grizzled jaw. "I thought you said you knew these ones?"

"We do." Cedric looked to the source of the screeching noise, saw through the darkness to where a door had opened at the side of the ship. "I did not say that we were on the best terms."

"Best terms," the old Human spat. "I don't like the sounds of that, and I won't lie and be telling you otherwise. We run a respectable operation, my wife and I, and I hope you're not preying on our good nature."

"Sir, I assure you, if we are not welcome here, we will not trouble you further." Cedric did not know how he would make good on that promise, but he did not wish to think on it now. Right now, the most important matter was to convince Bauchan.

Humans called out orders as quietly as they could from the large boat, and Edward answered them in hushed tones, as well. The result of their combined efforts was the placement of a long walkway between the two vessels, which, under cover of darkness, a few Fae shapes made their way across the expanse.

"Why do they not just fly between?" Cerridwen grumbled. Cedric did not reiterate the danger of their situation; if she did not realize by now how very close to Human discovery they were, she would never realize it.

Bauchan was the head of the three Faeries that joined them on the little boat. He looked them over with a bland expression. The two that followed him flanked the walkway, as if guarding it. Perhaps they were meant to stop them from rushing onto the ship without permission. Cedric smiled at that. Only someone like Bauchan would feel the need to make such a display of strength, someone who had so little to begin with.

"I was expecting Flidais," Bauchan said finally, with a little shrug, as though he was not as put out as he had expected to be and was a bit relieved at that. "Where has she gone?"

"Dead." Cedric answered, and prayed the ferryman would not know enough to correct him. "Along with Queene Ayla."

"I am sorry to learn of her passing." Bauchan bent his head in reverence. "She must have been prepared for the consequences, though. Anyone who chose to stay in the Underground must have realized it was suicide."

From the corner of his eye, Cedric saw Cerridwen stiffen. He reached for her arm, took her hand at the wrist, hoped it would be enough to signal how crucial calm was at this moment. "Queene Ayla understood the danger, but thought it cowardly to abandon her subjects. It was her last wish for your good Queene to take the Royal Heir into her protection."

"The Royal Heir?" Bauchan's eyes, instantly alight with greed, fell on the unlikely shape huddled in the blanket. "We have met before, at your mother's audience," he said smoothly, bowing before her. "It is an honor to be in the presence of so great a beauty again."

Cedric cleared his throat. "She is wounded, and will need healing. There is only so much that mortal medicine can accomplish, and I fear that limit has been reached. Also, she comes with this small entourage of advisors. I trust that this will not be an imposition, either."

"Advisors? What need has the Royal Heir of advisors, if she is entrusted to my kind and attentive care?" Bauchan looked over the guards with a critical eye. He was looking for the trick, for some crack in the lie, but he was not intelligent enough to see it beyond the wealth on the Faeries' backs.

"She will need help managing the meager fortune she brings to sustain her, of course. And one cannot expect the Royal Heir to personally handle the duties of setting up a new—if somewhat diminished—household in Queene Danae's Colony."

"Yes," Bauchan agreed, smiling what must have

been the single most insincere smile in the history of all the Fae. "I do think it will be quite a change for her, but a positive one, for all involved. Queene Danae will not see this as an imposition, but a blessing for her *Court*. And you, were you not one of Queene Ayla's advisors? Do you wish to maintain that position within the Royal Heir's household?"

Cedric remained stone-faced in contrast to the Ambassador's oily graciousness. "Your kindness is appreciated. I travel with the Royal Heir not as an advisor, but as her betrothed. It was decided not long before your arrival at Queene Ayla's Court that Cerridwen and I should be mates, and the Queene thought it would be in the interest of all involved if such an agreement was not thrown over just because of present dangers."

Bauchan's smile faded a little at that, and it pleased Cedric. No doubt that upon setting eyes on the Royal Heir, Bauchan's mind had spun with all the possibilities for advancement that such a prize could bring him. He'd likely already imagined the reward he would get from Danae for delivering the direct Heir to Mabb's throne. From there, it was a simple seduction and a carefully constructed revolt to overthrow Danae and make Cerridwen Queene, and him to rule as King beside her. It did not surprise Cedric that Bauchan would be among the many who would seek to gain from the tragedy of Queene Ayla's death.

Perhaps that ambition would cool a bit in the face of competition, though Cedric doubted it was so.

"I congratulate you both on your good fortune.

Rarely have I ever seen so splendid a match." Bauchan bowed again, and Cedric was certain that the Faery vowed it would be the last time. There was such an air of finality in the gesture that the Ambassador might as well have stamped his feet out of disappointment.

"Then, we are welcome at Queene Danae's Court?" Cedric motioned to their meager group as a whole.

Bauchan waved a hand. "*Of course,* you are welcome to join our trooping party. We have very little space, so accommodations will be quite... cramped. And we will be long at sea. Five days, perhaps more, they tell me. But you are lucky, to come to us so close to our departure. The rest of us have been languishing here in the harbor, ready to fly into the hands of the Enforcers by choice."

Bauchan nodded to the ferryman and pressed something into his hand, but Cedric did not see if it was adequate payment. Guiltily, he did not pursue the issue. They had so little, themselves, that paying the Human seemed a burden. At least he'd gotten something of value for his troubles. Cedric nodded to him as they filed up the walkway.

Bauchan walked ahead of them, and Cerridwen behind him. Cedric noted the way her shoulders hitched as she breathed, the way her feet shuffled, uncertain, on the narrow plank. Two rails fell easily at waist level, and she clung to these as though they alone kept her from plunging into the waters below.

"Easy, now," Cedric murmured close to her ear. "Stay steady, and you will soon be back on surer footing."

She blew out a shaking breath and nodded, increasing her pace incrementally.

"You have already had a run-in with Enforcers, then?" Cedric asked Bauchan, tightening his grip on the railings himself as the plank shook from the weight of the guards behind him.

Ahead, Bauchan had nearly reached the opening in the other ship. It was as if the unstable Human contraption did not worry him in the slightest—he had lighted across it as though it were a fallen log on the forest floor.

"No run-ins yet, thank the Gods," he answered, waiting for them in the muted light from the doorway. "They have been aboard the ship, but we are well concealed, should they raid. A few of the earlier refugees from your Court have not made it, or so we hear, because Enforcers were out on patrol."

Cerridwen made it to the end of the walkway, and eagerly accepted the arm that Bauchan offered her. Too eagerly, Cedric judged. It was out of fear, he knew, but he wished she would not provide any further fuel for whatever twisted schemes the Ambassador no doubt entertained in his fevered brain.

Once Cedric joined them on the ship, Bauchan relinquished his hold on Cerridwen's elbow, and smiled at her warmly. "There, no need to fear. Our hosts aboard this vessel care very much about their cargo. They do not undertake a mission from my Queene lightly."

Cerridwen did not answer him.

"The Royal Heir is very tired," Cedric said, pulling her close to his side. "Are you not, my…flower?"

She looked up sharply, confusion and anger on her features. Then, as if in defeat, she nodded. "I am. Very tired. Ambassador Bauchan, if you would please show us to our quarters for sleeping—"

"Quarters." He laughed. "Oh, I wish I could offer you such luxury. We are all bunked in the lowest hold. Though I am certain some arrangement can be made for your privacy and comfort, given your station. I do hope you do not come to us with high expectations for this voyage. It is a meager freight ship, after all."

"I am sure that she wishes for nothing more than a flat place to lie and a blanket to keep warm." Cedric chuckled as heartily as he could manage and plucked at the coarse material that covered her shoulders. "And we have half of that already."

She jerked away and pulled her blanket tighter, as if it were armor. He'd made her angry, that much was obvious, but he did not have the energy, nor the inclination, to soothe her now. Nor was this the proper place, as soothing her would only bring to light a weakness of character in her.

Bauchan led them through a round door a Human would have to stoop to pass, and bade them watch their steps. "These Human vessels are built so strangely. The stairs are steep, and there are constantly barriers underfoot."

"Give me an old wooden craft any day," Cedric agreed as they followed him down the narrow ladder, just glad that he wasn't returning to the depressing concrete surroundings of the Underground.

The lower hold was vast and open, brightly lit, and cluttered here and there with huge steel containers anchored to the ship with heavy straps that bolted to the floor. It was by no means crowded with cargo, but it was crowded with Faeries. Many of them, Cedric recognized from Court, but by their faces only. They no longer looked as fine and self-important as they had when Queene Mabb or Ayla ruled. They wore rugged traveling clothes and crouched protectively over bundles, saying little to anyone but the three or four Faeries who might share the small spaces they had staked out as their own.

He had not seen Faeries behaving so distressingly since he'd stayed on with the Winter Court, long before the Veil had torn. The summertime had always been a time of celebration and plenty, and he'd continued to travel with Mabb's trooping parade long after the fires of Samhain had extinguished. But with the turning of the year had come a stark, depressing change over most of that Court. They'd become greedy, distrustful hoarders.

As if sensing his thoughts, Bauchan nodded, but he did not comment on the scene. "I know exactly where you will be comfortable," he declared, striding across the metal floor, his footsteps ringing out as he went. "Back here, this little corner is perfect."

The space was small, barely long enough to lie down in, but it was protected from prying eyes—and prying ears, hopefully—by two of the large cargo containers and the side of the ship. The guards would have to find another place to rest, ideally not too far from them, but at least it would offer some hope of keeping the Royal Heir safe and away from the betrayers of the Court.

"Here?" Cerridwen sniffed the air and made a face. "It is so dark back here. And close. I do not like close spaces."

"You skulked about sewage tunnels with your Elf," Cedric said quietly, near her ear so that only she would hear. "You can deign to sleep here."

"I will bring you some extra blankets," Bauchan went on, as though she had never argued. "The crew has been exceedingly generous with their things. They are…sympathetic to our plight."

"Our *plight*." Cedric could not help but scoff at the words. Then, he waved an apologetic hand. "Forgive me, I am tired."

"Of course." Bauchan bowed, like a Human fop. "If that will be all, then, I can have your companions settled, as well."

He would not give them a moment alone to confer. Already, he suspected some plot, saw that the guards were not truly the nobility he had dressed them up as.

One of the guards puffed up his chest and clutched the satchel he'd carried tighter. "I do not wish to seem ungrateful," he began, in tones that sounded comically similar to Bauchan's, "but it does not appear as though our—we *courtiers*—our possessions will be safe among the rabble."

Cedric spared a glance toward Cerridwen. She stared, mouth agape, at the guard, broken out of her sullen reverie for a moment. It was almost enough to make Cedric laugh.

"You could leave your things with us, then," he offered, quickly stifling the amusement that he was certain had shown on his face. "We seem to have a most isolated spot, and of course you can trust the Royal Heir."

The guard played it hesitant; time at Court had afforded him an uncanny ability to imitate the behavior of his "betters." Finally, with a heavy sigh, he handed over the satchel. "From the looks of things, I would advise you all to do the same," he said with a courtly flourish as he stepped aside. The others entrusted "their" belongings to Cedric a bit too easily, but Bauchan would not argue. It would not have been Court manners.

"What a generous offer," the Ambassador said with a smile as sickeningly sweet as spun sugar. "You are truly fit for your role as Royal Consort."

"Let us hope it should never come to that," Cedric said with a humble bow.

Bauchan, the rage practically radiating from him, returned the gesture and quickly ushered the guards away.

When Cedric turned to Cerridwen, she had already lain down, the blanket pulled sullenly over her face.

Two

꧁꧂

The hold of the ship was cold, and dark, and noisy. Though the lights had been put out an hour before—or so Cerridwen was guessing; time passed so slowly with nothing to occupy it—the rustling and whispering of hundreds of Faery bodies echoed off the steel walls.

Though Bauchan had an underling drop off more blankets, enough to build a respectable nest for themselves on the hard floor, Cerridwen still shivered. The temperature of the sea seeped through the ship's metal body, up through the layers of blankets that Cedric had arranged for her.

She searched through the darkness, her eyes grateful for the reprieve from the harsh lights of the past few days, to find him. He sat with his back against the huge cargo container that blocked their corner from view, his legs stretched across the slight opening that made an entrance to their makeshift dwelling. He did not sleep, but stared into the darkness, no expression on his face.

She turned her head back to the wall of the ship, examined the crude drips in the white paint that covered every rivet and seam. This place smelled like Humans. Human bodies, Human goods, Human chemicals. It was almost too much to bear, even for one with Human blood in her veins.

She thought of her mother, whom Cedric spoke of as though she could have lived. Had Ayla felt so uncomfortable around mortals? Obviously not, as she had kept one at her side for all those years of Cerridwen's life.

As if to remind her, the wings at Cerridwen's back stirred of their own accord. She shifted restlessly on her pallet. Her mother had kept Cerridwen's parentage a secret, even from her, for most of Cerridwen's life. When Cerridwen had discovered the truth—that she was not the daughter of the late King Garret, that instead her father was a strange mortal creature from the Darkworld—it had been too late to confront her mother about it. And where was Queene Ayla now? She had believed that the Veil had begun to mend, that the dead moved on to a Summerland kept hidden from the Faeries who had once inhabited the Astral in life. If that were so, where was her guiding hand now? Could she not spare her daughter a sign, something to explain why she had kept such a secret for all of those years? Did she not realize, wherever she had gone, what the revelations of the past days had done to her?

"Are you well, Cerridwen?"

Concern, but from the wrong source. She squeezed

her eyes shut against the angry tears that welled there. Cedric had thought it so comical, to keep up the charade of their betrothal. Well, it was a farce, and had been since the moment her mother had sprung it upon both unwilling parties. But he'd also had great fun in pretending that they would bow to this False Queene Danae once they stepped on the shore.

"I am fine," she said through clenched teeth. Let him leave her alone, then, if he wanted a ball of clay to mold to his liking. She was not so stupid that she would endanger herself, or him. She knew what was at stake. A pretender was about to absorb her mother's Court, would likely force Cerridwen into some position of servitude to suit her ego. Let her. There was nothing left for her now. Her mother was dead, her father was a mere Darkling, and she had no claim to the crown. No desire for it, either.

"Why did you not introduce me as Queene?" She did not whisper; whispers attracted attention. It was something she learned long ago, a part of daily life in the Palace.

Cedric crossed one leg over the other, shifted as though he could possibly get more comfortable in the position he was in. "I did not, because we do not need to declare our intention for you to rule in Danae's stead. You will not be safe if we do."

"You do not trust me to say the right thing, or act the way you wish me to act. You do not trust me to make the right decisions." Not unfairly, she reminded herself quietly. She had betrayed her mother, and that betrayal had ultimately caused her death. But if

Cedric judged her as she judged herself, he would see that she was a selfish creature, and that she would not harm her own interests.

The thought gave her little comfort.

"It is not a matter of trust." He moved toward her now, settled himself on the pallet beside her, but he did not look her in the eye. "If it were, that would mean that I thought you capable of avoiding the traps certain others might set for you, but you are not."

"Certain others?" She scoffed. "Bauchan, you mean. You think he is too clever, that I cannot see beyond what he really is?"

"I think that he has much more practice at deceit than you, and is a master of it. Besides, it's not just a matter of *seeing* his deceit, but knowing how to react to it, and how to prevent it, too." The disgust in Cedric's voice was as chill as the air around them.

Cerridwen burrowed deeper beneath her blankets. "If you had simply told him that I am Queene now, perhaps he would not think to trick me."

Now, Cedric looked at her, his eyes blazing with anger. "If you believe that, you are far more naive than I could have ever imagined."

"I would not be so naive if the people around me did not treat me as though I were a child, incapable of understanding!" She lowered her voice. "You do not wish for him to know I plan to be Queene, because you believe that will make me a sweeter plum for Queene Danae. Is that right?"

"It is." Cedric rolled to his side, propped his head on his hand. "If this Danae gains the support of the

Court members that Bauchan brings her from the Underground, we will be on our own. And it looks as though there is enough desperation here for exactly that to happen. We do not know Danae's temperament. She might be merciful, and allow you to stay on at her Court as a lesser noble, if you pledge your loyalty to her. Or she might chose to view you as a threat, and have you executed."

It seemed almost absurd to suggest such a thing. "How could I be seen as a threat? I have nothing. I've never actually ruled. I have no real power."

"And that is even more true if you are not the Queene," Cedric interrupted. "The only Faery you have known well was your mother, and perhaps your governess. But your mother was part mortal, and born in the Underground. The way most Faeries are—the way they were before the Veil was torn—they behave in ugly ways. These Faeries we travel with now will no doubt turn back to their old ways. Danae is probably very much like one of them. We must be certain that she will cause you no harm if you choose to pursue your throne."

Cerridwen lay on her back, stared up at the ugly ceiling above them. "You were not born in the Underground. You fought beside Queene Mabb during both wars with the Humans. And you are not vain and petty, as you assume this new Queene will be."

"I am…glad that you do not find me vain and petty." He stumbled over the words, as though he knew he must acknowledge them, but had no idea why she'd said them. "But we must not trust that

Danae will be the same. She keeps company with Bauchan. That does not recommend her character over much."

It struck Cerridwen then that Cedric spoke to her now not as though he were scolding her, not as though he believed he knew better, but as though she were of equal intelligence and capable of rational thought. As though she were not a child. So rarely did that happen, the feeling was still a novelty. She was but twenty, while Cedric—and most Faeries—were untold hundreds or thousands of years old.

Unbidden, her mind returned her to the night she'd left the Palace, intending to betray her mother's plans to the Elves. She'd been so besotted with the Elf she'd met on the Strip, she'd followed him into the Darkworld, had pretended to be fully Human just so he would not be repulsed by her. Now, she understood what Faeries meant when they said someone was elf-struck. Sickening.

But that night, before she'd stupidly taken flight from the safety of the Palace walls, Cedric had made good on his promise to tell her all that was discussed in her mother's private Council. Of course, he had made that promise only to keep her from causing a further scene in the Throne Room, in front of the entire Court. But he had come to her and told her the dire news—that her mother intended to attack the Elves rather than wait for them to unleash the Water-horses, horrors of the deep that had been summoned to destroy the Faery Kingdom of the Lightworld—

and he'd done so without warning her that she did not wish to hear, or that she would not understand.

A pang of homesickness gripped her stomach and stole the breath from her lungs. How she longed to be back in the Palace, in her chambers, in her own, comfortable bed. To feel Governess's cool hands on her forehead, soothing her to sleep after a bad dream. To know that her mother slept safely down the hall.

That, she missed more than anything, because she had not appreciated it then. She'd hated her mother, had raged at being treated like a child. And though she enjoyed being spoken to as a capable Faery who was full grown, she would have gladly remained a child-princess forever if she could have her mother back.

Only when Cedric asked quietly, "Are you crying?" did Cerridwen realize that she was. She wiped her eyes and shook her head, rolled to face away from him.

This was not a nightmare that she could wake from to find Governess at her bedside, ready to soothe away her fears. "Cerridwen," Cedric began, but he said no more. He laid a hand on her arm, patted her uncertainly.

She wanted to shrug it away, to isolate herself once again with her misery, for it had always helped in the past. Now, though, she could not stand the thought of being alone with such grief, though it could not be truly shared.

So, she let him keep his hand there but did not acknowledge him, and she cried herself quietly to sleep.

* * *

The ship sailed in the early dawn. Exhausted, Cedric had not noticed the sudden churning of the water beneath them, or the subtle feeling of movement. Perhaps it had even soothed him into deeper sleep. He would not complain. Only rest would ease the trials of their flight from the Underground, and all that preceded it.

No, not all. Some wounds would never heal, only seal off with time, waiting to split open and spew forth their pestilence again. He carried several of that kind. The freshest had not yet begun to close, and the pain was constant, even when he thought of other things.

When he'd first boarded the ferry and looked over the side rail into the ocean, he'd imagined the bodies of the Gypsies floating in their watery graves. He'd seen Dika's face, too, unscarred but ashen blue, her hair floating around her submerged head.

When he'd come aboard the ship and watched the Faeries with their packs, for a moment he'd seen the panicked faces of the Gypsies as they had fled to the center of their camp, ready to leave the Underground entirely. A trip none of them would take.

He wondered if he was as doomed now as they were then, but unable to see it. The entire Kingdom of Queene Ayla was destroyed by Waterhorses from the deep, from beneath the sort of ocean they now traveled upon. And the ship's hold reminded him of the Underground and the Darkworld…as if an echo that would not end.

He'd woken to find Cerridwen sitting beside him,

her knees pulled to her chest, rocking as she stared blankly ahead. She'd looked frightened, but when he'd asked, she'd denied it.

"Sick again, from the motion of the ship," she'd insisted, though why she would continue to rock, he could not fathom, as it seemed it would only make it worse. But he did not wish to have an argument.

"If you are staying here, I will go and see what other facilities are available for our use." At first, he'd been uncertain whether or not to leave her, whether or not she was able to defend herself and her possessions, but after only a moment's consideration, he'd realized that he could not spend the entire voyage in their hiding place. There was no time for her frailty, and perhaps leaving her to fend for herself would shock her out of her incapacitation.

Had Ayla been there, or Malachi, Cedric would have discussed his worries with them. But they were gone now, and he had never truly shared his fears with anyone, not completely. He was not sure which realization hurt him more.

The morning brought more of the same in the lower hold. Faeries, reduced to their primitive, trooping states, regarded Cedric with suspicion and hostility as he walked among them. It took incredible strength not to respond in kind; he did not wish to become like them, but the fear, and the pull to his old nature, were almost too strong. That was what had happened to them, and he did not wish to follow them down that way.

He found the door they had entered through the

night before. Now, it was closed, and when he tried the handle, it did not open. A momentary panic gripped him. What if the Humans had lied to Bauchan? What if the ship sailed to some port where Human Enforcers would await them? It took all of his will not to claw at the steel, to calm his mind.

"It is an unsettling thing, is it not?" Bauchan's voice behind him did nothing to soothe Cedric's nerves, and he closed his eyes a moment to force away his panic.

"It is." His voice scraped out, betrayed the turmoil inside him. He took a deep breath. "I had forgotten how very stifling the Underground was, until I stood under the sky again. Now that I am enclosed once more…it is unpleasant."

He turned to face Bauchan, found the Faery as clean and unrumpled as he had been the night before. He smoothed back a matted rope of hair with one ring-encumbered hand and nodded lazily. "Unpleasant, yes. I fear this entire journey will be one of unpleasantness. But we have endured hardships far greater in our time, have we not?"

"Have we?" Cedric narrowed his eyes as he surveyed the other Faery. Bauchan had never lived in the Underground. His skin was not translucent white from a lack of sunlight, his eyes not dull for want of starlight. He outfitted himself with the trappings of Human luxury, and dared stand before one who had remained faithful to the Fae race and claim hardship.

Almost faithful, Cedric reminded himself, and felt another pang of sorrow at the remembrance of Dika.

Bauchan disregarded his comment—though he reserved his offense for a later time, Cedric was certain—and motioned for the other Faery to walk with him. "The captain of this vessel came to speak with me this morning. He believes that once we have put the harbor behind us, it will be safe for us to leave the hold and go to the upper deck. I have asked him, on your behalf, to provide extra rations at mealtime for the Royal Heir. She did not look well."

"She is well enough." The last thing Cedric needed now was to have to protect Cerridwen from Bauchan's scheming in the guise of kindness. "What can we expect, in terms of rations, though? I do not worry for myself, but for some of these Faeries, who are near feral already. I have been out trooping, and I have seen how it can affect the weaker of our race."

"You assume they are weak?" Bauchan's eyes glittered with humor or malice, Cedric was not certain which.

He fixed the Ambassador with a gaze that was not threatening, but could not be misconstrued. "I believe that if they had been stronger of will, they would not have left with you."

Bauchan took umbrage with this, true feeling finally visible in his expression. But only for a moment. A tight smile that grew a bit more relaxed, a bit more natural with each passing heartbeat, until it was nearly impossible to tell that he'd been angered in the first place, spread across his lips. "You will forgive them their weakness, I hope, now that you have joined them."

"I have joined them out of duty to my Queene." He did not wish to argue, but the man drew him into it so easily. The journey would be most interesting, as would its culmination. "I still have my own reservations."

"Reservations," Bauchan repeated with a soft laugh. "Yes, I understand. You fear that your mate will be in some danger from my Queene. And I do not begrudge you those fears. If I did not know Danae the way I know her—and that is to say, very well—and I were in your position, I might have the same fears."

It was a well-rehearsed speech, Cedric credited Bauchan for that. "You can assure me, then, that she will not be a trophy for your Queene? That she will not be viewed as a threat, or that she will not be pressed into slavery in order to appease Danae's ego?"

"My, but you Underground Fae are a ruthless kind, are you not?" Bauchan laughed through his expression of mock horror. "To have thought of such a thing!"

Cedric smiled with him, but his patience wore thin. "We are not newborn Humans, Bauchan. We are Fae. Born with a capacity for deceit far greater than any other species on Earth or in the Astral. It would be very unwise to forget that."

"So true," Bauchan agreed easily. "But then, why should Danae be threatened by the Royal Heir? She does not seek to make an issue of her…title, does she?"

Careful now, Cedric cautioned himself. He'd already given away enough to make Bauchan doubt their intentions, if not suspect the truth outright.

They came to the end of the aisleway, on the

opposite side of the ship from where Cedric had left Cerridwen, to another row of shipping containers. A blanket stretched over a gap between two of them, and Bauchan gestured to it. "Come inside. I have nothing to offer to you, but then, you would not take it anyway."

At least the Ambassador did not think him so thick as to fall for being gifted into service by a few crumbs or a cup of water. He followed Bauchan through the gap. Past the huge cargo containers, a space that spanned the width of the ship opened. Though it was large, it was crowded with all manner of objects so that it was nearly impossible to walk. Cushions, chests, even Human furniture of sofas and chairs, covered all of the floor space, and atop all of these perched Bauchan's retinue.

"I had wondered where you had hidden them away," Cedric said, picking his way carefully through the space between an ornamental table and a chest overflowing with silks and jewelry.

"We had much more room on the journey over." Bauchan waved a hand apologetically. "We like to travel in comfort. You cannot blame us, can you?"

He could blame them for any number of things, but kept silent.

"It is a pity your Queene would not leave the Underground and join us," Bauchan continued. "She would have had this whole chamber to herself."

"And her life. But Queene Ayla did not require luxuries. She was a commoner before she took the throne, after the death of her mate, King Garret."

Cedric took care to speak of Cerridwen's lineage. Though he did not wish to give the impression that Cerridwen would press her claim, there was no reason to let Bauchan forget that Cerridwen was—as far as the Court believed—a descendant of Queene Mabb.

Bauchan nodded. "Yes, Flidais told us the tale of how, exactly, Ayla came to the throne. We were quite enraptured by it, were we not, friends?"

A few murmurs of approval came from the Faeries draped languidly over the furnishings. They appreciated the blood and horror of the tale, nothing more. It sullied what had happened in the Underground, sullied Ayla, if they believed she were anything like them.

"She did what she had to do, in order to save the Kingdom." A bit dramatic, but the truth. Garret would have turned the Faeries of the Underground into what Bauchan and his fellows—indeed, what Cedric expected all of Danae's Court to be—had become. They had already been as weak-willed and self-indulgent. The Fae grumbling and desperate in the stronghold were lacking from this retinue in only one regard: access to material wealth. The selfishness was the same.

Bauchan's eyes widened, as though he had meant no offense, had not meant to trivialize Ayla's reign as he had. "Oh, and we greatly admire her for it," he insisted. "Do we not?"

"Do not do that," Cedric snapped as Bauchan's companions began to mumble their agreement. "I am not impressed by such displays."

"Nor would I expect you to be," Bauchan agreed smoothly. "Not with the experience you have *behind* you. After all, if Queene Ayla saw fit to entrust you with her daughter, not only as a mate, but to be kept safe in her absence, you must be not only loyal, but highly intelligent."

Cedric did not know how to respond, so he stayed silent while Bauchan made a show of pacing the small bit of cleared floor he occupied.

"But I wonder at how loyal *you* are to *her*," Bauchan continued. "Was there no command from her that you should… Excuse me, I do not wish to pry into affairs that do not concern me."

Cedric could not help his laughter at that. "Why would that concern you now, after you have meddled so thoroughly?"

Bauchan ignored him. "Ah, but I must know. Why did the Queene not charge you with returning some of her subjects? Surely, she wanted to see the Light-world Court flourish even after her death?"

"My Queene had but one mission, the one entrusted to her by the Gods." Cedric chose his words carefully, wanted no misunderstanding.

"But it would be so easy," Bauchan pressed on. "Our journey had not even begun and they were discontent. It would have been no trick to lure them back to the Underground."

"I did not come here to upset your plans, nor the plans of your Queene," Cedric stated firmly. "Nor do I care what her plans might be, so long as Cerridwen will not be harmed by them. With all the troubles that plagued my Queene and the Faeries of the Underground, I do not believe the destruction of the Lightworld to be any great loss. I only wish it could have come without the expense of ones I cared for deeply."

Bauchan nodded. "To hear you say such a thing brings me great relief. I must admit, I feared some trickery on your part, especially when Flidais did not return. But knowing that you speak earnestly, I no longer fear your presence, or what actions I might have had to take to prevent you from harming my Queene."

Cedric hoped that this would be the end of the conversation, even turned to go, but Bauchan's voice stopped him. "And please, be sure to impress upon the Royal Heir that I am her servant on this journey, and upon our arrival at Queene Danae's Court. I do not wish her to feel…friendless there."

"She will not be friendless," Cedric assured him, hoping that the icy weight of threat he pressed into his words would not be lost on the Ambassador. "I will be at her side every moment. I am, perhaps, the greatest ally and protector she has at this time."

Three

~~~~~~

In most ways, the days on the ship were long and more dull than any Palace banquet had ever been. Still, the first day at sea had lifted some of the fog of sorrow from Cerridwen's mind. It had helped, strangely enough, that the other Faeries had eagerly abandoned the hold and went above when given the signal that it was safe to do so. Many of them had taken their possessions and set up camp under the sky, leaving the hold less crowded. It had been a strange feeling, after so many years at Court, to be left alone, and it was a good feeling, as well.

Cedric had asked her to accompany him up to the deck a few times. He spent his days at the edge of the upper deck, staring down into the water, the same grim expression on his face. A few times, something had broken the spell the waves seemed to have over him, and he'd asked Cerridwen to walk with him, to keep up appearances, she supposed.

But he'd sworn only to protect her, not to keep her entertained, so she did not approach him during his times of deep melancholy. On those rare moments when he'd sought out her company, they'd found little to talk about, anyway. She did not wish to discuss what had happened, and it would not have been wise to, but they did not know much of each other beyond the horrible times of the past weeks. She was most glad for the nights, when they would sleep, or at least pretend to, so that she did not have to think of things to say to him.

There was no doubt in her mind that Cedric would keep her best interests in mind as they embarked on this strange journey. But whether out of concern for her, or out of obligation to the promise he had made her mother was a mystery in itself.

She wondered why it mattered. It should not. But he had kept her safe when Malachi had fallen in the Elven fortress, and during their flight from the Darkworld. He had not coddled her—in fact, he'd been angry—but he had truly seemed to care whether she lived or died.

More than that, he had treated her with respect when the rest of the Court had discounted her as pretty decoration.

Perhaps he had not lost that respect for her, if he did blame her for her mother's death. He had loved her mother as a close friend, and Malachi, as well. That was more than Cerridwen could ever hope anyone would feel toward her, now that she knew herself to be a selfish, reckless creature. But she hoped that Cedric cared enough that he did not view her as a burden, and that he would not continue to feel obligated to her when they arrived at the Upworld settlement. If he returned to the Underground, if that were even a possibility, perhaps she would not have disrupted his life irreparably. If he stayed in the Upworld settlement, he might find a mate there and be happy. But he should not feel indebted to her, and to her mother, forever.

It had occurred to her that morning, when the movement of the ship had woken her, that she could be embarking not only on a journey to a new home, but to a new life altogether. If the events of the past few days had not unfolded as they had, she would still be in the Underground, living out her days there. Mated to Cedric, if she'd bent to her mother's wishes, or living in the Darkworld with her Elf, Fenrick, had he not turned out to be a spy against the Fae.

Now, though, the future was not so sacrosanct. It frightened her, but it was not nearly so frightening as knowing that her life had been decided for her. Though her heart was still wounded from Fenrick's betrayal, she wondered at the type of Faeries who made up Danae's Court. If they were as handsome as Bauchan, surely she would find someone she did not find objectionable.

She wondered, too, what role she would have in this other Queene's Court. Whereas before she had been hidden away and taken out only for special occasions during which she was meant to be seen and not heard, she was a Queene now. Or, she would be, if she had her way. If they failed, though, and this Danae let her live, she might be just like any normal Faery. That promised a sort of freedom, and freedom held for her giddy fascination and terrible fear.

No matter what might happen, she knew that she would always be haunted by what she had seen in the Underground. Not just the horrible violence of her last few days there. She would never forget the sickening rush of exhilaration she'd felt at the sight of battle, or her sorrow at watching her parents cut down before her; those images would force themselves into her mind every time she closed her eyes, and chase away any happy thought she might begin to feel, she was certain. But she would always remember the awfulness of the lives lived by the creatures there, the scrabbling for sustenance, the very real possibility that something could come out of any one of the shadows and end the life they struggled to lead.

She would not live in such a way, nor would she allow anyone she cared about to, if she could help it.

If the days were interminable, the nights were only slightly less so. But the evenings, they were nearly pleasant. Once the sun set, a change would come over the Fae. Probably relief. Cerridwen felt this every day that passed. The setting sun showed them that they were one day closer to their destination, that soon they would be quit of the ship and one another, free to seek out new companionship in the Upworld settlement. Free to set up new lives not encircled by walls.

A few of the Faeries had brought instruments in their flight from the Underground, drums and whistles and pipes, and a harp. They assembled on the deck, under the night sky dazzled with stars, and played until the dawn lit the sky. Sometimes, the Human sailors would come and watch them, but always from a safe distance, always wary.

Cerridwen watched, as well, because she was not fool enough to think that she could truly be a part of it. But being near the others was enough to make her feel less lonely, and so she watched them celebrate their journey's progress.

On the fifth night, Bauchan approached her, practiced smile in place. "And where is your mate? I have not seen him any night yet, when everyone else is here."

She would not let him goad her into giving anything away, not even her unhappiness. "He is tired," she said with a shrug. "And he does not care for parties."

"Too tired to dance with his lovely betrothed?" Bauchan clucked in disapproval.

"Too tired for disrespectful celebration in the wake of terrible tragedy," she replied coolly.

The humor fled Bauchan's face, and his eyes glittered like those of the great, sleek sea creatures that bumped and brushed against the hull of the boat as they slept at night. "Tragedy, yes. The death of your mother, the Queene."

"And countless others, and the destruction of our way of life." She held his gaze, hoped he would see something of her mother in her.

"But no such a tragedy for yourself? You will be Queene, after all."

Be cautious, she warned herself, but her anger was far stronger than her restraint. "Not all of the Fae in the Underground have survived," she snapped. "Many of them died at the hands of the Elves and Waterhorses because they would not turn their back on their true Queene."

She had said too much, but she did not care. Her hands trembled, her chest jerked with her angry pulse.

"I have upset you." He tried another harmless smile. "It seems I cannot say the right thing when I am near you."

"I am sure it is not just me." She would give him no foothold. "Why does anyone fall for your obvious manipulations?"

Hatred, she had learned long ago, looked especially ugly on a beautiful face. Bauchan was more beautiful than most, so on him the effect was terrifying. "You should watch your step, little one. I may have underestimated you, but I know exactly the kind of creature your Cedric is. I can turn him from you in a moment."

She laughed at the absurdity of his arrogance. No power on Earth, the Upworld or the Underground, could make Cedric betray the last promise he'd made to her mother.

"You do not believe me?" Bauchan's voice was as cold and deadly as a blade. "I turned Flidais, ever faithful Flidais, from your mother."

"I would be careful if I were you," she warned.

"What will you do to me?" Bauchan had the nerve to laugh at her. The fool. "You have no allies. No real power. If you do intend to overthrow my Queene, and I suspect you do, you have no army and no Court."

"I do not need an army! I can easily do what I did to Flidais, to you and anyone else who stands in my way!"

The music stopped; the dancing followed.

They could not have all heard. Soon, she knew, a ripple of whisper would begin, growing and spreading until their outraged voices would be louder than the instrument had been.

Bauchan looked so pleased with himself, she wished she really could do to him what she'd done to Flidais. The red haze of her anger was so similar to what she'd felt in the battle in the Elven Great Hall. A family trait, she thought with pride. Her mother had been a skilled assassin. Her father—her true father—a great warrior. She did not falter under the accusing stares.

Bauchan called for quiet, and the crowd fell silent. He stalked forward, so close that if she'd had a knife, she could have easily sent him the way of that treacherous Fae.

"And what did you do to Flidais?"

It was too late now to keep from telling everything. And that must have been his plan all along. To push her to this. He was, indeed, very good at this sort of trickery.

Still, she would not let him see that he had beaten her. "I killed the traitor Flidais. Before we boarded the ferry, I killed her with a dagger in her throat, and I have not thought twice about it since!"

A gasp went up, and she turned to address the Faeries that had formed a circle around them. "I dealt with Flidais the way we should deal with all cowards and traitors. She lied to you, working with Bauchan to deliver you as playthings to his Queene. You would not be here, on this boat, bound for an unknown future, if she had not promised this man something in exchange for your presence!"

Bauchan smirked at Cerridwen and looked around. "You would not be free of the oppression of your Queene, who would not let you decide for yourself whether or not you wished to stay buried underground," Bauchan countered. "Give up this foolish argument, little one. I have won, my Queene has won. You no longer have a Court to support you, *Your Majesty*."

"Bauchan! What is the meaning of this?"

Cedric appeared out of the air, it seemed, and stalked through the crowd of Faeries around them. He did not look at her, did not divert his focus from Bauchan.

She'd seen him look this way before, when he'd stood, blood-drenched in the thick of battle. He was no less terrifying now. He stood between Bauchan and Cerridwen, so that she could not see his face, but the tone of his voice told her that she would not want to see it, anyway.

"Step away from my mate," he growled.

Four

~~~ଵଵଵ~~~

Cedric had been nearly asleep when the guard had burst through the blanket that partitioned off their sleeping quarters. It was difficult, he found, to sleep with another body beside his. Twice now, he'd woken to find that he'd put his arm around Cerridwen as she slept, had dreamed she was Dika lying asleep in his arms.

He was not sure which was more acute, his embarrassment with himself at touching her so intimately, or his pain when he woke and remembered that it was not, could never be, Dika. He was relieved when Cerridwen had begun to linger with the Faeries on the deck, so that he could steal a few hours of rest without fear of frightening her.

Or worse, leading her to believe something that would never be.

He squinted at the intruder through sleep-bleary eyes. "What is it? What's happened?"

"You should come above. Immediately." The guard's tone and expression were enough to jolt Cedric fully awake. In an instant, he was on his feet, pushing past the guard.

He did not ask what he would find above deck. Bauchan would be involved, he had no doubt. They passed no one on their way, so there was nothing to flee from. It gave him no clue to what he might find. Had Cerridwen fallen overboard? Had she made some pact with Bauchan? He did not wish to know; at least, not before he had to. So, he did not ask.

But he had not expected to see the scene on the deck of the ship, a ring of Faeries crowded around the two that he had already known would be involved.

"Bauchan!" he shouted, and it was enough to draw the attention of the Faeries away from Cerridwen's words. He shoved one last Faery from his path and strode into the center of the circle. "What is the meaning of this?"

At the sight of him, Cerridwen began to tremble. If it was from her anger, then he could top it. If it was out of fear of him, then she was wise. She'd revealed too much, and come far too close to disaster, even after his warnings. The very sight of her sparked an intense desire to wrap his hands around her throat and choke the life from her. He turned his back to her as he stepped between her and Bauchan, and directed all of that rage toward his real enemy. "Step away from my mate."

Bauchan smirked and made a mocking bow. "Of course, Your Majesty."

A twitter of nervous laughter rippled through the crowd. Cedric turned to address them directly. "You laugh, yet you do not accept that you have been led to this place by a trickster, a jester? You abandoned your Queene, who fought to protect you, in order to follow this wretch?"

"What Queene did they abandon?" Bauchan laughed. "Your Ayla was a half-breed, a half-Human, with no more right to the throne than you, or any of these Fae."

"Queene Ayla carried the Royal Heir, who stands before you now as Queene, descended from the line of Mabb. What right does your Danae have to call herself Queene?"

"Her Majesty Queene Danae has never lost a battle against the Humans. She has never allowed herself to be forced underground. What good is a bloodline if it stems from a source as powerless as your Mabb?" Bauchan smirked and turned toward the crowd. "You were not coerced. You made a choice. And Queene Danae will reward you for it!"

As the Faeries mindlessly clapped and cheered, Cedric spared a glance at Cerridwen. She did not look queenly. She looked like a terrified child, with her head bowed and shoulders sagging as she hugged herself and trembled.

The desire to throttle her faded somewhat, replaced by the instinct to comfort her. But that would not help her. Silently, he willed her to look more dignified, to revive her anger, if that was what she must do in order to appear less weak.

If she would not fight back, he would have to. "How will they be rewarded, Bauchan? With the privilege of bowing to your Queene's vanity? You promised you would deliver them from the threat of the Waterhorses, and you've done that. But you've not made any of your other intentions clear to them."

"They will be rewarded by living at a Court where the Queene does not permit lawlessness, and does not indulge in it herself." Bauchan leveled a finger at Cerridwen. "And she will not excuse traitors like this one. She will pay for the death of Flidais, who only sought to protect innocent Faery lives."

This brought Cerridwen to life, animated her with pure hate. "Your Queene has no authority over me! I name you traitor, and if you turn your back on me, even for a moment, I will carry out my own sentence upon you!"

"Cerridwen!" Their position was too precarious here. He wanted her to display some courage, but not foolish bravery. They were surrounded by an easily swayed crowd, who would think nothing of tossing them overboard—and who knew how long their wings would hold them above the endless ocean, if Bauchan let them? Bauchan wanted to see them humbled at his Queene's feet, and a reward for himself—but Cedric could not let this continue.

She snapped her head to face him, the rage in her eyes flaring to new intensity. Her mouth opened, to issue a challenge, no doubt, but she thought better of it.

Good. She had no one else, and she should tread

cautiously with him, as well. Especially now, after what she had done. She may have ended the royal lineage of Mabb—and her own life—with her actions. One an ancient dynasty, the other barely beginning to sprout.

He took her by the arm, aware that by humbling her in this way, he contested her authority and damaged her in the opinion of the Court. But the Court was a shambles now, and any real chance of ruling had died with her mother. Now, he merely sought to save her life.

"She has threatened me. They all heard it," Bauchan shouted, finally losing his infuriating calm as Cedric pulled Cerridwen through the throng. "You cannot simply leave!"

Cedric composed his features into an impassive mask before he turned to face the Ambassador. "Do you think we will run? To where? If you wish for some kind of justice, if her words have caused you some damage, if you so respect the law as you claim to, you can pursue the matter when we arrive at your Queene's Court. For now, I am removing her from your company, until you can treat her with the respect that the Queene of the Fae deserves."

Bauchan moved forward, as though he would follow them, but the Faeries, seeing that the evening's entertainment was now finished, began to scatter, blocking his path.

"You're hurting me!" Cerridwen cried, digging in her heels as soon as he'd pulled her through the door and closed it behind them.

He flexed his fingers, and she whined, jerking her arm from his grasp. "I am glad!" he shouted, not caring at this moment who heard him. "But there is no way I can hurt you more than you have hurt yourself tonight! How could you be so stupid?"

She shoved him with enough force that, combined with his shock at her action, he stumbled backward. It gave her time to get past him, to run down the steps to the lower hold, her hair like a banner behind her as she whipped through the door at the bottom and out of his sight. He did not pause in his pursuit of her. She would go to the place where they slept, because there was no other place for her to flee to. She was as trapped here as she had been in the Palace, he thought with mean satisfaction, only this time she could not as easily run away.

"What did you think to accomplish with that display?" he asked as he pushed past the blanket partitioning their space from the rest of the hold. He had shouted the words, and now the echo rang off the steel walls, taunting him with a reminder of how silent, how close, the space truly was. He lowered his voice and continued, "Do you really think that you have the power to rule these betrayers?"

"Of course not!" Cerridwen was not as conscious of the possibility of eavesdroppers, and she shrieked like the Bean Sidhe.

"What, then? Did you think Bauchan would simply hand over power to you?" A rage burned deep in him, oddly protective and perhaps even jealous at his next thought. "Did he make a promise to you?

Did he seduce you with pretty words? I told you that you could not trust him!"

"You think me so stupid as to fall for such an obvious trick?" Tears sprang to her eyes, and her antennae drooped on her forehead. "No, his manipulations were far more clever. Even you would have been impressed."

"What do you mean by that?" Now, the rage that had been directed toward Bauchan turned ugly and pointed to her.

Though her words had been intended to cause a fight, there seemed to be none left in her. Her breath left her in a long, shuddering sigh. "Why are you here?"

"Because I made a promise to your mother." It was automatic, simple, and not, he realized, the entire truth.

She slumped to the floor and stared at the floor. Her hands lay limp in her lap. "My mother is dead. You need not honor that promise any longer."

How to explain the concept of honor to her? If she had not learned it from her mother or her father—two of the most loyal beings he had ever known—perhaps she was destined to never know it. "I cannot abandon you."

But it was not just his promise to her mother. In their flight from the Elven hall, he'd hated Cerridwen, and had seriously considered leaving her for dead. It had been only his promise to Ayla that had stopped him. But in the time that had passed since then, in the time since he'd made yet another promise to Ayla that her child would not be harmed, he'd learned something about his charge.

She could not survive on her own.

It might have been the way she'd been raised; in the Fae tradition, the Royal Heir was never truly expected to inherit the throne. Mabb had gained hers only when her mother had stepped down. That Queene was still out in the world somewhere, but she'd merely tired of ruling her subjects. She'd prepared Mabb for the job, though. No one had prepared Garret. What kind of a King could he have been? Ayla, a complete outsider, had learned what she needed to know about life at Court in such a short time, but she had come armed with the cool, logical head of an assassin. That she had not prepared her daughter to come into her title was not a surprise; she'd left behind what should have been the more dangerous life.

If Queene Ayla would have been able to see ahead, to know that her rule would be so short, she might have instructed her Heir in the ways of the Court. Not the manners, for as surly as Cerridwen could be, and the poor choices she could make, she knew the graces of the Court and could also make herself a pleasing addition to a gathering. But she did not understand the games, the intrigues, that one needed to be aware of to maneuver at Court. Not knowing, one could not rule, not successfully. And success was measured by how long one could reign before someone stuck a knife in one's back.

The truth was, as he had marched through the crowd on deck, he had not seen Cerridwen standing there, but Mabb lying on her bier, limbs twisted to withered branches by death. When Cerridwen's face had replaced hers, he had known what he was called to do, not simply because of a *geis* made to a dead Queene.

"I cannot abandon you," he repeated, forcing the image of Mabb's cold face from his mind, "because if I did, you would not survive long."

He was not certain how she would accept this explanation. He expected anger, and a heated denial. Instead, she looked up at him with wide, tear-filled eyes, and said in a near whisper, "Then you should abandon me."

It was some mortal trait, surely, to wish for one's own death. He could not think of hearing an immortal creature long for the end of their life. In fact, they feared such an unnatural event. He recoiled without meaning to, and she looked down again, as if his disgust were another weight added to her burden.

"You should not say that." He tried to sound comforting, but she had frightened him too much, and it came out stilted and insincere.

"I should not say it, because it makes you uncomfortable, or because it is true?" A bitter, mocking laugh came from her, as if coming from another body altogether. "I have destroyed them, Cedric. My parents, my fellow Fae. I am nothing, was nothing. If I had not been Garret's daughter, I would not be the Queene now. I would be some worthless halfbreed dying on the Strip, or in the Darkworld tunnels. But I am not Garret's daughter. I am more mortal than Fae, and somehow, by being both of those things, I am less than either. You should let Bauchan's Queene kill me. I can bring only despair to those I touch."

He raised his hand to stop her. "Cease your self-pity!" he barked, jerking his head toward the curtain, hoping she understood his sudden change in mood.

Her head lifted, eyes going even wider as she looked at the curtain. She saw the silhouette of someone standing, listening, on the other side of the partition.

He spoke again, louder, and inched toward the curtain. "And your lies. Garret might have been a worthless King, but you cannot distance yourself from the stain of his ignoble lineage with a falsehood!"

Cedric turned and launched himself at the figure on the other side of the curtain, but he knew the moment he moved that he would not be successful. He tumbled through the cloth, arms full of empty air, and saw Bauchan fleeing. In the next instant, he saw Cerridwen's feet as she leaped over him, and he ducked his head to keep from being hit by them. He called after her, but she did not stop. "He heard everything!" she shouted back.

It took him a shocked second to realize what she'd done, and what she intended to do. It was an increment of time he hoped to make up as he chased after her. If he did not reach Bauchan before Cerridwen did, the Ambassador was dead.

"Cerridwen—*stop!*" he shouted after her as Bauchan fled out the door, down the hall that lead to the stairs that took them above deck. Bauchan was halfway up that steep rise, and Cerridwen on the bottom. Cedric knew he was too far when he saw the curved flash of the Elven knife. "Bauchan, look out!"

Even in his days as a young, untried warrior of fifty years, he would not have done something so foolish. To shout out a warning to someone already engaged distracted them; for Bauchan, it was a fatal distraction. Even as Cedric blanched and heard the echo of his mistake off the metal walls, Cerridwen brought the blade down, down into the base of Bauchan's neck. The point of the warped blade appeared nearly level with the handle as it protruded from Bauchan's throat, and Cerridwen jerked it free with a grunt, releasing an arc of blood that sprayed her, the floor, the ceiling, the wall.

Bauchan opened his mouth to scream. That was unmistakable. The gaping mouth, the ropey lines that stood out against his jaw, as he struggled to make a sound that would not come.

Cerridwen stepped back, still gripping the knife as though he might attack her. But it was too late. Crystals of ice stole up Bauchan's face, covering his visible skin like frozen diamonds. From his open mouth, a breath of snow unfurled in a wintery gust. The blood that flowed from him came as clear, crystalline water, and he fell against the steps, shattering as his eyes rolled back into his head and closed over like ice on a pond.

Within moments, Fae surrounded them. Ones who had heard the commotion from the deck and had come to investigate for themselves, and ones who had seen the confrontation begin only seconds before and had followed. Rough hands grabbed Cedric, jerked him backward with his arms pressed up tightly between his wings. Cerridwen tried to fight her way free with the knife, but lost it embarrassingly quickly. Two Faeries gripped her by the shoulders and forced her to her knees. The meaty sound of a booted foot connecting with flesh cut through the riotous noise, and Cerridwen's cry cut through him more effectively than her blade ever could.

"What the hell are you lot doing?" A Human fought his way into the fray. Stocky body, hard, lined face. He would not choose sides. He was afraid of all of them, and that was far more dangerous, Cedric realized, than the murderous horde surrounding them.

One of Bauchan's retinue, a sickly thin-looking thing with long, green ropes of hair, called out, "This is none of your concern, Human!"

Her vehemence startled Cedric; he feared what reaction the Human would have now. He might produce one of those Human weapons, with the devastating projectiles, and kill them all out of fear or malice. He might be moved to contact the Enforcers.

More Humans arrived. One of them seemed to have more authority than the others, as the rest of them stood down when he barked his command. "Where is Bauchan? I demand to see him!"

"Then see him, Human!" the green-haired Faery hissed, sweeping her arm and brushing the other Fae away as though they were flies.

Cedric followed the Human's gaze to the ground, where Bauchan's robes lay in a puddle of melting ice that used to be his body. But it was an uninteresting sight, and he used the distraction of the crowd to look for Cerridwen.

The Fae that had taken hold of her had dropped her. She lay, unmoving, on the floor, her body turned in on itself so that he could not see her face to tell if she was conscious.

Anger churned in him, flaring red at the center of the tree of life force inside him. Some of it was still directed at Cerridwen herself, for her rash actions. Some was reserved for Ayla, for forcing him into a promise that he could not keep since she had not bothered to teach her daughter to rein in her temper and recognize the consequences of her actions. But those were diminished in the face of the rage that made him wish he could do to these Faeries exactly what Cerridwen had done to Bauchan.

"What is this? Is this some sort of joke?" The Human looked to Cedric on the ground, at Cerridwen, and back to the green Faery. He recognized her as the representative of the Fae. Cedric ground his teeth.

The green Faery straightened her long back and tossed her matted hair over her shoulder. "This is no joke, Human. Bauchan is dead. Killed by these traitors. And we will punish them as we see fit."

"Bauchan owes me money," the Human said. How like a Human, to be unconcerned with anything but monetary gain. "Is this a trick?"

"You will be paid," the green Faery spat. "Do not trouble yourself with that worry."

The Human's gaze moved over Cedric and Cerridwen again, and he flicked nervous eyes back to the green Faery's face. "I can't have any nastiness aboard my ship, you understand? What's to stop their people from coming after me if they die here?"

"They have no 'people.'" The green Faery sneered down at Cedric. "They will not be missed."

The cold efficiency in her voice told Cedric that she truly believed this, and he could no longer idly watch. "You can explain to your Queene, then, why she has been denied her prize."

The green Faery turned flashing eyes toward him. "Have I asked you to speak?"

"You know that Danae would not permit the death of the Faery Queene. Not when she could parade her in chains for her own pleasure."

The Faery's eyes narrowed. Her lips pursed. She said nothing.

"Queene?" The Human frowned. He'd lost control of the situation when he'd lost the green Faery's attention, and he aimed to get it back. "This one here is a Queene?"

"A Pretender Queene," the green Faery snapped.

"Queene of the Faery Court, descended from the line of Queene Mabb." This would mean nothing to the Human, Cedric realized. A bolt of inspiration struck him. "One of your Human poets told of her. Shakespeare? Do you know what I speak of?"

The man made a noise, which was neither an affirmation or denial. It did not matter to Cedric which it was, because now the Human's focus was trained on him. "She killed Bauchan?"

Cedric nodded gravely. "She did. He committed a great offense against her, and it was her royal right."

"Liar!" The green Faery struck his cheek with a stinging slap.

Moving faster than Cedric had ever seen another Human move, the man stepped between them and grabbed the green Faery's arm. She hissed and thrashed and spat, but he kept ahold of her. "There's going to be none of that!" he roared, pushing her backward. She stumbled against the rail of the stairs and glared up at him. "This is my ship, and if anyone's going to be dealt with, it'll be me doing the dealing. Understand?"

The man considered Cedric for a moment, then turned his attention to Cerridwen. "She hurt?"

"I do not know," Cedric answered truthfully. If she was, he would make those who had done it pay.

The Human nodded to his crew. "Get her up. Check her over. Then throw her in the brig."

Cedric did not know what a brig was. "She cannot be separated from me."

"Fine. You go, too." The Human gestured to another man. "Take him, too."

"And when we arrive at our destination?" The green Faery climbed to her feet, still seething. "Will they be returned to our custody?"

"Once you are off my ship, I don't care what you plan on doing with them. So long as I get my money." He nodded to Cedric and Cerridwen. "Get them out of here. And the rest of you, clear off."

Cedric locked eyes with the green Faery. Hatred and malice blazed in her eyes.

If they were friendless before, he realized, things had become far worse for them.

Five

~⚬⚬⚬~

Clouds covered the sun, made the world a gray-white that was neither night nor day, but a perpetual in-between time that pricked the edges of consciousness as though in warning. Mist shrouded the floor of the clearing, as if the forest had come to life and exhaled too-warm breath into the chill air.

Blinking as she strained to see through the sinuous vapor, Cerridwen rose from the grass, felt the cool, wet air envelope her as though she'd dived into a pool.

A dark shape materialized in the mist, growing more distinct as it moved toward her. It was a female, a Human female, or so Cerridwen thought until she saw its face, flanked by two identical ones on either side of its head. The thing that was not a woman, but three in one body. It wore a long cloak of black feathers that rustled in a breeze Cerridwen could not feel. Beneath the blanket of feathers, metal armor glinted. Tall, armored boots rose past the woman's knees. In her hand, she carried a spear tall enough to touch the ground at her feet and rise above her head, the gleaming silver of it stained with rust-colored rivulets of dried blood. Under her arm, she carried a helmet of silver, shaped like the head of a raven and so finely detailed that it must have come from the Court of the Gnomes. A strip of feathers rose from the crown of the helmet and spilled down its back in a mimic of the hair on the woman's head, which was shaved but for a knot of ebony in the center that fell in a gleaming tail behind her.

It spoke with all of its mouths at once. "Do you enjoy killing?"

An aura of menace surrounded the thrice-faced woman, but it did not touch Cerridwen, and she spoke without fear. "I do not enjoy it. But it was necessary."

The head nodded, all six eyes closing in slow appreciation. "This is a lesson many warriors take time to learn."

"I am no warrior." It embarrassed her to be called such, after seeing the bravery displayed by the Guild members in the fight at the Elven quarter.

"You are a warrior." The answer brooked no quarrel. "You have blood on your hands, three times, blood on your hands."

More than three times. This woman with three faces did not know that she stood before the Faery who had destroyed her own kind, killed her own mother and father through her foolishness. She did not need a blade to kill.

The three mouths continued to speak in unison. "The blood of your enemies. The dark one. The traitor. The deceiver."

The Elf, and Flidais, and Bauchan. "They all had to die."

"I will grant you a boon." The woman dropped her spear and used a finger to trace the symbol of three spirals, connected in a triangle, the same as Cerridwen had seen in her dreams, in the air. Mist conformed to the shape, twisted into something more tangible. It turned to fire and steel, cooled to a stone and dropped into the woman's open palm. She held it out, as if offering it, but when Cerridwen reached for it, she turned with sudden violence and threw it into the trees. It was lost in the mist and the darkness on the forest floor.

"Why did you do that?" Cerridwen cried, feeling entitled to the thing that had not been hers a moment before, had not even existed.

The woman shrugged, three bland expressions on her faces. "You will find it when you need my aid, and I will come." She turned and walked toward the darkness of the trees, the fog clearing like courtiers bowing out of the way for their ruler to pass. She halted and cocked her head so that one face looked back, shrewd eyes looking Cerridwen up and down. "Wake up, Sister. Wake up."

Cerridwen woke to darkness. There was a disconcerting moment in which she did not remember what had happened, and then the memory returned, horrible in its clarity.

She had killed Bauchan. She had done the right thing. No one would convince her otherwise. But when they'd seized her…when they'd hit her, the last thing she'd heard was Cedric, shouting her name.

Her hands were bound, but she tried to grope through the darkness, her breath coming faster and faster as she remembered the words that had drifted to her through her semiconscious fog. They had wanted to execute her, and Cedric; and the Humans had been concerned only with money.

"Cedric!" The panic she felt overrode any thought to what dangers might befall her if they discovered her awake and alive. If they had killed him—

"I am here." The sentence was cool and perfunctory, no attempt to comfort or reassure her.

But he did not sound damaged, and that outweighed any concern she might have had for his demeanor. "Where are we?"

"We are in a prison."

Had she slept that long? "They've taken us off the ship, then?"

"We are in a prison *on* the ship." His words seemed to come from behind clenched teeth.

Vaguely, she remembered him chasing after her, shouting for her to stop, but her head ached and she did not want to examine her actions, or his reactions to them, now. "Why would someone need a prison on their ship?"

There was a rustling in the darkness, and the sound painted a picture in her mind of Cedric, wriggling against his bonds in an effort to free himself.

"Perhaps in the event that someone loses all sense and reason and murders a fellow passenger?"

Absorbing that anger, she said softly, "You could have stopped me."

A spot of red flared in the blackness. His antennae. The illumination gave her a clearer idea of where he was. Close to her, but not close enough to touch if she stretched out her bound hands. He sat upright, and the red glinted off the metallic surface of the wall behind him. In the glow, she could see the top of his head, but nothing else, none of his expression.

It was probably best that way. "You could have stopped yourself! You must learn, *Your Majesty,* that only you are responsible for your actions. Your stupid, rash actions!"

Though he meant to chastise her, she could not feel guilt over her actions. She ran the moment of Bauchan's death through her mind once, twice, a third time. Her palms remembered the vibration of the blade in her hands as it sank into Bauchan's body. The scent of his blood, dried onto her skin like war paint, tainted each breath. It had all been real, and it had all been her doing. But she could not lament it.

"I take responsibility for what I did. Of course, I do. But you must have wanted him dead, as well. He knew the one thing that you did not want him to know. His death must be a great relief to you."

"A relief? To be imprisoned?" His voice rose in pitch, almost comical in his outrage.

"A relief, because now we are safe when we arrive at Danae's Court. Bauchan can tell no one what he heard!" They were not safe from execution for murdering Bauchan. How to avoid punishment for that still escaped her.

Metal thudded dully. Cedric had kicked the floor in frustration. "There were other ways, ways that might not have gotten us killed!"

"Bauchan could not have been bought." As if struck by lightning, a realization came upon her. "No one can truly be bought. If they are willing to trade their loyalty for gold or power, someone will always have a better offer."

"So, all enemies must die, is that what you're saying?" Cedric's bitter chuckle sounded as though it would gag him. "I had no idea you were so naive."

If he had looked into her most private fears, he could not have found words more able to wound her. "I did what had to be done!"

"Yes, I'm sure Danae will accept that at our trial—if she bothers to have one!"

Their anger filled the silence with hollow, rasping breaths. As if she'd brought that coiling, insidious mist with her from the dream world, something nebulous expanded in her, pushed out words that did not need to be said. "What do you think Danae will do to me? Imprison me? Execute me? Permit her to do it! I would welcome anything that would take this burden from me!"

"A burden you created!" he snapped back.

At once, the heady vapor that had fueled her rage fled her. She was empty, nothing but a husk of sorrow again. She'd forgotten that she'd felt this way before the exhilaration of Bauchan's murder. Would it always take being the instrument of death to fill that void she'd created? She'd felt at peace again when she killed Flidais, but it had not lasted. And the Elf, that death had given her the illusion of putting things to right. With each death, the wound in her grew deeper, and the balm did not deaden the pain as long as it had before.

Cedric had heard her restrained crying, and a soft, masculine sigh rumbled between them. He did not apologize for what he'd said; no Fae would recant what they believed to be a true statement, not if they valued the sentiment of it too much. Instead, he said, "You would not welcome death."

"You cannot know what greeting I would give such a sentence." *You did not kill your family with your deception.*

"I should not have laid all of the blame on you." A thud, a rustle. He tried to move closer. "You are to blame, for some. But there were more lies at work than a Faery no older than twenty could have dreamed up on her own. You may have hastened the end, but you weren't the only instrument in that respect, either."

The noise of his movements continued. He was nearly beside her now, but she held still. She would not meet him. "It is easier to blame myself for my part, than to point a finger at those who were ultimately wronged most."

She felt the heat of him beside her, and she wanted to lean on him, to feel the reassuring presence of him against her body. But he'd hurt her, and he'd been so angry only moments ago. She could not use him as her refuge now, as she had in the nights since they'd come aboard the ship.

"There are so many things that are not in our control in our lives. We cannot hold ourselves responsible for them." He sighed and leaned back on the wall. "You killed Bauchan, and Flidais. You lied to your mother. But your lies did not make Flidais betray her. You did not make Bauchan come to the Court with ill intent. You did not loose the Waterhorses upon our people."

She rocked herself from side to side, tried to sit up, but the motion yielded no result save for exhausting her. She lifted her head and tentatively laid it in his lap. She did not want to take such comfort in him if she had no guarantee that they would not part once things had been settled with the Upworld Queene. And she did not wish to admit that that knowledge frightened her more than any sentence that Queene Danae could pass against her.

"You say that, because it is easy for you to say it and feel that you've done me some service by your words." Her breath heated the fabric of his robe beneath her cheek. "But if I said them to you, you would not believe them."

"I have nothing that I blame myself for," he answered too quickly, with too much false confidence. "I am fulfilling my vow."

"To me." She did not know where these words came from, for she could not have thought them herself. "You fear that you failed someone else."

He took in a sharp breath, and the muscle of his thigh tightened beneath her cheek. "Who told you such a thing?"

"No one told me anything, explicitly. But I could read the truth of it in your face as you gazed on the water." A sudden, cold shock proved it. "You looked at it as though it were your enemy. You gazed into the depths as if you hated and feared it, but could not look away from it."

He took another breath, ragged, as though he held back with great effort something that he would not allow to be heard out loud. It was a struggle he could not win.

When he spoke, it was from a place as shrouded in fear as the clearing from her dream. But this time, the dread did touch her, so palpable was it in his words.

"The night I came to you, when I…fulfilled my promise to tell you of what transpired in your mother's Council…" He halted, swallowed audibly. "You were not the only one to have a Darkworld lover. There was a woman, a Gypsy woman. She was a girl, really, perhaps younger than you. I never asked, and she never told me. They are timeless, ageless, her people. At least, they seemed so. She had asked me to go with her, to flee the Underground and stay with her always…."

The words struck her like a weapon she did not see coming, and the wound in her deepened, split anew by the pain in his voice. If her hands were not bound, she would have covered her ears to keep from hearing, for she knew what would come next.

And, as if knowing that his own sorrow would cut her to her core, he sharpened his words, formed them carefully and slowly. Perhaps he said them for the first time. "All of her people were killed. By Waterhorses. And her, as well. I left you that night and found them slaughtered."

Her mouth was thick, as though the moisture there had fled to become the tears that filled her eyes. "If you had not come to me, would you—"

"No!" He threw the word down like a gauntlet. "You cannot blame yourself for their deaths. You cannot involve yourself in it, and do not play at it as though you could possibly share my pain!"

She squeezed her eyes shut, let a tear fall. Not because she believed she had any connection, no matter how superficial, to his tragedy, but because in her connection to him his hurt was too much to bear witness to.

"Anyway," he began, softer now, "it was too late. They had been dead for some time."

Striving to keep the sound of her tears from intruding, she said, "I am sorry. Not because I imagine myself a part of your pain, but because it hurts me, to see it hurt you."

"Empathy is a Human gift. Cherish it." In the silence, his heartbeat was audible, and fast. "As I cherish it in you."

The sentiment was so intimate, it shocked her. The cold slap of recognition she'd received before repeated itself, a battering ram of truth against all she thought she knew. If they had not been bound, he would have put his arms around her. Kissed her? She thought so. If he could have, he would have touched her, and it would not have been out of obligation to his *geis,* or to keep up an appearance of their false betrothal.

Her heart hammered against her ribs, and something quivered there, beat itself against her from the inside. She was too conscious of her breathing, too aware of her closeness to him. She clenched her thighs against the crude, primal ache that flooded the space between them, and prayed silently, *No, do not let me feel this. Not now. I cannot bear it, and I cannot be trusted.*

"Cerridwen." His voice was low and dark, meant to be spoken much closer to her, as the maddening inches of separation closed up between them. But it could not be that way, and it seemed futile to hear him now. "Cerridwen," he said again, and then was silenced as the little room flooded with light.

The door scraped open, but her eyes were still blinded when the Human entered. "On your feet. You're going ashore."

Six

❧━━━∽❀∽━━━❧

Faeries lined the corridors as the Humans marched Cedric and Cerridwen out of their prison. They wore expressions of smug hatred, of ill intent. Some of pity. They felt sympathy *now?*

The door they had entered the night of their arrival was open. Through the portal, Cedric glimpsed sky, and farther, over the expanse of sea, a thin, blue-gray line on the horizon. Land. *Éire.*

Recognition of the place beat through him. It was a shimmering jewel, a cradle of magic. It was not his home, not the only place that held magic, but it drew them all there, to the place the Old Gods chose as their throne on Earth.

They pushed Cerridwen ahead of him, toward the open door. She dug her heels in, and the Human behind her laughed. "Time to go, sweetheart," he cackled, and pushed her through the door.

Cedric broke free from the hands holding him,

fueled by a morbid flash of memory that replaced Dika's drowned face with Cerridwen's, blue and pale beneath the water.

"Don't worry, you're going, too," said the Human who'd pushed Cerridwen out. Hands seized him again, and he saw through the door that the surface of the water was dotted with boats. In the one directly below the door, a Faery helped Cerridwen to stand, and the craft rocked from side to side. One shove, and Cedric fell, as she had, crashing to the floor of the wooden craft.

"Human slime!" The Faery in the boat shouted up at the ship as she helped Cedric to his feet, as well. She turned to him, violet eyes wide with empathy. "Are you all right?"

"You would know, as well as I," Cedric said, nodding.

"You recognize me for what I am." The Faery tossed matted, sand-colored ropes of hair over her shoulder. Her skin color matched; she looked like a stretch of desert landscape, amethyst eyes nestled in the dunes. "That's good. Proves you haven't become totally Human, living below them."

He opened his mouth to tell her that Humans had treated him far better than his own kind, of late, but Cerridwen spoke before he could. "What does she mean, you recognize her? Have you been to Queene Danae's Court before?"

The Faery's sly eyes moved from Cedric to Cerridwen and back, a smirk bending her lips. *Proceed carefully, Cerridwen,* he willed silently. "She is an

Empath. It is a gift some Faeries receive, the ability to feel the emotions of others. Right now, she can feel our fear, and our confusion."

"Among other things." The Empath darted her hand out, faster than a lightning strike, and grasped his wrist. "Your anger. You do not like me."

"You have not made a very good impression." He nodded to Cerridwen. "Guard yourself. Danae would not have sent this one without a reason."

The Faery smiled; she admired him now. He did not need the gift of Empathy to tell him that. She glanced at their bound hands, then turned back to the ship. "You have given me prisoners. Where is Bauchan?"

A Human sailor leaned out of the door, scratching his head below the brim of his knit cap. "Dead. Them killed him."

The Empath turned, her face twisted in anger. "Is this true?"

"We will discuss the matter with your Queene, and no one else," Cedric said, seating himself on the narrow bench in the middle of the boat.

"You will tell me, or I will dash your brains into the sea!" She raised the oar she held, as if preparing to make good her word.

Cerridwen still stood, and she did not shrink at the threat. "He speaks for me, and you will not harm him."

The Faery sneered. "And who are you, who addresses her captor so?"

Cerridwen's back straightened. If her hands had not been bound, she would have looked almost royal. "I am Queene Cerridwen of Mabb's lineage, descended from Queene Ayla and King Garret, brother of Mabb, daughter of the first Faery Queene and King."

The Faery's expression did not change, and she turned to Cedric. "No wonder she is so afraid."

The Empath said no more as she slid the oar through the water and pulled the boat away from the ship, to the other side of the congregation of vessels.

Though she put up a brave front, sitting still and straight on the seat beside him, Cedric could sense Cerridwen's fear. The Empath could likely taste it. He had to take her mind off that fear, replace it with some new emotion.

Just as he needed to take his own mind off the traitorous feelings he'd experienced in the Humans' prison cell. He nudged her with his shoulder and nodded toward the land in the distance. "Do you see that? Those cliffs, and the beach below?"

Cerridwen nodded mutely.

"That is the scene of a very important battle. The last battle against the Human invaders on Éire." He glanced quickly at the Empath, and saw that she studied him with suspicion. "You have seen the tapestry of Amergin's defeat of the Tuatha De Danann in your mother's Throne Room?"

"I did not pay attention to the tapestries," Cerridwen said flatly.

"You should have," he said, jovial, as if they were on their way to a pleasant destination and not a likely execution. "You would have learned something."

She stared at him as though he'd gone mad.

"You see, those cliffs, right there, are the very same

cliffs that the Mílseans approached in their boats when they came to avenge the death of Ith." He paused, remembering the approach of those boats as if it had been only a few years before. He'd been young then, excited to be a part of Queene Banbha's Court, and ready to fight the fragile Humans who sought to take their land. If he had known then that it would not be the first time he would defend his race from Humans, that there would be a time in the future, under a much different Queene, he would not have relished the battle so. "When the battle terms were drawn, it was agreed that Amergin would lead his ships nine wave lengths from the shore, to give the De Danann time to assemble their forces. To give them a fair chance. When they returned at the agreed upon time, we raised such a storm as you could not imagine."

"I cannot imagine any storm. I was born underground," she reminded him sullenly. Then, as if resigned to her history lesson, she asked, "What happened then?"

"The Old Gods were not with us that day. Amergin charmed them with his words, and they gave over the battle to him." The failure stung as much as the failure to contain the Humans underground, hundreds of years later.

The Empath slapped the water with her oar, startling them both. "Liar!"

"Were you there?" he asked, knowing that she had not been. He remembered the faces of each and every Faery that had stood on those cliffs. "If you were not, how can you know the tale in its truth?"

She brandished the oar like a weapon. "The Fae are never defeated! Queene Danae will not tolerate such insolence!"

Young, then. Perhaps younger than Cerridwen, if she was so naive as to believe revised history from a false ruler. He let her feel pity, twisted with disdain for her foolishness. "The Fae have been defeated before. Many times, in cities all around the world. They have been forced underground, like rats. You might choose to ignore that, but that does not make your delusions true."

She cursed and beat the oar against the side of the boat, but she did not pursue the matter further.

"Listen to the wind, and the water," Cedric said softly, recapturing Cerridwen's attention. The fear in her made her eyes dark, the rapid beat of her heart visible in the black pools within them. "They will tell you so much here."

She shook her head. "They have never spoken to me before. Why should they now?"

"Because you were never here before. This place is magic. There is not magic in it. It *is* magic." He closed his eyes and saw the winds, shimmering, rose-colored, as they twined playfully together above the waves, which stabbed up, more blue than any color he could have seen with his eyes, as though they sought to steal the sky's place above the horizon. And, in the distance, the green of Éire, pulsing like a beating heart. "Can you not feel it?"

When he opened his eyes, he saw that hers were closed. Her sightless face lifted to the sky, and her eyelids, creased with concentration, smoothed as her mouth curved into a smile. "Yes!" She looked at him, stars of amazement replacing the fear in her eyes. "Yes, I can feel it!"

"Enjoy it," the Empath snapped. "You will not have a chance once Queene Danae passes sentence on you."

Cedric concentrated on his annoyance, so that the Faery would feel it, and not realize that he knew she was right.

It seemed they waited hours in the blinding sunlight for the rest of the Faeries to depart from the Human ship. They squeezed into the boats, five, six of them, with all of their belongings, so that the carved wooden hulls dipped low in the water.

"They will fly, once they are close enough to the shore," Cedric had told Cerridwen when she expressed her concern at this. "Some of them have not flown for hundreds of years, and will not pass up the opportunity."

She watched as the Faeries who had come aboard as her guard retinue jumped down to the boats, bearing packs on their backs. She wondered how much of what she had brought aboard had been recovered, but it seemed a small concern, knowing they would likely die for her actions. Once all of the Faeries were off the ship, the boats began to move, theirs leading the procession, toward the land in the distance.

The boat she and Cedric occupied was much the same as the other boats, carved from wood so thick that it appeared as though it should be too heavy to float, with intricate designs of chains and knot work etched into the surface. The center scooped low to the surface of the water, and the two ends rose up into high, curved points. They looked like something out of the tapestries in the Palace. She had paid attention to them, though she would not admit it to Cedric. In truth, she'd wiled away many hours staring at the picture-stories of the heroes who'd come from the island they now approached, and she felt a particular shame at coming to the place as a prisoner.

The boats cut through the water with surprising speed, considering that only one Faery manned the oars in each. The water grew more treacherous as they came nearer to the land, and each wave tossed them a bit higher before dropping them down again. Keeping her balance became difficult, with her arms bound.

Cedric did not appear to be having the same difficulty. "Lean against me," he said quietly, and she complied, though not just for the stability. His wings rustled and snapped open, providing surprising strength at her back, as fragile as they appeared.

"I don't want to break you," she whispered, laying her head against his shoulder. She closed her eyes. It intensified the feeling of rising and falling as they battled the waves, but it was less disorienting.

He chuckled at that. "You will not break me. And if you did, it would not be worse than if you fell into the sea."

A phantom of what she'd felt in the prison cell teased at her. She'd been so sure then that he had been close to disclosing something, something that she did not wish to hear. Now, that seemed foolish, and egotistical of her to think that…that what? That he had fallen in love with her? So soon after losing his Human love? After the Faery Court had been destroyed? How stupid, to think that anyone had time for something so frivolous as love.

And how stupid to believe that, even if they were in the Underground, and they were truly mates, he would love her, anyway. She was a spoiled child. He was wise, anciently so. He would have no reason to feel that way toward her.

Even less so now that she had all but condemned them to death.

The feeling that someone was watching her pricked the back of her head, and she turned to find the Empath's piercing violet eyes fixed on her. She knew. Cerridwen's heart dropped to her stomach and she turned away, mind racing with panic that was only made worse by the knowledge that the Empath felt it, too. Was nothing safe?

She forced her mind to what lay ahead, but tried to view it with cool and calm. When they arrived, there was sure to be some sort of trial. She had never had to address a Queene who was not her mother. That might work in her favor. If she were to die, she would like to do so with a dignity she could paradoxically muster through youthful impertinence, and that dignity would likely contribute to a death sentence, as it would be gained by not cowering in the face of a False Queene. But it had not been Cedric's hand that had wielded the dagger that killed Bauchan. He should not be punished, but her angry words might condemn him, as well. Or, according to her own logic, being seen as an enemy, Cedric would likely be killed in any event.

She wished there were some way to communicate with him, some moment they could have alone to plan what was to come. It was almost certain they would not have that time.

The Empath shook her head and shot an angry glare at them. "Enough of your confusion! Can your simple minds comprehend anything?"

"She is angry because her gift cannot be turned off as she wishes," Cedric said with a smirk. "Whatever you are feeling overwhelms her."

"As if you are not feeling the same as she is right now." The Empath turned back to her rowing, her head held high.

"I am not." Cedric spoke with such certainty that Cerridwen was left with no doubt. He knew what she felt for him, and he did not reciprocate those feelings.

The land in the distance grew steadily from a gray line to a gray line that radiated green above and gold below, finally coming into shape before Cerridwen's eyes. The cliffs looked more like wood than rock, grained as they were with lines of different color. The dominant gray layered with shimmering tan, brilliant white, and the dull green of wet moss. Dots of black flickered over the surface of the cliffs in some places, and Cerridwen rubbed her eyes. "What is that?" she asked, wishing she could point, not caring how childlike that would seem.

"A bird that nests in the rocks." Cedric looked down at her with an expression of sadness. "Much different than the ones you would have seen in the Underground."

It was as if it had struck him just now that she had never been in the Upworld, had never seen animals beyond those companions to the Humans in the Underground. She was not certain if she should be pleased by this ability to surprise him, or just embarrassed. She did not like to appear foolish, but somehow, it seemed she should not feel foolish when it was him noticing how little she knew about the world above.

An unexpected pang of sadness came over her. She had expected to be separated from him when they reached the Upworld settlement. Had looked forward to it, even. But she had not foreseen that it would be so painful, so terribly lonely.

It was almost a comfort that she would probably be put to death. She thought she might prefer that to being cast into this new world alone.

It seemed there would be no place for the boats to land. What had appeared at first to be a beach was quickly swallowed up by the water. "The tide has come in," the Empath said, whether to them or herself, Cerridwen could not tell. "We must increase our pace."

"I am sorry, but I cannot help you," Cedric replied serenely. "Perhaps if you untied us—"

"Untie him!" Cerridwen shouted, too eager, she knew in hindsight. She swallowed and licked her lips, tried to calm the hysteria she felt. "He did not kill Bauchan. It was my hand that held the blade. He is no danger to you."

"Cerridwen—" Cedric began, but something in his face registered that he suspected she might have thought her action through, no matter how quickly those thoughts would have had to have come.

Trust me, she pleaded with him silently. *Just trust me.*

He stopped himself and turned to present his bound hands to the Empath. "She speaks the truth. If you wish to reach the beach before the tide comes in, I suggest you cut me free."

After a reluctant moment, she did, setting aside the oar and pulling a sharpened stone blade from the belt at her waist. Her hand moved fast, imprecise, and Cedric winced. When he brought his freed hands in front of him, blood dripped from a slice along his arm.

But he was free.

If they walked into the settlement bound as prisoners, neither of them would be heard, not in seriousness, and both of them would face the executioner. If Cedric were free, walking straight and tall, trusted by someone who was obviously important to the Queene—important enough to retrieve Bauchan—he might save himself. A wild part of her dared to hope he might be able to save her, as well.

Cedric reached for her and pulled her to sit on the floor of the craft, so that she would not pitch over the side as they rowed over the increasingly hostile waves. She met his gaze as he did, urging him silently once again to trust her, and, as if understanding, he nodded.

They sped for the beach, tossing more perilously with every stroke of the oars. Before, it seemed the waves carried them closer to shore. Now, they prevented them from coming closer.

"We have reached the ninth wave!" the Empath shouted as a violent swell broke over the front of the boat. Above them, the sky turned to menacing darkness.

"Look!" Cerridwen shouted, at once afraid of and enthralled by the surge of power that split the sky like white fire. "Cedric, look!"

"Lightning," he called back to her. *"Éire welcomes you home!"*

As if he had forgotten about the death sentences that hung over them, he turned his face to the sky, and lifted his arm in greeting, waving to the black clouds that boiled through the air like ink in water.

No, not to the clouds, she saw as she followed his gaze. A figure, robed in white, stood on the cliff above, waving back.

"It cannot be," Cedric said, gaping in amazement. The Empath gave him a distrustful, sidelong glare, but said nothing.

As quickly as they had risen, the clouds rolled back, following the exact pattern they had fanned out in. The waves calmed and died. The sea became as flat as glass, and the wind became so silent that the voice of the robed figure could be heard, even as far away as they floated. "Hurry! I cannot stop the tide forever! She is far too insistent today!"

"I cannot believe my eyes," Cedric said, taking up his oar with renewed fervor.

His excitement was not mimicked by the Empath. "Believe it. There are many of them. So many, we are overrun, even as we rule this island."

When they reached the shallow waters near the beach, Cedric and the Empath jumped out, splashing into the sea up to their knees to pull the boat ashore. Thick chains protruded from the bottom of the cliff, and they strained to pull the craft over the sand.

"This is far enough," the Empath said, out of breath. She attached a chain to the boat while Cedric lifted Cerridwen out and set her feet in the sand.

She stumbled as she took her first steps, the strange sinking of the ground beneath her feet throwing her off her balance.

"Go slowly," Cedric advised quietly, while the Empath was distracted. "You'll get used to it soon enough."

She lifted her eyes to the cliff face. "How will we get up there, to the land?" She hoped they did not expect her to fly.

Cedric nodded to a crack in the rock. "There is a path, through the cliffs. It will keep us hidden, if there are any Human Enforcers about."

"There are no free Humans on Éire," the Empath snapped. She jerked her head toward the cliff. "But yes, we will walk."

The other Faeries had landed, as well, and a steady stream of them crushed around Cerridwen and Cedric as they passed under the narrow, pointed arch of the crevice in the cliff. The Empath shuddered as the cool darkness passed over them, but for the first time in days, Cerridwen was able to breathe freely. The damp air, tinged with salt and the clean smell of the sea, was not like the air at home, in the Underground, but it was close enough. At times, the walls allowed only enough room for them to walk two-abreast on the upward-sloping path.

In the dark, Cedric's arm slipped around her waist and pulled her close to his side. She peered through the blackness, aided by the yellow light from her antennae, the blue from his. He stared straight ahead, expression grim. All the joy of the sea and sky that she had witnessed had disappeared from him, once he was underground again.

They walked for a long time, until the sand beneath their feet gave way to rock, and then, inexplicably, to soil. The incline became sharper; with her hands tied, Cerridwen leaned into Cedric's hold, dependent on him to keep her from slipping down. The darkness abated as they went, misty light creeping up around them, until they reached the end of the tunnel and stood once again under the open sky, through another crack in the earth directly above their heads.

Two boulders with little space between them jutted from the earthen walls; with surprising speed, the Empath darted from one to the other, up and out of the hole.

Cerridwen looked up at Cedric, saw his fair brow crease as he worked out the problem of how to get her out, as well. But then the Empath's face appeared at the hole, and her reaching arms. "Hand her up to me," she ordered.

Cedric gripped Cerridwen at the waist and tossed her up, catching her around the knees as she wobbled precariously in his grasp. The Empath took her by the shoulders and dragged her out of the opening, scraping her along the rocks as she did so. Once she was free, the Empath tossed her down like a sack of flour and walked away.

"Let me help you," a kind voice spoke at her side, and she looked up, into the lined face of a Human male. His features were dissimilar from Malachi's, but, at the same time, very similar, as though all mortals must look alike. He had the same patches of white at his temples that Malachi had had, but his dark hair was more coarse, his face less handsome.

Cedric had emerged from the tunnel mouth and rushed to her side. "Are you all right?" Seeing the Human, his mouth split into a wide grin. "Amergin. How have you returned?"

"The same way that you could." The man's voice was deep and gravely. "When the Veil split, I wound up here, the same as you."

Cedric's brow furrowed. "Did it happen to all of you?"

"Only those of us worshipped as heroes." He gave his answer without embarrassment, but there was no pride in it, either. "You have brought a prisoner?"

"We are both prisoners, actually. The Empath cut my bonds so that I could help row us ashore." He lifted his wrist and displayed the slashed skin there. "None too gently, I am afraid. But I hope to lose the impression of captivity before we meet Queene Danae."

He said it as though it were his idea. Cerridwen fumed silently at his nerve. She tried to make herself taller, more imposing, to the Human. "I am Queene Cerridwen of the lineage of Mabb, descended from Queene Ayla and King Garret, brother to—"

The Human spoke over her, as though he had some authority where Faeries were concerned. "My, but you have the look of your grandmother about you."

In the moment that Cerridwen's mouth hung agape at the Human's disrespect, Cedric said, "This is Amergin, son of Míl. Known as the White Knee to the Fae."

"Do not be stupid," she snapped, irritated at suddenly being treated like a child once more. Amergin, the one that Cedric had told her of on the boat over, would have died centuries before. "It is impossible, he would have to be—"

"Immortal?" The man's cheerful brown eyes sparkled. "I am Amergin, the very same who turned a storm to calm with my words and came to steal Éire from the Tuatha. Such deeds turn to legend, child, and legend can make a man immortal." His expression turned serious as a group of Faeries approached them. "For all the good it does me now."

The four Fae that surrounded them were all male, all dressed in rough garments, their matted hair bound in tails that fell down their backs.

The Empath did not greet them, but addressed them with orders. Her clothing, Cerridwen saw, was the same as the guards, but hers, embellished with shells and stones, marked her out as superior to them.

"Those two are prisoners. Take them to Queene Danae immediately. The female claims to be Queene of the Underground Court." Her cold purple eyes raked over Cerridwen. "She killed Bauchan."

"Good girl," Amergin said under his breath.

One of the soldiers pushed her, indicating she should walk. Cedric and Amergin walked ahead of her, neither of them sparing her a glance as they followed the guards that led them.

"How far?" Cedric asked Amergin, and the Human shrugged. "We will not reach her until night-fall."

Tired, her feet aching, Cerridwen tripped over the stony ground. She glanced up. She had learned a little at sea about the way the sun moved through the sky, and it was not near dark, nor would it be for some time.

Miserably, she watched as Cedric and Amergin moved on. A guard at her back shoved her. "Go," he commanded gruffly, and she forced her feet to move, resigned that her loneliness and fear would be her only friends on this trek.

Seven

By nightfall, they had traveled far inland. The landscape was different now than the last time Cedric had seen it. That had been before the last war with the Humans. Buildings, and their burned-out shells, had stood abandoned by the Humans driven off Éire. By now, those places had crumbled back to the Earth. Coarse grass and scrub had grown over the roads, pushing up the pavement and breaking it down into stone once more.

"The Humans never managed to keep their hold here," Amergin said beside him. "They reclaimed the East, but they have not managed to gain and keep the West."

"Since when?" If he did not look closely, Éire was as unspoiled as the day Amergin and the Mílseans had invaded.

"Since Danae led her forces here against them in the last war. She has a constant battle keeping them out, but she does it. Killed a hundred and forty Enforcers just two months ago. But she has done her best to keep Éire free in a way that the Humans were never able to." There was a grudging admiration in Amergin's voice that Cedric did not like. "She can thank me for that, at least in part."

"She is defending the isle magically, as in the days before your people? If I did not know better, I would think that you support this Queene who keeps you hostage." He glanced cautiously at the guards, but they did not listen. They were soldiers; they did not care for politics, so long as their side was winning.

"You assume I cared for your Queene, as well." Amergin sniffed, and then, apologetically, said, "I was sorry to hear of Mabb's death. Although we often found ourselves on opposite sides of an argument, I had nothing but respect for her. And I know how much she meant to you."

"She meant less, as years went by." He did not feel the need to explain further. Another Human might have taken such a blunt statement of Faery sentiment as a breach of etiquette. But Amergin had lived among the Fae, on the Astral Plane, not as a deceased Human, but as something in between Human and divine. He remembered what it was to be mortal, and would, Cedric recognized with some sadness, always believe he was Human, but he had broken past the barriers of that limited mind. He had the wisdom of the Old Gods, and would accept Cedric's words for what they were, not judge them by a Human standard or feel the need to respond.

"Your next Queene did not sit on her throne for long. Less than an eyelash's weight in time," Amergin mused. "And her King, far less than that. Was it terribly violent in the Underground?"

"Violent, yes." It was a shameful thing to admit. "Violence of our own making."

"If Mabb had not moved against the Humans so quickly, if she had not spread her forces so thin..." Amergin waved his hand. "Ah, but after Paris, there was no hope for any of us, was there?"

Cedric's mind wandered back to that time, in the city where the Humans had risen up from under the ground and overtaken the immortals who had put them there. And Mabb had been so certain of herself then.

"It was her vanity that trapped you, and kept you trapped," Amergin continued.

"As your new Queene keeps you trapped, old man," Cedric told him, putting a warning in his voice. It did not bode well for him, if even one so wise as the White Knee could be kept under Danae's thrall.

"And as *yours* keeps *you* trapped. You do not see it yet." Amergin increased his pace and walked on, as Cedric stopped, tried to find what it was in the man's words that bothered him so.

He looked back to Cerridwen. It had been torture to keep ahead of her, ignore her stifled sobs when the guards shoved her or when she tumbled onto the rocky ground. But it was for both of them that he did not go to her aid. If he were bound, treated like the prisoner he still was, no one would speak for him, perhaps not even Amergin, and then there would be no one to speak for her. If he could somehow move Danae to spare her…

It seemed more hopeless than it had before as he watched the seemingly endless line of Fae trooping across the hills they had already trod. Danae would be overwhelmed by so many coming to her for aid.

The loss of two would ease that burden somewhat. Even the loss of one. Yes, that was an argument she would never buy.

Cerridwen's robes were stained with blood from the many times she'd fallen to her knees. She walked hunched over, arms tied behind her, the picture of pain and defeat that Bauchan would have relished presenting to his Queene. He thought of Caesar parading the Gaul King around those eons ago. The Human Druids had not been pleased at that.

She looked up, caught his gaze, and the accusation of betrayal in her face pierced through him. For a moment, it seemed so real that he almost went to her. Then, he remembered the Empath. Was it possible that Cerridwen played a role to trick the Fae spy?

He knew then what Amergin had meant, and he had known it since he had knelt with her beside Malachi as he died, watching her become something other than what she had been when she had run to the Darkworld. In that tunnel, he had seen a glimmer of something in her that he could care for. Stupidly, he turned his back on that spark, and it had burst into flame, raging away at his defenses. He had not seen the damage until it was too great.

"Cedric, are you coming?" Amergin called, as

though he did not know what a profound revelation had been born from his words.

He knew. There was no way such a thing could have escaped his notice.

Again it took a strength Cedric actually found pride in to turn away from Cerridwen and not run to her aid.

She would forgive him for this. She would have to.

The old Druid had been correct when he'd said they would not reach the settlement until nightfall. He told the time almost as well as one of those shiny Human clocks Mabb had coveted. The evening star had only just appeared when they reached a copse of trees that Cedric did not remember.

"The old oak forest?" He reached out in wonderment to touch the bark of one of them, his agony over Cerridwen momentarily put aside. "But they were gone centuries ago!"

"As I was?" Amergin responded. "After the Humans were banished, the trees sprouted again, from nowhere. They thrived off the magic here, and now look at them. As if they'd never gone."

Under the canopy of the trees, the darkness was almost as thick as it had been inside the crevice of the cliff. There was no road and he resolved to go slowly, to find some excuse to stay closer to her, to keep any of their guards from exacting their own justice in the cover of the forest.

Anyone could go missing in the depths of the old oak forest, he realized with a shock. He could grab Cerridwen and disappear into the night before anyone would see them.

Just as he had the thought, a guard called out, "Torches!" and immediately the woods were illuminated with flames carried by Danae's soldiers. He had missed his chance. It was just as well. If what Amergin told him was correct—and it likely was—there would be no place on Éire that was not controlled by Faeries, and those Faeries would be controlled by Danae. He had to accept that they were trapped for now.

As they moved deeper into the forest, signs of inhabitance began to reveal themselves. Light appeared from torches planted in the ground. A sudden, crude road wound through the trees, and the shadows of bodies crossing it ahead of their party stretched impossibly tall on the ground. A cracking twig, and his gaze snapped to a slender Human slipping between the trees, a jug of water balanced on her shoulder.

"Humans? You said there were none to the East," Cedric said, keeping his voice low as he followed behind Amergin.

"I said they had not managed to keep a hold on the island." His jaw set hard, angry, the sharpness made more severe by the flickering torchlight. "They are slaves. They aren't even the children of Éire, mostly. Many of them came here, thinking the Fae would welcome them. It's as though they paid no attention to the events happening around them for the past two hundred years, preferring instead to believe what Humans have always believed about your kind."

Cedric did not have to ask what that was. Humans had believed, might always believe, that the Faery folk were harmless, mischievous…childlike. They took Human-drawn conclusions about the nature of Faeries and believed it as truth, made the Fae into a race of toothless, even friendly beings who wished nothing more than to enchant the lives of Humans.

He stamped down his rage as the water bearer passed by, unchained, unbranded. *"Slaves?"*

Amergin nodded, appreciation glittering in his shrewd eyes. "To their own desire to touch the beautiful, the favorites of the Gods."

The Humans deserved their fate, Cedric decided, but he would not say such a thing to Amergin, who yet had some feeling for the creatures. Although, it was ironic: the Fae emulated Humans, and the Humans worshiped the Fae. No wonder the Veil tore, with everyone clamoring to grab hold of beauty.

The road led to a village. The dwellings were simple, constructed out of wood, with thatched roofs. They were small and placed in groups of threes, each triad arranged around a common area with a fire and cooking pot. There was a familiar, unpleasant smell to the place.

"The Human quarter," Cedric said, and Amergin nodded, though he had not sought confirmation from him.

Humans, far too happy to be slaves, stopped in their nightly rituals to watch the new Faeries pour into their camp. Some of them cheered, others held children on their shoulders to see the spectacle.

"Is that the Faery Queene?" a Human male called to the guards. "The one who wants to take Danae's throne?"

Though he had not believed Bauchan's insistence that they had come to the Lightworld meaning no harm, the blatant confirmation of it turned Cedric's hands into stone fists and pushed every rational thought from his mind. It would take considerable willpower not to kill Danae with his bare hands.

He looked back to Cerridwen. The guards treated her more roughly now, shoving her more often, shouting at her, all a performance to bring the Humans to a frenzy. It had been Danae's plan to display her might over the Underground Faery Court by humbling Ayla, but she would be as satisfied with Cerridwen.

How humbling a beheading would be, he thought, and a chill raced up his back, between his wings.

The road forked many times as they followed it. Some paths snaked like serpentine tendrils across the dark forest floor, others lay as straight as though mapped by the angular shadows of the trees on the loam. Always, they stuck to the main road, past stretches of dark trees that gave way to an isolated Human dwelling now and again or the larger group configurations that seemed fairly common. Through the trees, a dome of light became visible. The heart of the encampment would be there, Cedric knew, and he held his breath. The moment was fast approaching, and he was not ready for it. He tried to calm his emotions; the Empath still followed them and would no doubt record every intercepted feeling to be used against them at their trial.

The village bore little resemblance to the Human homes they had passed. These were the Faery dwellings, the kind Cedric had lived in, the kind they had all lived in on the Astral Plane. The structures were little more than canopies of thatched panels anchored between trees, the walls fabrics of all kinds and colors draped from those. The light was different, too. Magical lights, Faery orbs, floated through the air, bathing the scene in gold. Fae hovered close to the ground, feet barely dragging the vegetation on the forest floor, while others flew and flipped through the air. Platforms ringed the trees, with more dwellings constructed on them, some stacked close on top of one another, high up in the leaves.

In the center of it all, that would be Danae's Palace. Before Mabb had decided to usurp a ridiculous amount of space in the Underground, before she had thought to imitate the grand and sprawling castles of the Humans above, this was the type of palace she, and her parents before her, had occupied.

It was a large structure, elevated from the forest floor on a low platform of split logs braced on the stumps of the trees harvested for the building. The platform was octagonal, as was the tent itself—and patched together from gauzy fabrics of numerous hues. The shapes of Faeries could be seen moving against the light within.

The Empath moved through their ranks, head held high. "Queene Danae! I have brought you prisoners!"

This was the moment that should have been Bauchan's. The Empath assumed his roll—and the credit for their presence—easily.

All motion in the tent ceased in a choreographed

display of surprise. Against the light, too intentionally bright inside the tent, a lone figure stood. Her profile was slender and graceful, and the other Faeries in her presence bowed, accentuating her tall, straight posture. She looked down, fingers steepled at her lips as though she composed herself, but the angle was so practiced that each of her fingers was made out against the light. A visible breath raised her chest, and she shook out her hair as she walked toward the door, her servants falling into place behind her.

Two sentries flanked the door to her Palace. They crossed the crude spears they carried, held them in a high point over the opening. "Her Majesty, Queene Danae," one of them barked out, his voice resonating to the treetops.

It was a show, her entrance absurdly theatrical and as rehearsed as anything he had ever seen in Mabb's Court.

Then, the Queene herself appeared.

Cerridwen beheld the spectacle of this new Faery Court through eyes rimmed red by exhaustion, dazzled by sights she could have never imagined and no tapestry could have ever rendered with such truth. She had walked through the forest lost in wonderment, forgetting the rope that bound her wrists and the near-certainty of death that lay ahead of her.

Until the moment that Queene Danae emerged from her odd structure.

Cerridwen's heart sank in despair when she saw her. The Queene looked every bit the part she acted.

She stood pale and straight, with dark curls that fell in long, unbrushed ropes beneath the gauzy veil she wore, held in place by a glittering silver circlet, like a medieval princess in a Human Faery story. Her wings spread behind her, vibrant orange framed in black, like the wings of the desiccated Upworld insect Governess had worn pinned in her hair. The vibrant gold of Danae's gown, tight sleeved and flowing simply from her shoulders in the style of that Faery-tale princess she evoked, lit the air around her with a warm aura.

She looked beautiful and kind, and her appearance was likely deceptive.

"Mothú? You are not accompanied by Bauchan?" A delicate lilt colored her voice, and her smooth brow lined only slightly as she frowned out at the crowd.

The Empath stepped forward, her stance triumphant. "No, my Queene. He is dead. Killed by this Pretender!"

"Killed?" Her voice was a delicately broken whisper. "No. It is not possible."

"It is." Mothú sneered. "Every Faery aboard the ship he traveled on saw his murder."

Cedric stepped out of the crowd to stand beside her. "That is not true."

"Who is this?" Danae asked, turning her dark eyes to Cedric.

The Empath did not seem to hear her. She strode toward Cedric, fists clenched. "*Liar!* Anyone here will attest to your involvement, as well! I have felt your panic. Not just for your mate, but for yourself."

"Silence!" Danae shouted. She never took her eyes from Cedric, as though she had been hypnotized by him. "Who is this Faery?"

"I am the former Court Advisor to the true Queene of the Fae, Queene Ayla, mate to King Garret. I am also the mate to this Faery, Queene Cerridwen, daughter of Queene Ayla of the line of Mabb." He gestured to the Faeries behind them. "These are her displaced subjects."

"Queene Ayla did not survive, then?" Danae spoke as though she had known her, as though she felt real remorse at the news of her death. It might have been a trick, but it seemed so genuine. Did a Faery exist who could care for someone or something sight unseen?

"This Faery killed Bauchan! There are witnesses!" Mothú cried, seeming less sure of her accusation as she looked from Cerridwen to her Queene.

"There are no witnesses," Cedric said calmly. "There are many who can attest to seeing Bauchan's empty robes, and the Queene beside them. But none can truly say what happened in that corridor."

Danae's questioning gaze, warm despite the suspicion that clouded it, fell on Cerridwen. "Is this true? Did no one see what happened?"

Cerridwen did not answer, because she knew that the question was not meant for her. And Cedric did not answer.

"Tell me," Danae said, scanning the Fae refugees that crowded the grove. "Can no one tell me that they saw her kill him?"

A ripple of outraged whispers went through the

crowd, until a lone voice shouted, "She admitted it! She confessed to the crime!"

"Is this true?" Still that pretended caring, that false kindness. "Did you kill Bauchan?"

Cerridwen's lies had never worked before. But then, why should she lie? She could not imagine a deed she was more proud of, or an action more warranted.

The hatred coming from the Fae from the Underground could scorch her flesh, so hot it burned. They had already forgotten who had kept peace in the Lightworld. The true Faery Queene. They had abandoned her, only twenty short years after they welcomed her onto her throne, only days after she perished while trying to protect them. Faithless, hopeless, pathetic traitors. Why should she wish to live among them a moment longer? And why should she care if they thought her a murderer? Were they not just as terrible, abandoning their fellows and her mother, who had served them so faithfully, who had struggled to keep them free of some foreign Queene's tyrannical rule?

Seeing her now, though, Danae did not look to be the tyrant Cedric and her mother had feared. Still, a kind appearance was not enough. Cerridwen had long heard how fearfully low the Humans were, how immoral and grasping. Yet her kind had fared no better.

She was not ashamed. She lifted her head and answered, loud enough so the entire clearing could hear her, "Yes. I killed Bauchan. He committed high treason against me. I sentenced him to death, and carried out his execution myself."

The moment of stunned silence that followed her declaration seemed to last longer than the lives of the trees stretching over their heads. Danae's face, so comically composed before, was frozen in shock, and her mouth hung open like the mouth of the fish on the Strip markets. She took a breath, looked almost as though she had regained her control, then lost it again to confusion.

Cerridwen could not look away from the Queene's eyes, but she could see, in her peripheral vision, Cedric had gone very still beside her. He did not move even to breathe.

Now would be the time that Danae would pronounce her guilty, and have her head sliced off. Those terrible words hovered unspoken in the air, like the ax blade poised to fall.

But Danae did not speak those words. She did not speak at all. She daintily lifted the hem of her gown and walked down the steps from her Palace, to stand in front of Cerridwen.

She was taller, only slightly, but enough to make Cerridwen feel like a child being treated as a fully grown Faery out of courtesy and pity. Danae closed her eyes and, with a shaking breath, threw her arms around Cerridwen's shoulders and embraced her.

It would have surprised her far less to be slapped or stabbed. Perhaps that was an indication of how diseased her own mind was, that she would not expect kindness. But when Danae's arms closed around her, Cerridwen's stomach dropped.

Danae stepped back, all pity and sweetness, her

gaze far too intense as it locked on hers. "I am sorry, Your Majesty, that my emissary caused you so much pain." Then, she bent her back in a sweeping bow.

The crowd seemed to gasp in unison, as Cedric let out a relieved breath. He was pleased to have delayed the inevitable. But her own heart was hollow.

She should have been relieved that Danae seemed almost certain to spare her. Perhaps it was that she was more shocked than the rest of them, and she could not yet believe it to be real. But when she searched her feelings, she found that she recognized the reality of the situation, and therein lay the real problem.

She had counted on dying. She had imagined an end to this empty feeling of displacement and grief. She had wanted to die. And that, more than any need to keep her secrets safe, more than a desire for revenge, had made her kill Bauchan.

If she crumpled to the ground now and wailed, what would they say?

Danae stood and motioned for a guard. "Cut the Queene's bindings! How shameful, that she was brought here in such a state. Let this never be recorded as such."

A guard stepped forward with a dagger; Cedric took it and waved him away. "You will pardon me if I do not trust your guards, after the way they have so disrespectfully treated my mate."

"Of course." Tears shone in Danae's eyes. "And for the way my emissary treated you both. What treason did he commit? No, do not tell me. I cannot bear to hear of his betrayal, and you do not need to offer me proof of it." She wiped at her eyes with the back of her hand and produced a tremulous smile. "When I sent out my Ambassadors, I prayed I would find more of our kind. I prayed I would find Queene Mabb. Bauchan passed along letters from Flidais, on the Queene's Council, and they informed me of Mabb's death and Queene Ayla's ascension to the throne. My heart breaks for her demise now as it did for Mabb when I read of her murder. You must forgive me, Your Majesty, but how wicked your father was!"

"King Garret was a King of the Fae in name only, never in deed," Cerridwen said, fearing the Empath and her strange abilities would catch on that Garret had not been her actual father. "Just as I consider him my father in name only."

"Your kind words are appreciated, Danae," Cedric said with a courtly bow, "but we are tired, and we require a place to sleep. As do all of our misplaced Court."

"Of course!" She paused. "But I fear that it would be impossible to move my entire household tonight. And my servants are intensely loyal to me. I would hate to think that they might, misguidedly, seek to harm you both in an effort to…defend my now-forfeit position. I can offer you a comparable dwelling until you are better established here. I will even provide you with my best guards—"

"We have our own guards," Cerridwen said, feeling like a child left out of a conversation. "They have traveled here with us, in secret."

Danae nodded. "Very wise, Your Majesty." She sounded sincere.

The six Faeries who had fled the Underground and served Cerridwen faithfully came forward. They had stayed close without her realizing it, and she felt a little better for that.

Danae ordered a Human to go ahead of them and prepare their quarters with a bathing tub and clean linens. If she had asked them to prepare a chest of gold, Cerridwen could not have been more grateful. "You will have Bauchan's home, for now," Danae said, a look of arrogant fury on her face. "And all of his possessions. He loved them, so do with them what you will. There would have been no more fitting punishment in life than to see all of his precious treasures given away. And in the morning, you will dine with me, in the Palace, and we will discuss the best way for you to assume control of your people here."

Cerridwen nodded. It was the only response she could muster.

"Stay close by me," Cedric whispered, sliding an arm around her waist as they followed Danae's guards through the crowd, which fell away from them as though afraid to touch them. "I do not entirely trust that Danae is willing to give up her throne."

Cerridwen did not care. She had come to this place willing to die. She left disappointed, and far too alive.

Eight

❧❧❧

Bauchan's quarters were exactly what Cedric had expected: far more opulent than the rustic surroundings of the village, as pretentious as Bauchan had been himself.

They had walked away from the central village and taken a path deep into the trees to find the tent, raised on a wooden platform like Danae's Palace, and nearly as large. Bauchan's home boasted its own fire and cooking pot, something Cedric suspected owed more to Bauchan's distaste for sharing anything with the other Fae than to any official need for privacy.

To his relief though, privacy was exactly what this place would offer. The guards could easily keep watch around the small clearing and roust out any spies, and there would be plenty of room inside for them to sleep when not on watch. There were trunks crammed full of bedding, from feather-filled coverlets to rough-woven mats, enough for twenty people, far more than any one Faery need own.

If Bauchan had come to Mabb's Court, he would have been welcomed by her as a kindred spirit.

Cerridwen trudged into the dwelling behind him, her steps heavy, her eyes not seeming to focus on anything but the floor before her. The child who had been the Royal Heir to the Faery Throne, used to such finery and deprived of it since their departure from the Underground, should have enjoyed her new acquisitions, but the Faery Queene seemed more intent on the bed in the center of the round tent than on the glittering copper oil lamps and delicate lightning glass sculptures. From the way she shuffled her feet as she made her way toward it, it could have been any bed, not one so fine as what lay before her.

"This is suitable. For now." He was unable to gauge her mood. Was she angry that he had let her be treated so poorly on the trek here? Certainly, that was possible, but had she not willed it herself when she had looked so pleadingly to him in the boat? It would not be unlike her mother, he thought grimly, to ask for one thing and be unpleasant when she did not receive another.

Cerridwen did not answer him, but lay down on top of the meticulously tucked covers on the bed, curling her legs against her body and folding her black wings over herself like a shelter.

Cedric motioned to the Human servant, a slip of a young girl who seemed all too eager to be close to the Faeries. She nodded and lifted a pile of linens from atop one of Bauchan's chests, and hurried to the bedside. "Your Majesty," she said timidly. "Would you like your bath? I can help you."

Far too meek, in Cedric's opinion. He doubted she had seen even eighteen summers, but perhaps it would be good for Cerridwen to have someone closer to her Earthly age to serve her. She wouldn't feel like she had a governess, then, though if she were to begin acting this way all of the time, she might need one.

"I will go outside to speak to the guards and establish our perimeter," he said to Cerridwen, not expecting a response.

Outside, the guards had already strung up strings of bells at ankle height between the trees and the eight corners of the wooden platform as some measure against Human spies. They had not forgotten, then, how to live among the creatures. They assembled around the cooking pot, which already held the beginnings of an evening meal simmering away, and apprised Cedric of their plans for the Queene's security.

"It goes without saying," he told them after they had finished their reporting, "that I am concerned about spies. Danae puts on a good show for her public, but I will not trust her from one compassionate display. Check the surrounding woods often, and make sure that this clearing is well-lit at night. That should discourage anyone from coming too close."

They all nodded and murmured in agreement.

"And it should also go without saying that none of you—not one—is to divulge any private conversations you might overhear to anyone, even a fellow guard in this very group." He watched each of their faces, looking for something, some tiny effect that might tell him which of them, if any, would be dishonest in this respect. When he was satisfied that he had seen none, he thanked them and excused himself while they sorted out the details of their watch.

The soft sound of a female voice turned his attention back to the tent. The light inside was low, so no shadow revealed to him what took place inside. He went to the opening in the tent's fabric and parted it, just a fraction, to peer inside.

The voice had belonged to the servant. Subdued in his presence, she talked quietly, but cheerfully, now that he had gone. Perhaps it was Cerridwen's silence that caused the Human to chatter on so, but whatever the reason, the girl had gotten her off the bed and into the tub.

From Cedric's vantage point, he saw the pale line of Cerridwen's back as she knelt in the water and the ebony wings that sprouted from her shoulder blades dipping down to touch the floor. Her hair lay in a wet mass between them, dark from saturation, and she stayed motionless as the girl dithered on and poured another dipper of water over her head.

He let the flap fall closed and stepped back, hand paused in midair. He looked guiltily back to the guards around the fire, but they had not seen.

Whatever had come over him was some after-effect of their harrowing journey, some twisted tribute to the horror they had experienced and the continuing strife they endured. He cared for her; of course he cared for her. But it could not truly be anything more than what he felt out of obligation. He had promised her mother he would watch over her.

Another concern bit at him, one not so easily denied. Cerridwen had only known the affection of her mother, for as long as she would be able to remember. Malachi had doted on her in her infancy, but he had distanced himself as she had grown. Now, there was no one in the world to care for the new Faery Queene. She was lonely, there was no denying, and that loneliness made her fragile. Even if Danae's theatrics were to be believed, as Queene in a new land, she would be isolated for the rest of her life.

From inside the tent, he heard the chatter of the serving girl as she dried Cerridwen's hair. He waited, listened for the creaking of the floor and peeked inside again. Cerridwen lay on the bed, wrapped in linen, in much the same position he had left her in.

Judging it safe to enter, he strode in and announced, "The guards seem to have things well in hand."

Cerridwen did not respond. The serving girl, however, did. "That's good to hear. With all these new arrivals, Queene—I mean, Danae's—guards will be quite busy, I expect."

Momentarily mute with astonishment at being spoken to so casually by a servant, Cedric had to pause to regain his senses. "I would like a bath, as well. Draw me one as quickly as possible."

"Of course!" The servant smiled brightly and dragged the tub across the floor, sloshing water as she went to dump the contents.

Cedric took a few steps closer to the bed, but something about Cerridwen's stone-still posture warned him to stay back.

"There should be something to eat soon," he told her cautiously, watching for any reaction. There was none. "I look forward to our meeting with Danae tomorrow."

Quiet. Unmoving.

"I know this must be a shock to you, never having lived aboveground, and growing up in the Palace. This must all seem very primitive. But this is the way we are made to live. You are closer now to your Fae heritage than you have ever been before. You may find it difficult, but this life is in your blood."

She did not respond.

It would take time. How long had it taken him to adjust to life underground? But that had been so different. That had been imprisonment. This was deliverance.

Remarkably, he had begun to feel better about their situation. He would never have wished to come here if he had known the price would be Ayla's death, and Malachi's. But now he was here, and he could not force himself to stay shrouded in mourning. He was Above, in familiar surroundings. Yes, they were on the physical plane. But it was so similar to what he remembered on the Astral that he could easily trick himself into thinking all was right again.

The serving maid was small, and too talkative, but efficient. It was not long before she had the tub filled and fresh linens set out for him. He eased his arms out of his robe and turned to see her still waiting, expectant. "I do not need you. You can leave."

"Supper will be done soon. Do you want me to tell you when it's ready?" She shifted from one foot to the other as she awaited his answer.

He frowned. "No. I will come out when I am finished here. Do not disturb me."

She'd only just disappeared through the tent flaps when another thought occurred to him. "Do not bother the guards, either!"

A talkative servant, distracting the guards and plying them with comforts, would make quick work of any security they thought to establish. Perhaps she would not be such a boon after all.

He shed his clothes and eased into the hot water. He had not felt such comfort since the night they had stayed in the ferryman's warehouse shelter. His muscles ached, from the day's long trek, from rowing the boat, from sleeping bound in the prison cell….

His mind drifted further back. *From carrying Cerridwen to safety. From tearing her from her mother's arms. From fighting to protect her in the Elven hall.*

His fist clenched and he pounded his thigh, splashing noisily through the surface of the water. These thoughts were sent by some evil force to torment him. Those memories inspired tender feeling, and he would have to be made of stone to prevent that. He could not give in to them.

Dika's image insinuated itself in his brain, her brown skin gilded by firelight. He could almost feel her warmth against him, her body enveloping him. How could he replace her so easily? How could he betray her with thoughts of Cerridwen?

Briefly, he wondered if this camp was what life with the Gypsies would have been like. But he could not fool himself. They would have constantly been in fear of the Enforcers, moving anywhere they could find even a single night of safety. And eventually, they would have been driven underground.

Would he have wanted that life? Imagining it now, now that he was safe and would never return to the Underground, he was not so sure. Maybe Dika would not have been enough to keep him happy, then. Maybe that was why he found himself wanting Cerridwen now.

It was Ayla, damn her! His teeth ground as he remembered that royal banquet where she had announced his betrothal to the Royal Heir. Without consulting him, without a thought for his feelings, she had planted the seed of corruption there. He would never have thought of Cerridwen in this light if not for Ayla's insistence that he should.

This could not continue. In the morning, when he met with Danae, he would admit that they were not truly mates and that he needed his own quarters. They did not have to be so fine as these. He might take to sleeping in tree branches as he once had. If he could be rid of the sight of her, even for one day—

"I wish she had killed me."

Lost in his thoughts, he'd almost forgotten that the object of his distress was there, with him. He looked to the bed. She still had not moved, but she had spoken. He had not imagined that.

"What do you mean?" He could not have heard her correctly.

"I wish she had killed me." The sound of tears shook her voice.

The water had gone cold. He reached for the linens the servant had left and wrapped one around his waist as he stood. He flared his wings to dry them and stepped toward the bed, clutching the cloth closed with one hand at his hip. "You cannot believe that."

Her back shook now, as though she tried to restrain her sobs. The trembling of the feathers on her wings speared through him, as though he could feel her pain.

But he could not. He would never be able to understand a creature wishing to end its life. He could not understand, even now, how Ayla had given up hers. She had been devastated by Malachi's death. She had not wished to live without him. He knew loss, and he did not like the feeling of it. But when he was reminded of Dika's death, he did not wish for his own.

Perhaps it was a mortal foible. If he were a man, and not a Faery, the thought of Dika's death might have driven him to take his own life. Now, he could not imagine anything so terrible.

And if it were Cerridwen dead? The thought stopped him. On the ship, when they had thrown her out the door, he had been prepared to follow her, hands bound, no way to save her or himself, into the water. He had been willing to die for her. Would he have died for Dika, if he had been there when the Waterhorses attacked?

He did not wish to examine the answer. It would not help him now, and it would not help Cerridwen.

"Please," he tried again. "Do not say that you wish to die."

"But I do." The ache in her words was almost too much to bear. "I endured all of this because it seemed there would be an end in sight. I expected her to end this! I hurt. I miss my mother. I miss my home! I do not understand this place, or any place that is not the Lightworld. And I thought it was about to end!"

"You will learn to understand this place." But he knew as he said it that she would not believe him. "You can be happy here."

"With no one but myself? I can be happy alone, constantly on guard from the treachery of these creatures?" She sniffed miserably.

"You are not alone." How ineffective that reassurance seemed. And how dangerous his next was. "You are not alone, because I am here with you."

She made a noise, as if she did not believe him.

"Cerridwen—" He stopped. He could not say anymore.

He placed a knee on the bed, hesitating for a moment to see if she would object. When she did not, he eased himself down to lie beside her. She folded her wings, but she did not look at him. Perhaps it was better that way. If she looked at him with her perfect, heart-shaped face, he might not be able to keep from saying what he almost had. He drew her into his arms and curled his body around hers.

Cedric had only intended to hold her until she

calmed and stopped crying, but when she did, he could not let her go. She did not move away from him, either. The lamps burned out, and they were left in the semidarkness of the tent, the orange light of the fire flickering outside.

He lifted his head, checked to see if she was asleep. She was not. "Do you want me to bring you some food?" he asked, praying that she would refuse, in spite of himself.

She shook her head, a small movement, and reached for his arm where it lay across her waist. She drew it tighter to her body, as though snuggling deeper into a blanket. "Don't leave me," she asked sleepily.

He dipped his head, so that his lips brushed the hair at her temple. "I will not," he whispered against the shell of her ear. "I will not."

He could not.

The dawn woke her, disoriented her. It filled the tent with feeble gray light, and seemed somehow colder than the night before.

At some point while she'd slept, Cedric had covered them with the soft blankets they had fallen asleep on top of, and now she lay, bare skin to bare skin, wrapped in his arms.

He still slept. She thought of how she might slip away without waking him. That seemed like it would be best. Perhaps then they would not discuss how they had woken this way, how intimate it all seemed in the daylight.

But how to leave without waking him? She

became all too aware of how closely they were entwined. One of his legs lay between hers. His arm rested over her waist, and the other cradled her head. His face, achingly beautiful, now that she truly looked at it, was mere inches from her. If she wished to, she could kiss him, the way she had impulsively kissed Fenrick that day on the Strip.

She did not feel those same, nervous flutters in her stomach when she thought of kissing Cedric. No, not the same. A thousand times worse.

It seemed so much more important now not to disturb him, and more impossible. She took a deep breath and let it out slowly, silently, willing her body to shrink.

Perhaps he was a deep sleeper, and he would not notice if she went quickly and quietly. She had not noticed him moving her beneath the blankets. Her face flamed at the realization that he must have been awake then, even if she had not been, and he would have seen her, every bit of her, as he had done so. Though she had never thought of herself as ugly, she did suddenly. Ugly and unworthy and desperate to escape him before he woke and realized all of that, too.

She shifted, just slightly, poised to spring from the bed, and, without opening his eyes, he said, "You are awake, then."

She froze.

"I could tell by how stiff you went beside me." Sleep roughened his voice, and the corners of his mouth lifted in a lazy smile. "Relax. Danae will understand if we wish to rest from our journey."

Relax! As if such a thing were possible like this.

He opened his eyes and peered rather seriously at her. "No more talk about wishing for death. Can we agree on that?"

Shame, and then anger at that shame, replaced it. "Am I still allowed to wish for it, then, as long as I do not talk about it?"

She shoved angrily at the bed, trying to gain purchase to get away from him. But the mattress was full of feathers, and the bedclothes too slippery, so she fell short of her intention to sit up and show him her back, to prove her anger. Instead, she ended up somehow diagonal to him, her legs still tangled with his. Reluctantly, she met his gaze, expecting mocking there.

There was none. "I would not have you wish it at all."

She wished she could argue with him, but she could not bring herself to speak, not when he looked at her the way he did now, with sadness and regret and something else, something she had never seen so openly and honestly in anyone before.

Desire. Usually, it was hidden, or disguised as something else. But Cedric did not seem able to keep it secret as he looked at her. His gaze fell to her mouth, and, with a shaky inhale of breath, her tongue darted out to wet her lips.

That one action seemed to snap any control he might have had. In an instant, his mouth covered hers. Though her mind was caught off guard, her body responded readily, lips parting beneath his. He sat up, knees folded beneath him, and pulled her onto his lap, so quickly that her head reeled from the sudden change. She gasped and clung to his shoulders, and that brought another gasp; she had never realized how hard his body was, how tightly the skin stretched over the lean muscle beneath it. The sensation of him against her, naked flesh ground against naked flesh, made her ache to be touched in that place that only she had ever touched, begged her to open her legs and welcome in that eager, male part of him that brushed against her belly. Her pulse pounded between her thighs, making her slick and hot with every beat. She rubbed herself against him, silently urged him to take her in that way, to stop the game of pretending to be her mate and actually commit the act. His fingers dug into the flesh of her back, below her wings, and he groaned against her mouth as though he could hear her thoughts.

There was a gasp that did not come from her, and a crash. Cedric opened his wings, blocking her from the sight of their intruder with a canopy of powdery blue.

"I'm sorry!" It was the little servant girl. Cerridwen peered around the edge of Cedric's wing and saw her there, bent over as she tried to scrape up shards of something broken and covered in its gluey contents.

"It is all right," Cedric said, though his tone of voice indicated he did not truly excuse the interruption. He eased Cerridwen off his lap and pulled the sheet from the tangle of bedclothes to wrap around his waist. "In the future, do not apologize. Do not draw attention to yourself. Simply leave and return…later."

Cerridwen's face flamed. She pulled the thick blanket around herself. As if it did not know enough to be ashamed, her body still ached for him. She tried for a surreptitious look at him, but he caught her. He looked away, and went to one of the trunks Bauchan had left behind.

"I made p-porridge," the servant stammered. "There's more…I just thought you might not want to go outside yet this morning. It's cold and there's fog—"

"We will be fine, thank you." Cedric's words were polite, but his voice was sharper than usual. "Please, go and see that the guards are fed."

As she watched the serving girl leave, Cerridwen held her breath. Once she was gone, she found she could not release the air in her lungs. She did not wish to do anything that would call attention to herself. If she could sink down and become a part of the mattress, or through it, through the floor, even, into the forest ground, she would.

"Your shoes were ruined from the walk yesterday," Cedric said casually, as if nothing had happened. "And your dress is far too dirty to wear today. I will have that Human go and get something from Danae that you can borrow until your gown is washed and mended."

"No!" She said it with such vehemence that she startled herself, and Cedric, too, so she lowered her voice. "No, I would rather not borrow anything from Queene Danae."

"Danae, Cerridwen," he scolded. As if he were her guardian and teacher once more, as if he had not just put his hands all over her and—

She had missed the rest of what he'd said. "What?"

He knotted the sheet at his waist and turned, an odd expression on his face. "I said, 'You are the Queene. Do not defer to Danae.' Are you all right?"

"I am fine. I did not sleep well," she lied, and instantly regretted it. He knew how well she had slept, dreaming peacefully in his arms.

He did not remind her of this, though, and turned back to the trunk. "Well, you have little option, in any case. Bauchan did not leave behind any gowns. Just borrow something from Danae. She will not deny you."

Cedric was probably right on that account. How would it look to her Court if Danae was not as gracious as she had been the night before? But Cerridwen did not want to wear any of the False Queene's finery. She was not as slender and Fae as Danae—too much of her blood was mortal—and she would feel broad as a Troll in anything from the Faery's wardrobe.

She would feel more like a Pretender, as well. How easy it would be for the Court to whisper about her if she were wearing cast-off clothing from a Queene whose throne she sought to usurp.

But she did not argue. The thought of arguing with him made her sick to her stomach. In fact, she could not stand another moment of listening to him speak to her as though she were a child. She lay down and closed her eyes, listened to the sound of him dressing, and forbid herself even one look, though her curiosity seemed as though it would kill her.

"Cerridwen, I am going out now. Do you want me to bring you something to eat?" He paused, waiting for her reply. When she did not speak, he came to the bed and gently shook her shoulder. She resisted the urge to squeeze her eyes shut tighter, knowing that would give away her ruse. After what seemed far too long a time, he left.

With him gone, she found it much easier to breathe.

Nine

The Human had been correct: it was cold, far colder than Cedric remembered it being on the surface. The sun would not show its face today, and a dismal, wet mist hovered over the ground. The gray daylight turned the green of the forest into sinister black. It matched his mood as he sat before the fire, watching the pathetic flames struggle ineffectually against the chill air.

The Human walked past, arms loaded down with firewood. "You need dead leaves, dead bark, get it burning hotter," he snapped, knowing he took out his frustration on the wrong party. In truth, the Human had saved him from doing something he would have regretted the moment the act was over.

He'd lied to himself the night before. At each opportunity he'd had to slip from the bed and leave her side, he had concocted some excuse not to. That she might wake in the night and need him, and be distressed at not finding him. Cerridwen was no child;

she would have come looking for him. That she might harm herself if he were not there to stop her. She might have the mortal insensibility to long for death when truly disheartened, but she had Fae blood. There was nothing she could have done to bring about her own death, short of drinking poison, which he was fairly certain she did not have.

No, there was no reason for him not to have left her. Their position was not as tenuous as it had been on the ship, with so many eyes on their every action. If one of Danae's spies found the royal couple sleeping apart, well, what of it? And Danae would have to admit to spying, to actually use that evidence, anyhow.

Assuming she had spies at all. This Upworld Queene was not all she seemed. She'd had the chance to do away with her rival, and she had not. Whatever treachery she might have planned would unfold another day.

"Good morning, Your Majesty," the servant said, and Cedric looked up. Cerridwen emerged from the tent, clad in items he had seen in Bauchan's chests. She'd taken his robe of crimson silk and slit it at the sides, tying the front pieces into a knot below her breasts. There had been a pair of trousers, obviously Human in origin, with many pockets and strange metal closures, and she wore these, rolled at the waist and ankles to close the gap between her diminutive height and the size of the garment. On her feet, she wore two different boots, too large for her, as well, but she walked in them with more grace than should have been possible. She'd piled her amber hair at the back of her head, and messy tendrils fell around her face and ears.

It was not the clothing, but that he knew what lay under them, that made him want to pull her back into the tent and finish the ill-advised relations he had impulsively begun.

You are supposed to protect her, the small part of him with self-control chastised, disgusted. The part of him wishing to throw her down on the wet ground and have her, right there, not caring who saw, whispered, *But Ayla intended for you to be mated to each other. She would not object.*

No, she would not object. Worse, Cerridwen would not object. The memory of the way she'd responded, the feeling of her, warm and wet against his thighs, turned his body to stone. He nodded to her and prodded the fire with a piece of kindling. "You found something to wear, I see."

She sat down on one of the stumps that ringed the fire. "You do not approve."

"On the contrary, I think you have done very well with the resources available." She would not look as grand before the Court as she might have in one of Danae's gowns, but it seemed the wrong time to make such a criticism. Females could be…sensitive about such things.

She stood and peered into the cauldron over the fire, and made a face. "What is that?"

"Porridge," he answered, unable to keep his own distaste hidden. "Humans eat it."

"Humans do much that I do not wish to experience

for myself." She sat back down. "I thought things were better on the surface."

"Things were better on the Astral Plane. Here, we do what we can with what is available, just like we did Below. You cannot judge life on the surface by a single breakfast," he admonished gently. He looked up at the sky, found it as bleak and boring as it had been when he'd last checked.

Cerridwen pressed the heels of her hands against the stump she sat on, drummed her fingers. "When will we go to see Danae?"

"Soon." He considered. "Not too soon. We do not wish for her to think you are too eager. She might feel that you are uncertain of your place, and use that against you."

"I am tired of trying to safeguard against what others might do." She stood, kicked at the ground. "I cannot control what Danae will do, no matter how cautious I am." She stalked around the fire, then to the edge of the clearing, then back again. "What is there to do here? Count trees?"

"Do what you would normally do with your day." He cleared his throat. "Before."

She picked up a stick and swung it against a defenseless sapling. The feathers of wings shivered red-black in the light. "I rather think disguising myself as a Human and running off to the Strip is out of the question now."

"You did that *that* often?" Despite how foolishly dangerous those actions were, he couldn't help but admire her ingenuity at escaping the Palace, especially when Ayla wanted to keep her in. Ayla's will had been formidable to the point of legend. He recognized quite a lot of it in Cerridwen.

Perhaps that would help him overcome temptation, keep him from putting his hands on her any further, if he recognized the qualities in her that were most like her mother. He would never have even entertained the thought of lying with Queene Ayla. Imagining her in Cerridwen's place should cure him of his lust.

With a sigh, Cerridwen returned to her stump and turned her bored gaze to the fire. "Why does everyone want to live up here so badly? There's no civilization, nothing to do—"

"Civilization is a Human concept," he cut her off in frustration. How could Ayla have let her daughter grow up with no sense of her true heritage? But then, Ayla had not known it, either. He looked out at the trees, at the mist curling around their trunks. "There is much to do, if you are connected to yourself as a Faery."

She gave him a bland look, as if to accuse him of being as out of touch with his Fae blood as she was with hers. She was right.

He stood, held out his hand. "Come on."

"Are we going to see Danae?" She slipped her hand into his and let him pull her to her feet.

It was a mistake, touching her. The moment their skin made contact, he felt all of his life's energy rush toward her. He dropped her hand, resisted the urge to shake the feeling of her off him. "No. No, I want to show you something."

He did not touch her again, but trusted her to follow him as he left the clearing.

As they walked, the thickness of the morning air gave the illusion that they weren't actually going anywhere. The fog and gray that hung like a screen between the trees was never quite tangible, no matter how much time they spent walking toward it. It moved, darting farther back and back, and Cedric remembered with a brief stab of panic how easy it was to become lost in a forest. But it was his years underground that caused that fear. He would never truly lose his way here, so long as he was still Fae.

Cerridwen must have had the same thought as she followed him, because she asked in a quiet voice, "Do you remember the way back?"

He turned to reassure her and saw that they had indeed walked farther than he'd intended. But still, he knew he could find his way back. Even if he turned around three times with his eyes closed, he would find the direction they had come from. "I have never been lost before," he said. "At least not aboveground."

"Is that another trait that I am supposed to have, but do not?" Cerridwen asked, her bitter mumbling reminding him of the way she had been in the Underground. If she adopted those mannerisms again, it should be much easier to control himself in her presence.

"Whatever traits Fae blood lends me, it also lends you." He turned toward the direction he'd been walking in, but his feet remained rooted to the ground, as if to say that this was the place, and going farther would not suit his purpose. He'd forgotten how insistent the land could be. "You must stop using your mortal ties as an excuse to deny your Faery existence."

"How do you propose I do that?" she asked, folding her arms across her chest. "I have never felt as though I were a Faery, not truly. Until we had left the Underground, I had never seen the sky without grates barring me from it."

"You behave as though I am asking you to undertake an impossible task," he scolded. "All I am asking is that you acknowledge what you are."

"You are asking that I become something I never was, in order to suit a group of Faeries I have never met, and others who betrayed my mother."

"Yes, they betrayed her. And they will betray you, if they feel that you are not a competent leader. To be a competent leader in their eyes, you must be truly Fae. Because you are part mortal, you must be twice the Faery they are. And because of what the Humans have done to them, you will have to gain twice the trust from them."

She stalked away, in the wrong direction, but he did not stop her. *Let her feel it for herself,* he prayed. The Old Gods might be missing, but the heart of the land was still there. Even on the Astral Plane, the spirit of the Earth had been a palpable force. It was what had drawn the Faeries to Éire a millennium ago, and what had kept them there when the Humans had invaded centuries later.

Please, he urged the spirit. *Let her recognize you. Let her recognize herself.*

She'd gone only a few angry, marching steps before she stopped. A frown wrinkled her brow. "This isn't the right way."

"No, it is not." He chose not to elaborate.

"Well, which way is it? I am angry, and I just want to go back—" She stopped before she said the word. "I just want to go back to the camp."

"Home," he stressed the word, "is nearby. You simply need to concentrate, and you will find it."

"I will concentrate, and I will become lost in the woods, and you will never see me again." She put her hands on her hips. "Tell me where to go."

"If I tell you where to go, it will defeat the purpose of coming out here." Somehow, her outrage became more endearing as it grew. He was having a bit more fun tormenting her than he should.

"This is a test then?" She did not sound pleased with the idea. "I did not ask you for your advice. I did not ask for a lesson."

"And yet, I am giving you one." He leaned against the trunk of a tree and peered up at the gray sky through the leaves of the trees, struck again at how peaceful and fulfilling it was to be in nature. The rough bark pricking at his clothes and the rustle of leaves overhead was almost enough to make him forget the hundred years underground. For the first time, it seemed the wounds his soul bore from that ordeal could actually be healed.

Cerridwen's wounds were of a more complex nature, and would not be healed by the simple touch of bark. She needed the essence of the forest brought to her, not just the material.

For a moment she looked as though she would shout at him, but that moment passed and all that was left was a tired despair. Her shoulders slumped. "Whatever lesson it is, get on with it. I grow tired of being out here. It is cold, and I am hungry."

Forgetting his earlier resolve not to touch her, he went to stand behind her and put his hands on her shoulders. She jumped. He decided it would be best to pretend that he did not know the reason for her skittishness.

"You cannot find the way because you do not know the land," he explained. "And you do not know the land because you have never been introduced. You have lived upon concrete and metalworks and those strange *plastic* surfaces. Humans believe they know their way, because they have maps and surveys. They find immovable markers and track their location by those. But those markers, no matter how permanent they are to Humans, change over the centuries. There is a better way, for our kind. Have you ever had a course in healing?"

She shook her head, eyes downcast as if embarrassed. "No, I did not. Well, I did, but I was not…"

"Proficient?" he supplied.

She twisted her hands together in front of her body. "I could not see the tree."

"The tree of your life force?" he clarified.

"Yes." Her cheeks burned scarlet. "It was one of mother's healers that taught me. Or tried. I informed her that I could not see this tree that she spoke of, but it did not seem to be a concern to her. Without knowing how to take that first step, the rest of her teaching was lost on me."

"Of course it would be." The foundation of Faery magic was the direction of energy, and that energy stemmed from the tree of life force inside every Fae. If Cerridwen could not connect to hers, she could not manipulate forces outside, or in. That she had gone without that precious resource for her entire life was a crime. "Close your eyes," he commanded her gently.

She did as he instructed, but scrunched her face up. "I do not think I have this tree. You are wasting your time."

"You have it," he said, not wanting to spend time on pointless negativity. "You have just never found it."

"If it is supposed to be inside me, there are not many places left to look." She gave a laugh, then fell oddly silent, her face flushing again.

He ignored her comment. It was for the best. "Any tree has roots in the ground. Imagine similar roots, reaching from the bottoms of your feet into the Earth."

"I have never seen tree roots. I wouldn't know what to imagine," she said, somewhat petulantly. "Until now, the only trees I have ever seen were the ones in Sanctuary, and I did not know their anatomy then, either." She sighed in frustration, her agitation rising again. "This is why it wouldn't work before, with the healer."

"It will work," he encouraged her. "We are in a forest. If ever there was a place to learn about trees, it would be here." He remembered the roots of the great tree that had broken through to the Gypsy quarter. He could describe it to her, but how? How could any Faery describe a sight of nature, which they should have been born to? The roots of a tree, clouds in the sky, the feeling of wind against wings. It was unexplainable. It simply *was*.

He would have to show her. "Come here." He took a few steps to a tree and knelt at its base. He cleared away some of the detritus atop the soil with his fingers, exposing the rich, black soil that was the flesh of the Earth. Shifting into the other sight, he saw sparks of energy, vibrant green, racing toward the branches of his fingertips. That energy left, became hands of its own, cut into the soil, parted it, so that when he shifted back into normal sight the ground had opened down to a bone-white tendril nestled in the earth.

"There," he told her, pointing. "That is the root of a tree. But there are many of them, for just one tree."

Cerridwen knelt beside him, fascinated not just by the structure of the tree, but the act that had exposed it. "You just moved your hand," she said, awe tingeing the edges of her words. "You just waved your hand, and you made the ground open."

"I did not make the ground do anything," he corrected. "I used the force of my energy to manipulate the earth. But if the forest had not wanted you to learn this lesson, it would not have cooperated with me."

She turned face to his. "And I could learn this?"

"You could learn more than this," he assured her. "You just need someone who is a better teacher than your previous one. Someone who is willing to work with you."

She stood and brushed off her knees. "Well, now I know what roots are. So, you were saying? Every tree thrusts roots into the ground?"

Cedric did not need to use the other sight to call his energy back to himself. When he did, the ground sewed itself shut, pulled the forest debris back into place, as though he had never been there. "Yes, every tree has roots. Including the tree of your life force. Close your eyes. Feel your own roots in the ground."

She made a face, but did as he told her.

"I do not feel anything," she said, after a few short moments.

"It might take time. You must be patient." He paused. "Try again. It is why your feet stay on the ground, why you do not float aimlessly above the land. You are as connected to the Earth as these trees above us. You root deeper, though. In the very spirit of the Earth."

He waited in silence while she continued to stand, eyes closed, pale face upturned to the even paler sky. As he watched, her expression of hopeless frustration gave way to the flickering of an uncertain smile. "I think I feel it," she said, swaying slightly, as though testing the invisible connection to see if she were really tethered there. "Yes, I can feel it!"

"Now, imagine what those roots look like," he instructed. "Unless you are gravely injured, your life force should be—"

"Green!" she interrupted. "I see it! It is green!"

Cedric could not help his own smile then. "You are seeing in the other sight. Good. The roots beneath your feet should be wild and tangled, but they should join into two ropes that enter your feet and stretch up through your legs. Do you see them?"

She nodded. "I see them! I see where they join. And I see—" She opened her eyes slowly. "A trunk?" she asked, as though her answer might be wrong. "And branches."

"Branches into your arms and head," he agreed with a nod.

"It is brighter at the center. I saw my beating heart." She closed her eyes again. "Why could I not see this before?"

"Because you did not know what you were looking for." He joined her in the other sight, and saw her standing next to him, the misty outline of her around the glowing green source of her life. "If you look closely, you can see your energy moving. It can take different forms. For some, it is sparks. For some, bubbles. Or liquid in glass. Others see it moving as light or fire."

"Great round bubbles," she said dreamily, lost in the other sight. "Moving so fast. Some toward the center, some away."

"You can direct them. It is all a matter of telling them where to go." He reached for her hand, pressed his palms to hers. This time, she did not jump at his touch, lost in the wonder of new discovery. "If you needed to heal, you could send energy to your injury. If it is minor, you could take care of it yourself in this way. If you were whole, you could help another…. Imagine I needed healing. Can you see my hand, touching yours?"

"I can," she said confidently. Her fingers flexed under his.

"See if you can move your energy toward me, flowing out of your hand and into mine."

She tried, and slowly her energy changed direction. Bubbles moved toward his hand, but when they reached the ends of the branches that were her fingertips, they exploded against the boundary of her skin with a pop. Cerridwen made a surprised, "Oh!" and jerked her hand away.

"No, you were doing well," Cedric encouraged her. "You simply have not mastered this skill yet. You cannot expect to do everything perfectly the first time." He took her hand again. "Now you know the difficulty of the task. Your energy can be fragile. It can burst. But rather than pushing it headlong, forcing it to break free of your physical constraints, imagine that we are fused together, and you are not sending life force *out of yourself,* but into a *temporary part of yourself.*"

He opened his eyes and saw lines of determination creasing her brow. He wanted to reach out and smooth them away, to cup her cheek in his palm. But he could not bear to distract her from her lesson simply because he had a weakened resolve.

On her second try, she managed to move more energy toward him, and the path of it was less stilting than before. When the bubbles reached the ends of her fingers, a few of them did break, but others continued on through. They entered his body with a white-hot shock, and he struggled to concentrate, lest he lose himself as the very essence of her flooded through him.

"Very good," he said, keeping his tone even through sheer force of will. "Now, give me your other hand."

Their palms touched, and his energy leaped at hers, eager to find an outlet now that his body was overloaded by the addition of hers. Her fingers trembled beneath his as the circuit completed between them. She gasped, a sound so like the ones she'd made that morning that her life force speared through him.

"Anything that gives energy can receive energy, and the same is true reversed." He forced aside a tremor of longing. "At times, you might need to draw energy from another source. Plants, rocks. Wind is more difficult—it can be capricious, and won't often bend to the whims of a creature tied to the earth element, like yourself."

"And animals? What about Humans?" she asked, eager with the promise of new knowledge.

"No," he said gently, sternly. "Animals are our equals, but they cannot give their consent. Their consciousness is different from ours. Plants, rocks, trees are not subordinate, but they are amenable to our kind and can communicate with us as animals cannot. The life force of a Human is weak. You will not feel it. And you must never take without their consent. To do so would be Vampirism, and we have nothing in common with the creatures of the dead."

Their hands were still linked, the energy still mingling and flowing between them. He opened his eyes. A sheen of perspiration sparkled on Cerridwen's brow, her perfect lips parted. The feeling of her mouth under his had seared his memory like a brand, and everything in him urged him to burn that recollection deeper.

The change in him would not, and did not, go unnoticed in the other sight. At once, she dropped her hands and rubbed them against her thighs, as if to remove the feeling of him from her palms.

So, she regretted the morning, as well. He should not have felt disappointed at this. It was for the better. His rational mind knew this, but it did not ease the sting of his need.

"You made light once," she said, a little breathlessly and without meeting his eyes. "In the tunnel. When Malachi—" She stopped herself. "When my father was injured. You made light so that you could examine him. How did you do that?"

"It was a trick, nothing more," he said dismissively, at once regretting how arrogant he sounded. "That is to say, it is something you could easily do, as well."

He instructed her to enter the other sight once again. This time, it came easily to her. It pleased her; he could tell by the bright smile that illuminated her face.

"Pull your life force into your hands." He stood behind her again, allowing himself to lean close to her ear to speak. He was not touching her, but the closeness eased his desire, somewhat. "Cup your hands, as though you were trying to contain water in them. And now, imagine that water to be real." Slowly, a pool of water formed between her hands. "Now, send your energy into the pool, filling it with light. Imagine the life force growing, until it is almost blinding. And when you feel you can pour no more of yourself without rupturing it, throw it high into the air. It will not rain down. You can use your will to influence the life force to stay, though you have disconnected from it."

He watched, and waited, while a tiny glimmer grew in her hands, transforming the newly made water into pure light between her palms. Just when he imagined that she could not contain it any longer, and her limbs trembled from the force of the energy flowing from her body, she flung her hands upward with a sharp cry, and the light she had built hovered over them, bathing the forest in the only sun it would likely see that day.

"Is it still there?" she asked, opening her eyes warily.

He did not answer her, but let her see for herself the undeniable proof that she had accessed her magic. More than that—that she was truly Fae.

She launched herself at him with a squeal of delight and flung her arms around his neck. "Thank you," she cried. "Thank you so much!"

Reflexively, he put his arms around her, squeezed her tight to him, laughing with her in her joy.

"I thought I was hopeless! I thought I would never…" Her words died off, killed by the realization that she once again stood in his arms. Immediately, he released her. She stepped back, gaze firmly pointed at the ground.

"We should return to the camp," he said, more for himself than for her.

"Yes, that is wise," she agreed quickly. "We should eat, and go see Danae before she thinks we are slighting her."

She tried, as he did, to talk herself out of lingering in this place, with the danger of each other.

"Should I find the way myself? The way you told me I should?"

He was pleased at her enthusiasm for her new skill and waited while she found a direction, followed her as she cautiously picked her way through the forest. She babbled excitedly about something, he did not know what. He could not hear her, consumed as he was by need. Every step he took closer to camp increased his despair. The presence of their guards and the meeting with Danae would provide a welcome distraction and help to keep his raging need in check.

He dreaded, and welcomed, what would occur later, after night fell and there would be nothing but his own will to dissuade him.

Ten

When they had left their camp, four of their guards set off with them. Two had stayed behind to keep watch.

"If we took all of them, would it not seem more…important?" Cerridwen had asked as they started out on the winding path through the forest.

"Perhaps," Cedric had said, as though he'd actually considered it. "But Bauchan still has allies here. I would rather our home be defended."

"Our *temporary* home," she had corrected. And he had smiled.

She longed for that smile now, as they made their way through the stares of Human and Fae closer to Danae's Palace. If there had been so much open hostility when they had arrived, Cerridwen had not noticed it. She had been too tired, too disheartened, to notice more unhappiness. But now, buoyed from that bleak mood by the discovery of her new skills, she felt each angry glare like a knife to her throat.

"They do not like me," she muttered under her breath.

"They do not know you." It was meant as an encouragement, she knew, but Cedric's jaw was tight, and he spoke through clenched teeth, as though he did not believe that what they knew mattered, one way or the other.

She was not inclined to believe that, either. If they knew her, they would know that she was not as kind, not as selfless, certainly not as beautiful as Danae. From their first impression, there was nowhere to go but down.

She wished she was back in the forest with its multifarious greens and blacks. It had been so easy to be confident there, to be proud of herself. These Faeries who judged her with every step she took would not be impressed that she could conjure a ball of light or find her way when lost. She would need to be vastly more skilled than them. The prospect began to leave her hopeless and hollow.

Danae awaited them on the steps of her Palace, surrounded by ladies-in-waiting. They were identical in appearance, their hair shaved close to their scalps, dressed in plain black robes that fell from their high, pointed collars straight to the ground.

"They look like a murder of crows," Cedric said, low enough that they wouldn't hear as they approached.

Danae, standing in the middle of them, her dark curls pinned in a tight roll behind her head, wore regal robes of blue and a torque of gold glittered with blue stones about her neck. If she was ready to give over her position as Queene, she did not look it.

"Your Majesty," Danae intoned, and she and her maids bowed in unison. If there were any irony in her tone, Cerridwen did not recognize it.

Cerridwen almost bowed back, but Cedric put his hand on her shoulder to stop her. "Lady Danae," he called out in response. "The Queene desires an audience with you."

"And I am honored to receive her," Danae said, her kind eyes glittering to compliment her smile. "Please, come inside. We have much to discuss, and it will not be a conversation for so many eager ears."

Danae and her ladies broke their cluster and allowed the pair to pass through their ranks. Danae bowed again toward Cerridwen. When they stood on the platform, two of the ladies-in-waiting opened the tent flaps for them. But Danae did not follow. She stood on the topmost step and cried out to the onlookers in the clearing, "Go about your business! This is a royal order!"

Inside, the tent was sectioned off by more cloth segments. The room they stood in was bare but for a rug on the wooden floor and a carved wooden throne.

"There is no place to sit," Cerridwen whispered.

"The Queene will sit on her throne, I assumed," Danae said, her voice close to Cerridwen's ear.

She had not heard Danae come inside, had not realized that she would be overheard. Cerridwen did not look her adversary in the face, and she did not move to sit in the ornate chair. "No, I could not—"

"Nonsense," Cedric said, gripping her by the elbow and steering her toward the throne. "You are Queene, after all. Danae will not expect you to make these overly generous concessions to her pride forever."

"Indeed, I would not," Danae hastened to agree. "In fact, I will have my things moved from the Palace this very evening. Two nights out in the wretched wild is too much for my Queene."

Cerridwen wondered if there was a polite way to tell Danae that the entire camp was a *wretched wild,* but something stopped her. Her day in the forest had softened her to Faery life, she supposed.

"And I look forward to returning to the forest," Danae continued, her expression going soft and dreamy. "I did not realize how very tired I was of this post until Her Majesty showed up to claim it. Queenedom is not for me. I prefer a simpler Fae life."

"On the contrary," Cedric corrected, "Her Majesty prefers the privacy of Bauchan's former quarters. She might keep a small staff here, and she would certainly conduct her business here, but she, also, longs for the simplicity of the forest, now that she has been freed from the tedium of the Underground."

The conversation was civil enough, but Cerridwen had been at enough of her mother's audiences to recognize the tension coiled beneath spoken words. Though Danae's entire manner was guileless, something shrewd glittered in her eyes. Though Cerridwen wished to believe that the former Queene was not practicing Faery trickery, she could swear that Danae meant to insinuate that she was more Fae than Cerridwen. It seemed that Cedric strove to show the Queene that he saw through her ploy and warn her that he found it weak and unacceptable.

A smile touched the corners of Danae's mouth. "Of course. I can only imagine how very disconnected from her true heritage Her Majesty must feel, having been born underground. And such a young thing she is, too."

"Yes, youth is one of her virtues," Cedric said with a wave of his hand, as if to dismiss the unspoken accusation. "It does lend her the advantage when trying to judge things with a fresh eye in an alien world the Fae have inhabited for but two centuries."

Though she hated being spoken of as if she were not there, or worse, as if she were a child and could not understand, she found the play between the two of them fascinating.

"No doubt her youth is what drew you to her," Danae said with a sly look to one of her ladies. "Your last mate was quite young, as well, wasn't she?"

"Last mate?" The question burst from Cerridwen before she could stop it.

"There is no last mate," Cedric said tightly. "That union was a false one. It was rent by Mabb, herself."

"Yes, Mabb was often fond of distributing favors to you." Danae covered her smile with her hand and turned away, to circle the room behind the ring of her servants. "How are your children? Do you hear from them often?"

"Children?" Cerridwen's chest felt as though it were caving in. She looked to Cedric for a denial, and he looked away; he could not meet her eyes.

Danae strolled lazily around the perimeter of the room, her skirts whispering as they brushed the wood beneath her feet. "There were seven, I think? That he knows of. Your mate was quite…social, in his youth."

"That is enough!" Cedric shouted, his antennae flattened against his head, the red glow of his anger illuminating his pale hair.

In the strained silence that fell over the room, Danae hid another smile by ducking her head, and Cedric's hands clenched into fists. But Cerridwen found herself surprisingly calm. She saw now that Danae was not the kind face she showed to the Faeries and Humans of her Court, but a viper, like so many of the Fae that Cerridwen had known in her life at the Palace.

She saw, too, that Cedric was not all he had seemed. The revelation of his past hurt like a physical blow, and that, she knew, was because of what had happened that morning. But now was not the time to let such a thing create division between them, as Danae had surely intended, and it should not, anyway; they were not true mates.

There were two roads she could go down now. She could attack Danae, screaming, casting her out. That would be the next turn in the long game Danae hoped to play, and it would make Cerridwen, already a murderer tainted by mortal parentage, more of a monster in the eyes of this strange new Court. Or, she could play a game of her own, and not participate by the rules Danae had laid out.

"Your handmaidens are quite interesting, Danae."

Cerridwen looked them over, trying to appear regal. "Are they loyal only to you, or to any Queene who takes the throne?"

"They are loyal to the Morrigan, Your Majesty," Danae said, her mouth quirked into a smile she did not try to hide this time. "They serve me because I am a warrior. The Morrigan—"

"I know what the Morrigan is," Cerridwen said, though she did not. The image of the three-faced woman from her dream flashed through her mind. The helm, the spear, the shield. "The Warrior Goddess, in triple form."

"Very good." Danae's eyes narrowed. "Her Majesty has learned of the Old Gods."

Cerridwen imitated Cedric's dismissive wave. "She visits my dreams from time to time, to offer guidance. I, too, am a warrior. I fought in one of the final battles of the Fae Underground. Against the Elves, and the Waterhorses."

Though the servants did not move, something about them changed. Perhaps she imagined it, but Cerridwen thought they admired her a bit more now.

"A warrior is tested many times, on many battle-fields," Danae said, coming forward with her gaze on Cerridwen's feet. She stopped a few steps from the throne and looked up. "I am sure that, if you live a long life, you will have other experiences, and earn the title of Warrior Queene."

"To speak of the Queene's life as an uncertainty is treason," Cedric snapped. "Especially an Immortal Queene."

Cerridwen did not address this. "I do not believe the Morrigan would appear to me if she thought me unworthy," she said, as though her spoken musings were of no consequence. "She seems too plain a speaker for that. I value plain words above artifice. Do you not agree, Danae?"

"I do." Her antennae stirred against her hair, but she concealed her irritation well. "So, let us speak plainly. I do not believe you are fit to be Queene. I have worked too hard and for too long to raise this settlement out of darkness. I will not see it imperiled."

"And you believe that *I* would imperil it?" Cerridwen shook her head. "You mistake me for a fool. I have no other home. No other Court. If this colony were destroyed, I would be destroyed with it." She turned to Cedric. "There must be some solution, some way we can put our petty differences aside, in order to do what is best for our race, and give them back their true Faery Queene." She gave Danae an apologetic smile. "I do not wish to offend, but you know, as well as I do, that you do not possess the advantage of lineage as I do."

"I know that there are rumors about your true parentage," Danae snapped, but then softened. "Still, I will not fight your claim."

"There is much that needs to be attended to," Cedric said with a heavy sigh. "But I suggest we break for the day and reconvene on the morrow."

"No." Cerridwen spoke firmly, though all she wished to do was crawl into bed and sleep until she forgot everything that had happened. "There is too much that needs to be done."

"And too much that needs to be discussed privately," Cedric pushed.

"It can wait." She tried to give him a reassuring smile, to let him know that she did not care about his past. She was not as good at playacting as Danae was; she could not mask her uncertainty and anger completely.

"Sadly, it must." Danae bowed, and this time it seemed genuine, not mocking. "I had arranged a celebration tonight, to welcome the new Queene, and the Underground Court. Nothing so glamorous as you've seen in Mabb's Court, surely, but there are so many preparations already under way, we could not cancel it now."

Once again, Cerridwen found herself trapped. She loathed politics. Still, she forced a smile. "That sounds...pleasant."

"I assume Your Majesty wishes to dress and prepare.... You will sit on the dais with me, and assert yourself as Queene, will you not?" She turned to Cedric. "And you will be there, as well?"

"I do not see a way to refuse," he replied, as though he would have, if there had been.

Danae faced Cerridwen again. "We have started badly. Know that, although I am still not comfortable with the thought of entrusting my Court to you, I admire the way you have conducted yourself today."

Cerridwen did not know how to respond, so she bowed, out of habit, knowing it was the wrong thing to do only after she had begun the motion. She righted herself and made no comment on her mistake. "We will speak again this evening."

After they concluded their polite goodbyes to Danae, during which she promised to send an appropriate gown and two of her maids to help Cerridwen prepare for the night's festivities, they left the Palace. On the steps sat Mothú, calmly twisting a knife into the wooden floor.

"Cedric," Cerridwen began, but he took her hand and squeezed it hard to silence her. By the time they reached the camp, other matters had pushed the Empath's presence from Cerridwen's mind.

There was so much she wished to ask Cedric. Had he been mated before? Did he truly have seven children that he had hidden from her? And why not tell her? Why hadn't her mother told her of his past? Had she known? But all of these questions burst when they reached her mouth, the way her energy had burst against her fingertips. She did not ask, because she did not wish to know, too afraid of the answers.

When they reached their camp, she went past the little serving girl, ignored her eagerness to help. Directly into the tent, every step full of purpose, and when Cerridwen reached the bed, she did not fling herself across it as she had imagined she would. Instead, she sat on the edge, hands resting lightly on the neatly folded covers, and let silent tears fall.

Cedric's footsteps alerted her to his entry, but she did not turn to see him. She would sob, in humiliation and anger. She would scream those questions at him, and they would not burst. She would force them into him, and pull the answers from him, whether it was his will or not. She could not stand to think of the consequences.

"You did very well." He did not come to her. In her mind's eye, she imagined him standing just inside the tent, looking as ashamed as he sounded. "I apologize for my behavior. I let her get the better of me. It will not happen again."

You do not apologize for lying to me? For lying with me, when you have another mate? She squeezed her eyes shut tight. He had not lain with her. He had barely touched her again since that morning.

Barely looked at her.

He owed her no explanation.

He took a few steps toward her. "I should explain myself, after what Danae said." He paused. "Your mother should have mentioned it, when she betrothed us."

"Do not blame my mother!" she shrieked, unable to hold back her rage any longer. "My mother did not deceive me! You did!"

He stood before her, and when she would not look up, he knelt down. "I was betrothed, as you were, against my will when I was very young. My mate…she won me through deceit, and when I discovered this, it was too late. I had entered into a contract of a year-and-a-day handfast. When it expired, I was out trooping, and Mabb saw fit to punish me for not meeting my obligation. She ordered us mated. I did what I could by Aidbe. And yes, I did father children. But after a century, Mabb took pity on me, and released me from my misery."

"You abandoned your children?" She swiped at her eyes with the back of her hand. She did not know if she could love him if he'd done something so terrible. Her heart clenched, then; it did not matter if she could love him, if he did not love her in return.

"I did not abandon them. They were grown, and none of them inclined to stay. They were unhappy in our home, and their mother had done what she could to poison them against me. I have not seen any of them since, and I think they prefer it that way." There was pain in his voice. "I warned your father once not to turn his back on happiness with your mother. That was because I have had so little, in my life."

"But you loved your Human," she protested. "You loved her, and that made you happy."

"Yes. For a time." He took her hands in his. "Our lives are too long to be lived alone, Cerridwen."

It was the time to tell him. To say the words. But once she said them, they could not be taken back. So, she said nothing.

"Guild Master!" A voice from outside interrupted them.

"Guild Master?" Cedric climbed to his feet. Halfway to the tent flap, he stopped and turned back. "Cerridwen, I—"

"Go." She stood to follow him. "This is more important."

More important, and less frightening.

* * *

Perhaps it was a sign from the Gods, wherever they might have gone, that this unnatural attraction he felt toward Cerridwen was not to be acted upon, Cedric though as he exited the tent. It seemed so many forces conspired against him on that subject—the serving girl, his past, this current interruption—that it could not possibly be meant to be.

Outside, six Faeries stood, held off by the guards, at the end of the path leading into the clearing. Cedric recognized one of them on sight. The others were more difficult to place.

"Stand down," he told the guards as he got closer. "What do they want?"

"They are from the Underground," one of the guards said, sneering. "Came over on the ship, or so they say."

"They did." Cedric folded his arms across his chest. "But it is their purpose here now that concerns me. Tell me, what would bring the group of you to my door?"

One of them, tall, willowy, with long brown hair, pushed back the braid that fell from her temple to display the Guild Mark on her neck. "We are Assassins. All of us. We come to declare our loyalty to our Guild Master."

"Your loyalty?" Cedric turned his head and saw Cerridwen standing at the top of the steps. "Did you hear that?"

She nodded and kept a coolly composed expression on her face. She was so skilled at this. It had come as a pleasant surprise. He'd feared, from the way she had behaved on the ship, that she would be as wildly impulsive as her mother. Growing up in the Palace had proven much better training than he had expected.

He turned back to the Assassins who waited there. "We do not need loyalty that only proves true when convenient. Best you go and find another occupation, for I will not employ you, and I do not believe Her Majesty, the Queene, will, either."

The leader stood straighter, her expression sharper, though no offense showed there. "Perhaps we could speak to Her Majesty herself, and pledge our loyalty there. Explain ourselves, and why we betrayed Queene Ayla."

"You admit you betrayed her?" Cerridwen came down the steps, her features carefully composed, still. "You admit that, by leaving, you turned your back on the Lightworld, and the entire Faery Quarter?"

"It certainly can be perceived that way," the Faery answered with a bow. The other five bobbed their heads respectfully, as well.

"It is not a matter of perception. It is a matter of fact." Cerridwen turned her back to them and started up the steps, as though she would go inside.

"We were lied to, by Flidais," the Faery called, and Cerridwen halted.

Cedric saw her spine go rigid, her hands form to fists. The sound of her blade, slicing through the traitor's throat, filled his head anew.

She faced them again, and remained silent for a long time. "Perhaps I have misspoken. Perhaps it is a matter of perception, after all."

They seated themselves on the ring of stumps

around the fire. The cooking pot had been put into service for the preparation of the night's feast, and small flames crawled along the embers, white with ash in the twilight.

The Faeries had, in turn, introduced themselves. The only female, the one who had spoken for the group, was Fionnait. She had brought with her Colm, Scathach, Prickle—a Pixie who Cedric had reprimanded numerous times in his tenure as Guild Master—Bardan and Hawthorn. They each bore the Guild Mark and seemed content to let Fionnait speak for them.

"Best state your purpose, rather than waste our time, if that is what all of your talk turns out to be," Cedric told them gruffly after they had finished their hasty introductions.

Cerridwen placed a gentle hand on his arm, as if to restrain him. For a moment, he was affronted, before he had the sense to remember that she was, indeed, the Queene, no matter what their personal dynamic might be.

"You may speak," Cerridwen said in her best impression of a Queene. Which was, Cedric realized with a shock, fast becoming her role, not an act.

"Thank you." Fionnait's cool blue gaze slid from Cedric to her Queene. "When the trouble started, when that miserable Bauchan came to the Underground, the Guild was, each and every Fae individually, fully set on staying and fighting whatever threat might arise from his warnings. But then, Flidais came to us."

"She came to the Guild?" Cedric shook his head. "I would have known if she had."

"She did not approach the Guild, but Assassins, individually," Fionnait corrected herself.

"There might have been more than just us, we are not certain," Prickle mumbled, unusually subdued for a member of his race.

Fionnait nodded in agreement. "She came to each one of us with a letter, seemingly by the Queene's own hand, with the Queene's seal—"

"My mother could not read, nor write," Cerridwen interrupted. "The letter could not have been from her."

Cedric leaned closer to her to say quietly, "Your mother's illiteracy was not widely known, not even in the Palace."

Fionnait sat forward, elbows braced on her knees, and spread her hands apart. She brought them back together, entwining her fingers. "Because it was from a trusted member of the Royal Council, we had no reason to doubt the origin of our letters."

"And what did they say?" A single glance at Cerridwen's face showed Cedric the impatience and anger inside her; he wondered if they could see it, as well.

"The letters told us all the same thing. That we had been chosen for an assignment of grave urgency. We were to accompany Flidais and Ambassador Bauchan, as their protection, on their journey to the Upworld settlement. We were to tell no one, not even our mentors, of our purpose, as there might be traitors in our ranks who would prevent us from leaving."

This was the moment that Cedric expected Cerridwen to explode with old rage at Flidais. She did not. "Why, then, did you not protect Bauchan when I killed him?"

It was an intimidating question, but Fionnait did not backpedal. "By the time it became clear that Flidais was not coming, and Queene Ayla had been slain, I sought out the other Assassins who had fled the Underground. Of them, only these five admitted, after much pressing, to being on the same assignment."

"So, the ones who sit before us are the ones who disobeyed orders they believed came from their Queene?" Cedric did not know how to think of this, but he would not pass further judgment until the whole of the tale was told.

Fionnait nodded. "Take from that what you will. If we had not, we would not have realized that we had been tricked. We approached Bauchan, but he would give us only vague answers. And then later we overheard him talking about the Waterhorses."

"What did he say?" Cerridwen leaned forward, as if her nearness could force Fionnait to produce an answer she wished to hear.

"That Danae had done well to send them, that they had destroyed many, in her words, *lesser* Faeries. That her manipulation of the Underground Elves was masterful." The Faery cast her gaze down, for the first time since the conversation had started. "I am sorry, Your Majesty, but your mother was murdered by this Queene."

Eleven

∽⟨⟨⟩⟩∽

"*I will kill her!*" Rage burned, hot and uncontrollable, through Cerridwen. She screamed the death sentence to the sky, not caring if Danae herself heard. "*I will tear her flesh from her bones!*"

Cedric stood, but said nothing. He was powerless, before these Faeries, to do as he wished, to tell her that she would not, could not, kill Danae. Not without demonstrable proof of her treachery, not unless they were to spark a war within their barely coherent Court. She felt how much he wanted to, felt it fairly vibrating off him.

Instead of berating Cerridwen for her impetuousness, Cedric questioned Fionnait further. "Why, then, did you not come to the Queene?"

"Fear." Fionnait shrugged her elegant shoulders. "We had no idea what manner of ruler the Royal Heir would be. We feared that her grief might lead her to act…irrationally."

"Fear is not acceptable in an Assassin," Cedric scolded.

Cerridwen's jaw dropped. They had just learned that Danae, twisted snake that she was, had sent those monsters into the Underground. That she had planned...

But how could Cedric stand there and deliver a lesson to these Assassins, when they should be marching this very instant to kill this Bitch Queene?

If he would not initiate it, she would. "Guard! Give me your weapon!"

Without hesitation, one of the guards stepped forward and handed over his sword. She hefted it in one hand, flipped the handle around in her hand a couple of times, as though she had wielded this blade before.

"What does Your Majesty need with a sword?" the one called Prickle asked, his wide, gold Pixie eyes narrowing in suspicion.

Fionnait elbowed him. "Do not question Her Majesty. Have you forgotten your *geis?*"

"I haven't forgotten that I don't like getting stabbed," he said, scratching his behind.

"You hold your tongue in the presence of the Queene," Cedric said sharply. Then, to Cerridwen, he said softly, "What do you plan to do? Kill Danae now, in full view of a Court that you do not have control over?"

"Yes." It should have been obvious, she had thought. She snapped her fingers, and the guard brought forward the sword's sheath. She wound the leather strap of it around her waist and tried, un-gracefully, to slide the weapon into its home.

The Assassins stood, almost in unison, each of them pulling out a weapon of their own. "We are with you, Your Majesty," Fionnait said, her eyes flashing. In them, Cerridwen recognized the desire for justice, and she admired it.

"No one will go *anywhere*," Cedric bellowed, dropping his obedient mate act. "My Queene, you are not thinking this through. If you kill Danae, you gain the throne through a military coup. You will not win the hearts of the Fae here."

"The only Fae heart I care for here is Danae's!" Cerridwen shrieked. She had lost control; it felt good. "And I will see that it beats no more—this night!"

He stepped to her side and angled his body so that the Assassins could not see his face. He spoke so low that they would not hear. "You will *not* do this. I will stop you."

"You will try," she scoffed, but the resolve that hardened his face cast doubt over her heart. She struggled to turn her anger onto him, but she could not.

The weight of this would crush her, she was certain. "I cannot go to this feast tonight and look into her eyes, knowing this," she whispered. "I cannot."

"You can. You are…" Frustration lined his brow. "I can do nothing for you at this moment. Dismiss your Assassins."

Everything within her demanded she fly apart, but somehow, she did not. Eventually, these reserves of strength, ones she did not know she had, would run dry. "Thank you. Your…services will not be necessary." She cleared her throat. "You will not only serve as the founding members of the new Assassins' Guild, but you will be my eyes and ears in those places where I cannot observe. That is your assignment tonight. Keep watch at the celebration. Protect me by uncovering any plots evidenced there."

"We are not trained as spies, Your Majesty," Hawthorn protested.

Fionnait did not elbow him, but cast him an angry glare. "Come, let us do as the Queene commands."

They sheathed their weapons and bowed, then left the clearing without showing their backs to her. Cerridwen stood beside the fire, which now illuminated the night that had crept up without warning, and felt the last of her strength leave her. She slipped the scabbard from her waist, feeling like a child doffing a silly costume.

Cedric stood by silently, watching. She could feel his watching. Now, after all that had transpired between them, he would become patronizing, try to lecture her as though she were one of his Assassins. She clenched her fists until her nails dug into her palms. The little bit of pain gave her a little bit of fight. "Tell me now what I have done wrong, so that I can go to bed and have done with it!"

It took him a long time to speak, but she did not flatter herself that he was shocked. "You did nothing wrong. You reacted as I wish I could have."

This, she did not believe. She rolled her eyes up to meet his gaze, then looked away with a noise of disgust. "You do not react to anything. You barely have emotions. You are, as my mother would say, truly a full-blooded Faery."

Another long silence. Perhaps she had hurt him. Good.

When he spoke, it was not to defend himself. "You said before that you could not go tonight and face Danae. But I know that you can. If you do not, the Fae here will see it as a slight. You do not care about them, I know that. But you will care, in the years to come, when it is said that you did not embrace your role as Queene, when your enemies use that against you.

"Do you believe that Danae truly wants you there, tonight? She wants to appear supportive of you, and eager for you to be restored to the throne. She wishes to show us the face of someone who wants only that which is beneficial to the Fae. We know now that she has lied. What kind of a Faery would send such foul creatures after her own, rightful Queene? What kind would even think to consort with the Waterhorses?"

"The same kind as would pretend to be a Queene, when she is nothing more than the half-breed daughter of a half-breed Faery," she said miserably.

"Then think on this—every moment that you are in her presence, Danae will feel you planning her death. She will not know what causes you to smile so sweetly at her. It will unsettle her, but she will not be able to find the reason for the sinister chill she feels when you are near." From the corner of her eye, she saw his hand clench to a fist, then flex open again. "If you kill her now, her death will be quick, before she has time to fear it. If you wait, she will know nothing but fear, for the rest of her days."

It was a pretty thought, but useless. "She has an Empath. You were there today! You saw Mothú spying! Danae will know, and she will destroy me."

"She will not." Cedric sounded so sure of himself, so confident, that Cerridwen was forced to believe him. "She will not find out, because you are skilled enough to conceal your emotions. You did it in the boat with the Empath. You tricked her into believing that you had feelings for me. You can trick her again. And while you bide your time, we will plan, and I assure you, Danae will be punished."

Cerridwen looked up at him, blinking back tears of mourning, and rage. Of course, he thought she had been clever enough to pretend her feelings for him. Perhaps that was what had spurred on his actions that morning. She wanted desperately to tell him how wrong he was, how much he did not know. But not here, in front of the only Fae who were on her side.

One of the guards at the path called out a warning, and she stood, wiping her eyes. "That will be Danae's murder of crows, then, coming to prepare me for the evening," she said bitterly.

He placed a hand on her shoulder. "And you will be beautiful, so that when you face Danae again, you will show her what a true Queene looks like."

The handmaidens arrived together, emerging from the darkness in an eerie cluster, looking for all the world as if they were made of the night itself. Their pale, bare heads seemed to float above their high-collared garments, and they paused just outside the dome of light cast by the flames, as though adverse to the brightness of it.

"Your Majesty," the one at the head of the group said, and they bowed together.

They had brought with them, in packs concealed beneath their long robes, dresses and jewelry and cosmetics, which they laid out inside the tent for Cerridwen to choose. She faltered a bit. She had no notion of what might be considered fashionable, no way to tell if this were a trick of Danae's, to make her look ridiculous in front of the Court. But Danae would not do something so blatant. She truly believed she had her rival fooled, and would do nothing to jeopardize that ruse.

Cerridwen chose a gown so snowy white it was almost blinding, made of a material that was heavy and soft and made a shushing noise when it moved. The sleeves fell in exaggerated points, almost to the floor, and the waist and squared neckline were embellished with gold cord. The handmaids expertly fitted the dress over her wings, and cinched the lacing between them so that the fabric clung to her tightly.

"Bring the mirror," one of the crows ordered the Human serving girl, who had been lurking and watching, fascinated but afraid. She brought forward Bauchan's long, oval mirror, and two of the handmaidens tilted it so that Cerridwen could see the whole of her reflection in it.

The person in the glass was hardly recognizable.

The weeks of imprisonment and constant flight had taken their toll on her. She had been fuller before, not quite plump, but not so frail as she appeared now, and never had such hollows ringed her eyes. Her wings…she had never seen them this way before. Underground, she had always hidden them. They had been a nuisance, something to be corseted tightly to her back, always ruining the lines of any clothing she might wear. Seeing them so exposed, while she stood dressed in such fine clothing—their abysmal black against the white of her skin and gown—made her feel more naked than if she stood with bare skin to the room. They were like ghosts there, and if she closed her eyes, she could still see them. In her mind, though, they were splashed with blood, patched with bits of metal, and attached to a dying mortal father whose face she would never be able to purge from her memory.

She gasped and opened her eyes, saw the shock on the faces of the handmaidens. "I feel…" she mumbled, and staggered back from the foreign reflection.

Pale, skeletal hands, surprisingly strong, gripped her and helped her to sit. Black fluttered around her, white faces peering at her in concern.

"Leave her, give her room," the one who appeared to be the leader ordered, and the other crows fell back, exited the tent bowing. The servant girl remained, clutching the abandoned mirror and looking as though she would like to hide under the bed.

"You may go, as well," the crow told her gently, and watched her scurry from the room.

"She is afraid of you," Cerridwen said, realizing how foolish she sounded, stating such an obvious fact.

The crow nodded, her fingers stroking idly, comforting, over the black feathers of Cerridwen's wings. "She fears us, because of our association with Our Lady, the Morrigan. Many do not understand her beauty, and see only death in her."

"Mortals fear death." Another painfully plain fact, but Cerridwen could think of no other reply.

"Some mortals," the crow replied pointedly. She smoothed down Cerridwen's feathers. "Sometimes you might say immortals fear it more, since it is so unnatural to their life cycles."

Staring up into the crow's face, Cerridwen saw what she had not noticed before, and felt suddenly foolish. No antennae sprouted from the woman's forehead, and a faint network of lines ringed her features. "You are…you are a Human."

The woman nodded again, patiently. "I am the High Priestess of our order, named Moira by my mortal parents, named Trasa by Our Lady. I came to Queene Danae guided by a dream of the Morrigan. You have had visions of her, as well?"

Cerridwen did not know how much she should reveal. If Danae inclined to send spies, surely her handmaidens would be ideally suited for the role.

Trasa put her hands on Cerridwen's shoulders and gently turned her on the stool she perched on, then dove her long, thin fingers into the thick waves of Cerridwen's hair. "We are loyal to only one master, Your Majesty," she said, as though she had read Cerridwen's thoughts. She hummed a little, combing through the copper strands. "That is Our Lady. We do no one else's bidding."

"I have…seen her once," Cerridwen admitted, wincing a bit as Trasa took a brush to her tangled hair. "In a dream. But it was so vivid, it was almost as if—"

"As if she stood before you. And when you woke, you were as certain that you had spoken to her as you are certain that I speak to you now." Wistfulness crept into Trasa's voice. "Our Lady does not grace us often with her presence, but when she does, it is powerful."

"Yes, it was." The uncanny way that Trasa had described the experience cast it in a new light, made it all the more real to her. Gooseflesh raised on Cerridwen's arms, and she rubbed them through the sleeves of her gown.

"We thought that you should know," Trasa continued, her words low and measured, "that although we have loyalty only to Our Lady, we believe that she wishes us to welcome you as our true Queene. We will not become involved in any plot against Danae, for secrets and lies are not the weapons of Our Lady. But we will follow the Morrigan's chosen."

As Trasa continued to fuss with her hair, Cerridwen struggled to control the trembling in her body. It all seemed to be coming together. Until now, she had been going through the motions with regards to becoming Queene of the Upworld, never truly believing—though she had not realized it—that she would ever actually lead this new Faery Court. But in one night, she had gained the following of a new Assassins' Guild, and Danae's own handmaidens.

Had the Goddess truly chosen her, then? Was that what the dream had been about? It seemed all the more heady, such a weighty responsibility when she thought it one handed to her by a deity so feared and long thought to have vanished.

She thought at once that she should tell Cedric, but an inner voice warned her away from that course. He would want to know; of course he would want to know. But it seemed far too private, and, strangely, as though she would be breaking a confidence held with the Morrigan herself.

When Trasa finished with Cerridwen's hair, she carefully applied color to her lips and cheeks, and produced a small hand mirror to show her the results. The face Cerridwen saw was more familiar now, painted beautifully, the weariness of her eyes concealed, the colors carefully blended to fool the eye into seeing robust health where little existed.

"I have this, as well," Trasa said, pulling a medallion from around her neck. It was a miniature shield, copper hairs winding into a protective knot at its center. The Human slipped the heavy chain over Cerridwen's head. "Wear it so that Danae will see it. You will not have to tell her of our allegiance to you. She will know it on sight."

Cerridwen clasped the pendant in her fist, tried to stop the pounding of her heart. "Then perhaps I should not wear it. Not yet." She pulled the necklace over her head and wound it around her wrist, concealed inside her sleeve. "Thank you, though. I will treasure it."

"Deifiúr Trasa?" Another of the crows peeked through the tent flap suddenly.

Trasa turned. "Deifiúr Siofra?"

The girl showed no deference to the age or station of her priestess, and this sparked Cerridwen's curiosity. Deifiúr Siofra motioned to the outside. "The Royal Consort has left for the feast. He thought we would make a more…suitable escort for the Queene."

"He thought he could force our hand and make us appear bound to the new Queene," Trasa said with a note of annoyance. She waved a hand in the air. "It does not matter. He is shortsighted, if he believed we would not have supported her without his machinations."

Cerridwen might have defended him, but to hear Cedric's actions described in such a manner made them seem indefensible.

Before they left the tent, Trasa helped Cerridwen push her feet into jeweled white slippers, and then they joined the rest of the handmaidens in the clearing. They nodded their approval of her appearance as she came down the steps, and clustered around her as she made her way past the fire.

She stopped them. Looking to the guards who followed behind, she ordered, "Stay here. I do not need protection. I do not need your weapons." She straightened her back and lifted her chin. "This is an entirely different kind of battle."

* * *

The clearing around Danae's Palace was lit with globes of light that dipped and swooped, controlled by the entertainers who had cast them. The brightness made it seem as though the sun had risen in this section of the forest alone and the huge bonfires that blazed all around seemed dim in comparison. Rows of trestle tables flanked a huge space cleared for a fire and more entertainers. Humans did acrobatic tricks and juggling for the enjoyment of the Faeries, who watched their antics in amusement at the quaintness of it all. One table sat apart from the others, on a dais in front of the Palace steps. Danae presided there on the carved wooden throne, watching over the festivities as though she were the Queene.

She even wore a crown.

Cedric could not help but grin at the pathetic gall of it. She truly believed she would remain Queene here, that her life did not hinge on his control of Cerridwen's murderous impulses.

Spotting him as he approached, Danae took his smile as a friendly greeting, and she, foul deceiver that she was, returned the expression warmly. "Your Highness," she said with a nod. "Please, do not take my position here as a slight against your Queene. I thought it would be a lovely symbol if I were to cede the throne to her upon her arrival."

"A lovely symbol," he echoed, as if in agreement. His palms itched for the dagger in his boot. This monster had colluded with the Upworld Elves and sent the Waterhorses to the Underground. His mind clouded with the memory of Gypsy screams he had not heard, blood he had not seen shed. He saw Dika's face under the surface of the water, and the image did not twist to show him Cerridwen as it had so often lately. The loss washed over him, as keen as the very moment he had first realized it. The very sight of Danae, knowing she had caused his pain, brought it all back.

"Are you all right, Your Highness?" Danae asked, her expression faltering. Her concern would have seemed genuine, if he had not known her to be a disgusting fraud. "You look as though you have seen a specter."

"The ghosts of worse days," he said with an mock apologetic smile, wishing he could leap across the dais and pull her throat out with his teeth. "We saw much hardship in our last days underground. All of this light and noise disorients me."

He sat beside the throne to await Cerridwen's arrival. "You will cede your throne, but not your power entirely?"

"I wish for the Court that has trusted me to know that I will always be there for them," Danae said with a kind half smile. "I do not think it fitting to go out of their sight entirely this night."

"We will see what Her Majesty thinks," he said, a tone of joviality changing the subject. "This is quite clever. Reminds me of the Human Courts after the sons of Míl invaded."

"I would not know." Danae struggled to warm the frost that crept into her voice. "I was not born yet."

"Oh, yes, I forgot." He waved his hand. "I have a very difficult time remembering that not everyone is so ancient as I."

"Such as your mate, I am sure," Danae said, eyes fixed on the gathering before her. "I say this with as much respect as can be applied in this situation. You are a fool to have mated yourself to one so young."

"It was arranged by her mother, the Queene." Cedric followed the path of a globe of light through the air, idly added his own contribution to it as it passed. "She thought it would be a good match. And it's proven so."

"I do not believe you, Cedric." Danae turned to him, her beautiful face composed into a mask of pity. He wanted to snatch it off her skull. "There is a shroud of misery around you."

Misery. She would know the cause of it. Everything he had known for the past hundred years had been destroyed on her whim. His friends, his lover, his life—all of it had disappeared the moment Bauchan had stepped into the Underground. He could tell her this. She would see through it. To be so vile, so reprehensible, one had to be shrewd enough to pull their schemes off. She would know that the misery he felt now had to do with the torment he felt every moment that he spent at Cerridwen's side.

"Much has changed lately. I am…struggling with it."

Danae placed a hand on his knee. He did not react. She leaned closer. "You deserve your happiness, Cedric."

"And you should teach your Empath to keep out of my feelings."

A hush fell over the clearing. Danae looked up, and Cedric brushed her hand aside.

And then he saw her.

Cerridwen strode into the clearing, luminous white like the center of the sun on a clear day. Her black wings separated themselves slowly from the darkness. Her skin glowed, her gown shone. Her hair was pulled away from her face, piled atop her head like a crown and raining fiery ringlets down her shoulders.

The cadre of crows that Cedric had mocked earlier followed behind her, almost obedient. No guards accompanied them; a bold move that Cedric would compliment her for, later. The Humans and Faeries they passed were struck dumb, only remembering to bow when she had gone far by.

The firelight gilded her as she passed. This close, the stark contrast of her black wings to her radiant white dress stood out even further. Cedric stood, bowed, forced his heart to calm its rapid beating. She was a hundred times more regal than Ayla had ever been, a thousand times more than Mabb. She let the maidens lift the train of her gown so that she could ascend the dais, and, with a secret smile that showed only in her eyes, she bowed to Cedric.

"Your Majesty," Danae said, overloud, so that the attention would turn to her. She stood and bowed. "How glad are we all that you are here with us on this day."

As though she had barely heard her, Cerridwen

slipped between Cedric and Danae, edging her carefully out of the way before seating herself on the throne. "Thank you, Danae, for entertaining Cedric in my absence. And thank you for the gifts you sent me."

Cedric covered his smile with his hand and motioned to the crowd. "How does Your Majesty receive this feast? Is it to your liking?"

Forgotten, Danae stood, stunned into silence, face taking on the hue of a polluted sunset. She cleared her throat and sat in the chair on the other side of the throne, folding her hands in her lap.

Cerridwen's gaze slid sideways, and Cedric knew she checked to make sure that Danae was appropriately humbled. "I like it very much. So far."

For a long while, the crowd seemed content to stare at their new Queene. For her part, Cerridwen appeared as composed and natural as if she had presided over Court functions every day for a thousand years, as though the combined attention of the hundreds gathered in the clearing affected her not at all. But even this new radiance of hers could not hold their attention forever. Soon, the food was brought on great platters, and the festive air returned.

"Your Majesty," Danae began in a tone of painful civility, "fifty sheep were butchered for this feast, and one hundred geese. We've used the last of our stores from the winter in preparing dishes for this welcome supper."

"That was foolish of you," Cerridwen said blandly. "I will hold you responsible, personally, for seeing to it that whatever remains in the morning is distributed for use for the rest of the week."

Cedric smothered a laugh with a gulp of wine. "The food *is* good, though, Danae."

In the years underground, even during Palace parties and feasts, there had not been such excesses of food, or such variety. Cedric helped Cerridwen select the best parts of the meat from the platters that were brought before them, and the sweetest berries. She ate daintily, another practiced act; he had never seen her at a meal that she did not practically inhale. It might have been the wine, but the grim feelings of the day seemed to lessen. He found himself quite pleased at the ease with which they had managed to insinuate themselves into the new Court.

After the platters had been cleared away, and after a short, but drearily boring masque performed for the benefit of the new Queene, a group of musicians, Faery and Human alike, started up a lively brawl, and circles of dancers formed around the clearing.

"I have not danced in so long." The longing in Cerridwen's voice squeezed Cedric's heart. He'd nearly offered her his hand when he remembered the work that still remained to be done.

"Go, then, and enjoy yourself. I am sure you will find many willing partners." He smiled and allowed himself to touch her face. But he could not dance with her, as though he had no cares.

Not when Danae had provided him the perfect opportunity to get close to her.

He had lied to Cerridwen when he had told her

that she would one day fell Danae herself. That was a revenge he reserved for himself. He hoped that one day, Cerridwen might forgive him. But for now, it was worth the risk.

Twelve

Cerridwen stumbled from the dais, hurt and confused, but she would not display those emotions to the Fae that she now ruled. Instead, she motioned to Danae's—now her—handmaidens, and they helped her to tie her long sleeves behind her neck and tuck up her skirt so that it would not interfere with the dancing.

So, Cedric thought she would find many willing partners. She moved determinedly through the crowd. She would find someone suitable. Not some high-ranking member of the Court. No. Someone low. Someone common, so that she could show Cedric how easily she could purge him from her thoughts.

At the edge of the group of musicians, a dark-eyed Human played a fife, tapping his foot in time with the music. He was beautiful, with sun-browned skin and dark hair tied back at his nape. He was exactly the kind of Human Cerridwen would have danced with at one of the Darkworld parties.

She surveyed the musicians with a merry smile on her face, and clapped her hands to them when their song was done. Then, with a grin that she hoped displayed charm more Fae than mortal, she beckoned the Human to her.

The musicians cheered and cracked wise to their friend, and he looked slightly embarrassed at having been singled out by the Queene. But he looked pleased, as well, and that made Cerridwen quite happy.

"For the Queene's first dance," the bodhrán player cried over the noises of the crowd. "A Rufty Tufty!"

The band started up the tune and Cerridwen breathed a sigh of relief. It was not a difficult dance, and it was one that she, thankfully, knew. She bowed to her partner and began the steps. "What is your name?" she asked, as she walked her half-circle about him.

"Christopher," he said, surprisingly confident for someone dancing with his Queene. He added, "Your Majesty," almost as an afterthought.

"Do you like dancing, Christopher?" She came to stand at his side, and they spun to the left.

"No, I do not, Your Majesty. I prefer to make the music, rather than dance to it." He took her hand and led her a few steps away, then back to the couple that danced beside them. Cerridwen linked hands with the male Faery beside her, and saw his partner make a face as she touched the Human Christopher.

In the moment that she was turned again to face the dais, she looked to Cedric. Did he seek to catch her eye? Did he appear unsettled, that she danced with another? But he was leaning close to Danae, who once again had seated herself on the throne, and they were deep in conversation.

"He is a poor mate, indeed, if he will not dance with you," Christopher said as he took her hand and led her in a long turn.

"Do not speak so to me, Christopher," she warned him, but her heart was not in it. "I would hate to have…your lips burned off with irons."

"My lips burned off?" He laughed at that, and she was forced to join him.

"It was all I could think of that might hinder your music-making," she said, face flaming. Perhaps it was the wine, but she truly was capable of enjoying herself without Cedric.

Then, her heart dropped. That was what he had intended all along. To show her that she did not need him, so that it would not hurt her when he left her. On the dais, Danae's hand rested on Cedric's shoulder, and he made no move to push it away.

Cerridwen marched through the rest of the steps mechanically, and when the music stopped, she bowed to her partner. "I thank you, Christopher," she said, her voice strange and strained to her own ears.

"You do not like the dancing, I think." He bowed again, this time in deference.

"Perhaps that one is best saved for later, when too much wine makes more complicated patterns impossible. For now, though, it is boring." She fanned herself with her hand, feigning warmth. The disappointment that had settled in her chest would keep her cold for many nights to come, though. She was certain of that.

When she looked back to the dais, Cedric and Danae had gone.

The Palace was dark, except for the room at the center. Low flames burned in oil lamps there, and mounds of plush cushions littered the floor. A side table was set with wine and two goblets. If Danae had imagined that Cedric would not guess that her plan had been seduction all along, she was terribly naive.

"This is very…welcoming," he noted with a wry smile. "I assume that this has all been done in my honor?"

Danae came to stand beside him, slid her hand between his wing and his shoulder. "It is only the welcome you deserve."

As quickly as she had sidled up to him, she retreated, going to the side table to fill the goblets. "I am surprised at your desire to stay in the woods with that…with your Queene and mate."

She thought she was being clever. He curbed the urge to grip her by the hair and pound her face into dust on the table. "She wishes for some normalcy. To have a real home, away from the prying eyes of Court."

"There are no eyes here." Wine deepened Danae's voice, and she came forward to press a cup into his hand. "Do not worry that any will see."

"Only you, and your spies." He lifted the goblet to his lips. "Is this poisoned?"

"You do not trust me?" She pouted up at him.

He slowly lowered the cup, then dipped his finger into it and brought it to her lips, tracing the bottom one in a lazy arc. Never breaking contact with his gaze, she opened her mouth to pull his finger in.

He pulled his hand back and tried not to show his disgust. "I trust you."

"That is a most dangerous thing to say to any Faery," Danae said with a smirk. "You have been away from our kind too long."

She took a few steps back, the tip of her tongue pressed to her upper lip, and giggled. "Why are you here with me?"

He took a sip of the wine. It would have been so satisfying to tell her the reason. *I am here to kill you,* he would say, and then, before she could fully comprehend, he would plunge a dagger into her heart.

The wine burned some sense into him. "I do not know."

"We can discover that together, then." Danae reached for the ties that held the front of her dress closed.

Before he could stop his hand, he covered hers, and she gasped in shock. "I am sorry, I cannot do this."

He could not touch her. Not only because the very thought turned his stomach, but also because he could imagine the hurt in Cerridwen's expression when he returned to her. The guilt would crush him.

He would turn and walk out. If his feet would obey him. He tried, found himself glued to his place.

"What have you done to me?" It could not have been poison, not to work this fast, and certainly not if she had tasted it herself.

From his finger. The cup itself…

"Corpse Water," Danae said, sounding far too proud of herself. "You truly have forgotten the old ways, to fall for such a child's trick."

Corpse Water. Water that had been used to wash the blood from the dead after a battle. Once it was on the target of one's spell, their will was no longer their own. He would be powerless to whatever Danae asked of him.

"You did not think I would…what? Align myself with you? Bed you? Offer to make you King to rule at my side if only something could be done about your pesky little mate?" Danae laughed. "And I would spill all of these secrets to you so that you could play along and expose them, as my final denouement? You must truly think me a fool."

"I meant to kill you," he said through clenched teeth. "I meant to spill your blood here and muffle your screams with one of these ridiculous pillows. And then I would hack your body to tiny pieces and feed them to your crows!"

"I would not threaten the Sisters so," Danae warned, no hint of mockery in her words. "But you are so eager for blood. You surprise me. Ah, well, I will help you slake that lust, but you will not kill me. That is a command. Go to Cerridwen, now. Take her back to your little sanctuary in the woods. Lie with her, tell her you love her. Tell her she is—" Danae snickered "—beautiful. And then, kill her. Before first light."

"I will not!" But the horror in him would not be enough to conquer this spell. "I will not do this!"

"Oh, you will. You will, and without a Queene to inherit the throne, I will simply have to take on the role once more. Things will return to normal, then." She took her own cup and reclined on one of the cushions. "One small favor? A command, really, so you will be bound by the spell. Obviously, you cannot tell anyone, Human or Fae, especially Cerridwen, what has transpired here. I would like her to feel ultimately betrayed in her last moments. The way she betrayed me, by taking Bauchan's life."

"You and Bauchan?" Cedric laughed bitterly. "I should have known. You make such an ambitious pair."

She hurled her goblet at him, but he could not move, not until she allowed it. It struck him, splashing wine across his robes. "You can mock me now, but you will not laugh so easily when you have her blood on your hands!" She took a deep breath and lowered her voice. "Go. Do it now."

He tried to force himself to stay. To dig his heels in and resist. His body, under the control of Danae's cruel command, ignored him.

He emerged from the tent, his brain screaming at him to do anything that would prevent him from finding her. But the thoughts did not come easily— Fling himself in the fire? Throw himself on the sword of a guard?—and then they stopped coming altogether.

There. In the crowd. Her shining white dress and

her hair like liquid copper. A sob of despair fought its way up in his throat, where it lodged painfully, bound there by Danae's will.

Cerridwen caught sight of him, and a smile came to her face. Then, it died. She had noted his absence. She thought he had betrayed her. She moved away, through the crowd.

He followed.

Cerridwen made her way to the path out of the clearing. The light and noise pounded pain behind her eyes. She had had enough of celebrating.

She closed her eyes and used the other sight, as Cedric had taught her, and felt her way toward her camp as a glowing heartbeat that grew stronger with each step she took. The noises of the celebration grew fainter. She abandoned the other sight, embraced the clean, cool night in the forest.

Cedric was behind her. She heard him following, quiet, brooding. She could not face him. He had done something he was ashamed of; she had seen it in his face as he had come down the steps from the Palace. The hollow pain behind her ribs teetered on the brink of true sadness. As long as she could ignore it, it would not push over that edge, and she would not have to endure yet another heartbreak.

"Cerridwen, wait," he called after her, and there was such desperation in the sound.

Swallowing her tears, she faced resolutely forward. She would not look at him.

That was the way the walk went. He would call

to her; she would ignore him. The pain in her chest would grow tighter and tighter, until she thought she would burst, and then she would force it away, until he called for her again. He stopped a few times, and she wondered if he would turn back and go to Danae. Panic flared in her then, for although she did not want him to follow her, she did not want him to go to Danae, either. But each time, he would start again, pleading with her to come back to the feast.

At the campsite, he stopped by the guards. Probably to order them to take her back to the festivities. She would love to see them try.

But when he approached them, he seemed...held back. As if he could not force his legs to move. When he opened his mouth, no sound came out at all.

She paused on the top of the steps and turned. "So, you do have some sort of a conscience!" She did not wait for his reply. Inside the tent, the little servant girl napped on a blanket on the floor. "Get up!" Cerridwen ordered, prodding her with her toe. "Get up and go to the feast!"

The girl blinked up at her wordlessly.

"*Go!*" Cerridwen howled, and that set the girl scrambling out of the tent, just as Cedric came in. "I will not go back there!" Cerridwen cried at him. She pulled off one jeweled slipper and flung it at him. "I will not sit there while you leave with her, in full view of everyone!"

He calmly dodged her other slipper. She pulled at the pins in her hair, but there were too many, and they were hard to find. She tugged at the sleeve of her dress, but it had taken more than one pair of hands to help her into the gown. She had no hope of removing it on her own. Her anger fading into tears, she sank to the floor. "I was humiliated."

Why was that easier to admit than her true feelings? Before she had come here, she would have died rather than say something like that out loud. The prospect of telling him the truth was far more degrading. How could she say that she did not care what the Court thought of her, no matter how desperately he wanted her to? That everything she did was only to please him, and it was all worth nothing if he were to pursue Danae?

She would drink poison before she would admit that she loved him with no hope of it being returned.

He took a step toward her, halted, then took another, the planks of the floor creaking as he moved. What made his steps so heavy and reluctant? "Am I really so disgusting to you, that you have to force yourself to approach me?"

"I think you know that that is not true." He knelt beside her, lifted his hand slowly, as though it weighed two hundred pounds. When he laid it on her shoulder, she barely felt it.

"You know what she did," she said, unable to control her tears. "You know what she did, and you still went with her—"

"And nothing happened!" He stood, stormed away. But his steps stopped as abruptly as if he had walked into a wall. He turned back to her. "We argued. I told her that I did not think it was right for her to stay on the dais, as if she were still ruling over the Court. She left in a rage, and I followed her. Then, she threw her wine at me. That was all!"

She looked up and saw, to her shame, that wine stained the front of his robes.

"You cannot believe that I would…" His fist clenched. "Cerridwen, Danae is a thing of pure evil. She has done more than you know, she has—" His words cut off abruptly. He swallowed, closed his eyes. "You must believe me when I say that there are more plots afoot. That you are in danger. And that I would never do anything, willingly, to hurt you."

"I know you would not." He had sworn to her mother that he would keep her safe, and he had protected her faithfully this far. How he could think that she would doubt him, after all that he had done, baffled her.

"But you thought I would, what, couple with Danae? Take her as my mate?" His words scraped from his throat so that they sounded raw and painful. "I would never…"

She looked up, into his eyes, his beautiful, clear blue eyes, expecting to see anger in them, but there was none. There was anguish.

"As far as my feelings are concerned," he continued, looking away from her, "I am not looking for a mate. I am…content. With the one I have already."

"What, *another* that you did not tell me about, from hundreds of years before I was born?" She almost laughed. And then he faced her, and his meaning became clear.

Her breath left her without seeming to go anywhere. Everything in her froze, and she was certain that if she looked at the tree of her life force, she would see the bubbles of her energy suspended, motionless.

"Cerridwen, I have fallen in love with you." He did not sound happy about it. "I tried, please believe me, I tried to keep my distance. I would never wish for you to think that I had tricked you. I was as unhappy about your mother's announcement of our betrothal as you were. I was prepared to leave the Lightworld, the Underground, entirely, to escape it. But then, circumstances being what they were, throwing us together...and you seemed so—"

"Pitiable?" Her long-held exhalation followed the word out, making her sound somewhat hysterical. "Did you pity me? Do you think you need to protect me, and your obligation has turned to love?"

"I admire you!" he shouted, his anger returning to him. "I see so much in you that you kept hidden in all of your years underground, living as a pretty but useless object. I see you facing tasks so daunting that previous Queenes, even your mother, would have shrunk from. And I admire that. I love you! I do not know how these things happen! I cannot dissect my feelings quite so easily as you seem to be able to! Either accept it or—" his expression changed suddenly, flickering to a burst of hope that was strangely incongruent with his next words "—tell me to go. Order me to leave here and never return! Banish me, and send me as far away from you as you possibly can!"

Her head swimming, her lungs caught in the vise of a fear that this was not really happening, she fought her way to her feet. Hampered by the folds of the gown, she fell toward, more than walked, to him.

Whatever conflict had held him back before seemed to have resolved itself as his arms opened to catch her and haul her up against his chest. He crushed his mouth over hers, unrelenting, so that she could not breathe, for an entirely physical reason this time. Gasping, she broke their mouths apart, caught his gaze and bent her head to his again. Only then did she realize he held her up, and she flared her wings to help him balance.

His hands splayed on her back beneath her wings, his thumbs brushing the dangling ends of the laces that crisscrossed between her shoulder blades. He managed to get hold of one without dropping her or breaking the connection of their mouths, but he could not pull it free. He moved forward, to the thick center post of the tent, and pushed her back against it, pinning her between himself and the wood. Then, before she could protest, he reached between them and ripped the front of the dress open in one swift motion.

Stunned and a bit frightened by the sudden violence of the action, Cerridwen was jolted into rational thought once again. What was she doing? This had seemed like such a terrible idea just that morning. Why could she not control herself now?

Then, his mouth moved to her neck, and those rational thoughts fled. She groaned, clawed at the post above her head.

There was no art in this, no seduction, and the

blatant, brutal nakedness of the act sped the blood through her veins, the energy throbbing at the center of her. He bunched the voluminous folds of the skirt around her waist, and the shock of the cold air against her wet, heated flesh pulled a whimper from her throat. He tore at his own garments, until they fell open. He lifted her again and pushed inside her. She was as eager for him as she had been that morning, more so after the torturously long day spent craving him. Still, her flesh was untried, and she cried out at the intrusion, digging her fingers hard into his shoulders, biting her lip to stifle another cry. He smothered her in another kiss, gripped her tight around her waist as he began to move inside her, the almost painful hardness of him tugging free of her body before plunging back. She lifted her hips, tried to match his movements, yet wanting him to cease, wanting him to stay buried inside her. She ground herself against him, arched, pushed away from the beam at her back.

With a groan, he staggered backward to sit on the bed, and she wrapped her legs around his waist. He braced his hands at the small of her back and she leaned into them, pushing herself tighter against him. Gasping, panting, she folded her legs on either side of his and used them to raise and lower herself, as he flexed up, deeper and deeper into her. But it was not enough, and she thought she would scream at the frustration that built within her, the feeling that intensified and swelled, the way her energy had built up and built up between her hands before it became too much to bear, and she had thrown it, bursting to light, into the air. Already this was too much to bear. Already, she wished she would burst.

She cried out in desperation, begging without words, and he pushed her off him, onto her knees beside the bed, and before she could complain at the desperate emptiness at his withdrawal, forced into her again, his hands covering hers, pinning them to the bed. His every thrust pushed her face into the bed-clothes, pinched and crushed her wings, but she did not care. He slammed into her, over and over, and she shrieked with each breath that jolted from her panting lungs. His fingers twined with hers, his breath heated her sweat-slicked skin to boiling. He laid his head on her folded wings, his movements faster, frenzied, until he pushed against her so violently that it was painful and shouted her name.

The tension in her did burst then, and she gripped the bedclothes, screaming, every part of her aflame.

Just as quickly as it had begun, it was over. He pulled her onto the bed and collapsed beside her, breath rasping as though he had just run harder and farther than he ever had in his life. The chill air bit at her exposed skin, and her legs trembled, too weak even to help her push under the covers. He gripped her hand suddenly, pulled it to his lips and kissed her fingertips. "It is not dawn yet, is it?" he asked, as though he feared the coming morning.

She turned her head, saw the guards' fire still flickering outside. "It is not." She yawned, and then she could no longer keep her eyes open.

* * *

She slept on her stomach, tangled in the tattered remnants of the gown, her hair, still pinned up from the feast, a mussed tangle on her pillow.

This was not how he had wanted it to be. No. He had never wanted it to be. He could have fought it, could have kept himself from ever revealing any of those feelings to her. It had been Danae's spell that had forced him to act out those emotions, though the emotions themselves were true enough.

"I am cold," Cerridwen mumbled in her sleep, clutching at the shoulder of the gown as though it were a blanket she could draw over herself. He pulled the blankets free and tucked them around her, the little good it did to show her tenderness, now.

He could not blame the spell for the fury with which he had taken her. That had been his own base desires fighting free from their tortured confinement. He had wanted her more and more with every breath. He would have taken her, despite the spell. But now, the deed was done, and he would kill her before first light, and he had not even managed to be gentle, to savor the act that would be their final moments together.

He tried again, with all of his might, to force himself from the bed, to get away from her and get her out of harm's way in the process. But he would not budge. He could stroke her hair and smell her skin, he could whisper to her that he loved her, but he could not do something so simply as stand and walk away from her.

When the spell wore off, which he still held out

hope would be before the morning, he would do more than kill Danae. He would torture her. He would torture her, almost to the point of death, but he would not let her die. She would beg for death, but he would not grant her that boon, not until he was satisfied at his revenge. If he killed Cerridwen under this spell, if there was nothing he could do to stop it, the day of Danae's release in death would never come. And immortal creatures could live a very, very long time.

As if the murderous thoughts in him controlled his hand, he reached for the dagger in his boot and pulled it free. But it was not time. Though the air smelled faintly of cold dew, and the fire outside died, he could resist the spell for at least a little longer.

He lay beside her, a prisoner in the body that would kill her, and watched with growing dread the night begin to recede outside the tent.

Thirteen

꧁ ꧂

The mist in the clearing was not white but bloodred, and it pulsed as it undulated around her legs. Cerridwen did not know how she had come to be in this place, but she was not frightened. She waited, watched as the sanguine mist tickled her ankles and waited.

She did not wait long. A woman, slender and beautiful, with long, straight slashes of pale blond hair, appeared. The simple dress she wore was as bloodred as the mist and clung to her, suspended from her shoulders by two thin cords. A matching red cord wound around her hand, tethered to the collar of a huge white pig that walked at her side.

Cerridwen blinked and stared. "I know you," she said. "I am you." Was that right?

"You are my namesake." The woman knelt in the mist and cupped the animal's snout, clucking to it affectionately.

"My mother saw you. She knew you." Cerridwen

pressed her palms to her eyes, but in this dream, she could see through her hands, and it did no good.

"And you know me, whether we have met or not." The Goddess, the one Cerridwen had been named for, straightened. "I come to the faithful, even if they do not know yet that they follow me. I came to your father, to help him find his way. I came to your mother, to guide her. And I come to you now, though you did not know that you need me."

"I—I did not call you," Cerridwen stammered. "I do not need help. I have handled everything myself, this far."

"Yes, it would appear that way. On the surface." The Goddess's eyes narrowed playfully. "But we are watching. We know things."

"Who is watching?" Cerridwen started forward, but the space between them did not alter. "My mother?" Why had she asked that? That was foolish. There was no one on the Astral. The Astral did not exist any longer.

But the woman nodded. "Your mother, yes. And she sends you a warning."

"My mother is dead. She cannot warn me of anything." *But you were so certain of her a moment before.*

"After I am gone, you must be patient. You are not my own. I intervene here on your mother's behalf. And she says that you must wake up, Cerridwen."

"Wake up?" Now, that simply made no sense. If she had no tangible body here, she could not be asleep here. "Wake up?" Her words echoed back at her eerily from the forest.

"I must go." The Goddess came forward, gripped her face, kissed her lips. "Wait for her!"

"Wait for *who?*" she pleaded, capturing the Goddess's hands against her face.

"You must *wake up,* Cerridwen!" The Goddess moved without moving, and suddenly she was across the clearing, barely distinguishable against the trees. *"Wake up!"*

Cerridwen shook her head. This was going all wrong. It was nothing like her other dreams. She looked down at her hands, ghostly white in the darkness. Blood welled on her skin in the form of the triangles she had dreamed of so long ago. And then her mother's voice rang out through the dream forest, clear and commanding.

"Wake up!"

With a gasp, Cerridwen opened her eyes. The dim light of the morning cast a blue pall over Cedric as he knelt above her, arms stretched over her, trembling with exertion. He held a dagger, fingers clenched on the hilt so tightly that blood dripped from them. His eyes were hollow, his lips white. "Run!" he managed, in a voice that did not sound like his own, like it came from someone far away.

Then he stabbed the knife down.

Cerridwen rolled out of the way, fell, wrapped in the bedclothes, and could not struggle free. "Run!" Cedric shouted at her, and again: "Run!"—a scream tearing from him as though ripping a part of him away even as he gripped her ankle, crushed the bones in his strong grasp—and she screamed, kicking at him with her other foot. He covered her body, a sick parody of the night before, and she could not fight him, pinned beneath him. He still held the dagger, and the blade of it cut into her palm as he held her hands down.

"I love you," he whispered against her ear, and she felt something hot and wet fall on her cheek. He rose up, and she saw the tears that flowed down his face.

The disparity between action and word was so unreal that she could not reconcile what she witnessed. She could not even plead with him to stop. Cedric raised the knife again, and she waited for it to fall, knowing that it would end her life.

The sound of the guards' footsteps as they raced into the tent sent a shock of reality through her, and she brought her arms up, together, to shield herself from the dagger. The blade tore through her flesh, but she pushed back, bucked her body, and through some miracle managed to free a leg. She planted her foot against his chest and pushed.

He fell back, screamed at her to run, even as the guards fell upon and disarmed him.

Bleeding, sobbing, she staggered back. Strong arms caught her. "Easy now, easy," the guard soothed, but when she glimpsed his face, he looked as though he would crumble as easily as she might.

"My hands," she whispered, raising her arms to show him, and hot jets of blood poured from her torn skin.

"Gods!" He grabbed her, lifted her in his arms, and ran her outside, into the growing light of the dawn.

She sat on a stump beside the fire, shivering as he cut strips from her ruined gown and bound her wounds, disinterested in the entire process. There was no sound from inside the tent. Had they killed Cedric?

"This is too much for me. Stay here, I will go and get the healers," the guard instructed her before jogging away.

She stood, not really feeling her legs, nor the pain in her arms, though she knew it was there. She pulled the gown onto her shoulders, held the torn front closed. She had come to the bottom steps of the tent before she realized she had moved at all. She had reached the top step before she realized that she did not want to look inside. She did not want to see Cedric, alive or dead. She did not want to see her blood on the floor. She did not want any part of this.

Sitting on the steps, she listened to the commotion inside. It did not grow in volume, though it seemed to inside her own skull, and she looked out to the forest. It was so peaceful, so dark. It could not be as cold and harsh as this clearing.

Climbing to her feet, she walked toward the trees. Her walk grew in pace when she reached the edge of the clearing. She caught her torn skirt to keep it from tripping her as she broke into a run. The trees came at her, faster and faster. She opened her wings and used them to push her ahead, catching them on branches. She closed her eyes. She would not collide with anything. She could not. And she could not stop. Because something would catch up to her, something that she did not want to think of.

She turned her head to see the thing that chased her, though she knew it was formless. It was something she carried with her. The trees obscured her view of the camp, and she realized with sick panic that she had come too far now, that she could no longer see the clearing....

What had she done? Gods, what had she done? She was wounded, bleeding, and she had run from help. What had happened? Cedric had tried to kill her.

Kill her.

For what?

She could not breathe, panic clawing inside her chest like a wild animal. She folded her wings before she realized that her feet no longer touched the ground. She fell and tried to open them again, only to snag one painfully on a branch. The ground rushed up to her with a sickening crack, and she lay, too weak to move, unable to do anything but scream at the agony that exploded over and over, unrelenting, in her shattered body.

Though no one would hear her, she screamed, bellowed like a wounded animal. Even after the riot of pain dulled some, into a white-hot, stabbing ache, she screamed, as though every sobbing breath expelled more of the pain in her wounded heart.

When her throat was raw, and the cold and fatigue had numbed her, body and mind, she stared up at the sky. First one cold drop fell, then another. Beside her face, a fern trembled from the weight of the drops. The forest filled with the dull popping sound of the falling rain, hypnotizing her.

With no strength to fight off the darkness, Cerridwen succumbed to it.

When the alarm sounded, Amergin was in the village center, watching from one of the tall tree houses as the Humans slaved to clean up the destruction wrought by the night's wasteful banquet. Faeries, half-dead from too much drink and too little sleep, stumbled out from the trees and dwellings and sat up under tables. Idiots, to think themselves so safe as to let down their guard. It would serve them all right if he had let down the wards and all the pretty magic that disguised their Kingdom and let the Enforcers come to their doorstep.

Not that he would appreciate being dragged off by them himself. Humans found consorting with magical beings were put to death. As he would be hardpressed to explain that he fell somewhere between the two races, he would likely endure several attempts on his unkillable body before they realized he was not going anywhere.

The commotion brought a flood of Faeries to surround Danae's Palace. The clever girl hadn't left it yet, obviously stalling to retain *de facto* control. Amergin understood the stubbornness of the Fae, possibly better than they understood it themselves.

A group of Faeries, heavily armed, but not outfitted like Danae's guards, wrestled a stumbling figure down the path. A sting in Amergin's heart told him the Faery's identity, without seeing his face.

Living as long as he had, in both the physical and

Astral realms, Amergin had learned a thing or two about large crowds. They would always look to the source of the disturbance, each individual believing that they could not be seen, so long as something held their—and everyone else's—attention. It provided Amergin with ample opportunity to gauge their reactions.

Danae, for instance, came from her tent with no hint of surprise or concern or urgency. She viewed the scene calmly, kept her eyes fixated on the Faery bound and hooded as his captors marched him toward her.

"Gods above, what has happened?" she asked, her face suddenly ashen. But she did not need to ask. She already knew what she would hear. It was clear from the way she held her body, as if anticipating the news.

"There was an attempt on the Queene's life," one of the captors called out, and the obligatory chorus of whispers rose from the crowd of bystanders.

"An attempt?" Perhaps Danae had not anticipated this, after all. She seemed genuinely surprised at the proclamation.

Or she did not expect to hear that her plan had failed….

It became clear, like clouds moving away from the sun. Of course. He had seen them, the night before, as he had hidden from the festivities and sat high above, alone with his harp. He'd seen the two of them in conversation, and then their disappearance into the tent. Cedric had emerged with wine splashed on his robes, but he had not looked like a man just engaged in an argument. His expression had been grim, determined.

"Bring her attacker forward," Danae ordered, and they pushed Cedric toward her. "I wish to see his face."

As if she did not know what face she would see. Amergin's mind raced.... Of course they had planned this. And last night, they had decided to act on their plan.

Sickness clenched in his gut. The new Queene was practically a child, and so lost when he had looked into her eyes. No matter how brave a front she had mustered before Danae upon her arrival, she showed fear, and deep despair. Harming her was destroying an already wounded heart. There was no sport in it, no honor. Certainly no dignity.

The guards pulled the hood from Cedric's head, which drooped on his shoulders, and his blood-stained hair obscured his face.

"Cedric!" Danae's hand flew to her chest in the kind of dramatic gesture Humans liked to use. She'd probably practiced it before a mirror. "Gods and Goddesses, *what have you done?*"

Cedric did not respond. Amergin leaned over the rail, then thought better of it. Though a fall would not kill him, he would probably wish it had.

"Tell me!" Danae snapped. "I order you to tell me."

"I..." Cedric sobbed, as if fighting back the words he did not wish to admit. "I stabbed Cerridwen. While she slept, I took a knife, and when she tried to fight me, I..."

"Enough!" Danae lifted her hand in a good show of anger. "Where is the Queene now?"

"We do not know," one of the guards admitted. "While waiting for the healers, she…disappeared."

"So, is she dead?" The eagerness in Danae's words would go unnoticed by any that did not know to look for it. But Amergin chuckled ruefully. My, how she wished for the girl's death.

"We do not know, Lady Danae," the guard said with a bow. "She may have gone into the forest. There were tracks, but they ended."

Danae considered a moment, her dark eyes scanning Cedric's humbled form. "Organize a search party! Every able Faery should scour the forests. Bring the Queene back to me, safely, and you will be richly rewarded."

This would never do. Amergin turned and ducked into the small tent. He had few possessions in this realm, but he would find what he needed in the chest that stood at the end of his cot. A pair of trousers, the heavy woven denim kind favored by modern Humans, to protect his legs from the whiplashing briars growing from the forest floor. Human "sneakers," thin canvas boots that only laced to the ankle but had thick, hard soles to guard his feet. He found a doublet spun from soft wool, and pulled that on, as well. A flashlight, which he would need if caught out after dark. Good thing he had bought it off the Human trader who had come during the last fair. So much easier than torches.

He also took the pack that he had cobbled together

long ago in case he ever wished to run from Danae's Court and stay hidden. Inside, all manner of food, preserved in aluminum cans by the Humans, strained at the seams, and a small plastic case with a red cross emblazoned on it held some meager supplies for patching wounds. To this strange mix, he added his wand, and slung the long handle of the bag over him so that it crossed his body.

Stepping back out of his tent, he could see that the village was, as expected, in chaos. Danae had known exactly what she was doing by ordering an immediate search. Some would object, others spring to action. Those who objected would do nothing. Those who were moved to act would clash with others who had plans of their own, and the whole of the effort would bog down in petty bickering. By the time a search got under way, the poor girl would almost certainly have bled to death.

He descended into the clearing on the rope ladder from his narrow porch and tried to make his way through the throng without attracting Danae's notice. But she always noticed him, the way one always fixates on the single guest at a party that they do not care for.

"Where do you go, wizard?" she called out.

He stopped and bowed to her. "To search for the missing Queene, as you commanded." He paused, then added, "Your Majesty."

Her chest swelled with an outraged breath. "You will watch your words more closely, wizard. There are many things I can think of to do with a body that does not die."

"I am sure there are."

And with that, Amergin slipped into the forest.

The rain had stopped, and the cold had become warmth to her. She opened her eyes, the great effort in that simple movement stabbing pain through her head.

Beside her face, the little fern that had been so battered by the water now stood straight and tall, its feathery leaves brushing her face. She closed her eyes and used her other sight. In that place, it did not hurt to look, or to breathe.

The tree of her life force had so many broken branches and snapped roots. Her energy, sickly yellow, moved like the sludge in the bottom of a Darkworld tunnel, and the dirty bubbles of it burst into nothing where they reached a fracture in their path.

Beside her, the little fern, buzzing with bright green like a swarm of angry bees, bent to brush against her chin again. The fibrous material shocked her skin, dripped blinding green-white sparks onto the surface of her. The energy sank into her own, green for a moment, then blending into the dim mix of her own. A similar prickle snapped at her elbow, another at her thigh. All around her, the plants of the forest touched her, gave her their strength. Was she doing it, or were they? Cedric had not taught her this….

…that name should have caused her pain, but it did not. She did not have enough strength to feel it.

She thought of that day in this forest, perhaps very close to where she lay now. Yesterday? It seemed like a lifetime. Perhaps it had been. She might have lain on the forest floor forever, caught between life and death, kept in the former state only by the scant help the plants could give her.

That was a happy delusion. The hours had not *seemed* like years, they *had* been years. The rain that soaked her hair and skin was not the same rain as had fallen before. No, she had been here for as long as it felt she had.

The plants around her trembled. A breeze brushed her face. And then, a voice, as if underwater, but unmistakably a voice, pulled her out of the other sight.

A figure, clad in strange, Human clothing, ran toward her. It knelt, features fuzzy as it loomed over her. "I'm here," it reassured her in a masculine voice. "I've got you."

"Cedric?" But it couldn't be, could it?

He lifted her into his arms, and the pain washed her into darkness again.

Danae had ordered him tied to the post in the center of her tent, in the same room where he'd fallen so easily for her trick. During the night, one of her crows came to cover him with a blanket. In the morning, they brought him water and something to eat, feeding him patiently. The rest of the time, he was alone.

Days passed this way. How many, he had lost count. He asked for Cerridwen. Had they found her? Was she okay? They ignored him, or merely shook their heads.

When he slept, images of her, head thrown back, panting, breathless, haunted him. His hands covering hers as she bunched the bedclothes in her fists. Her slender legs quivering where they wrapped around him.

Always he woke still bound, body aching from lack of movement, tormented by wholly different images in the light. Her confusion, her screams, her pain. The knife blade sinking into her arms, over and over, blood splashing against her linen-pale skin.

Whenever they brought him food, he prayed it was poisoned. He prayed for an end to the spell that kept him prisoner. Neither death, nor relief, came to him.

He had heard Danae, all during his captivity, pretending to be concerned when the searchers returned with no news, gloating later to her faithful handmaidens that it would only be a matter of time before she was Queene once more.

All the time he had listened to her his hatred had grown. He had never imagined such an abhorrence. It consumed him like fire, leaving only ashes behind, and yet even after it had used up the last bit of his will, still it burned. No matter what vengeance he might exact upon Danae—and he prayed that he would, someday, claim that revenge—it would never wash away the foul loathing of her that blackened his heart.

It was almost nightfall when the False Queene came into the room, dressed all in black, her hair unbound, hands clasped in a unified fist against her stomach—she looked the picture of a somber mourner.

"What do you think?" she asked, her voice full of tears. "Will this be convincing?"

He tried to spit at her, but his mouth was dry, and the motion was useless. Pathetic. He hung his head.

"The searchers have given up," she declared in a more cheerful tone. "They have found their answer."

He looked up, to her hands, outstretched and cupped. In them, feathers. Black, tinted red in the low light of the oil lamps.

"Good work, Cedric," she said with a cruel smile, and turned her back to leave.

A cry woke Amergin, a scream that sent a chill to his immortal bones and echoed through the treetops like the anguish of a dying animal. It repeated, tugging sympathetic pains from his chest. Any creature that could hear such a sound and not shudder in agony in unison with the creature that had uttered it was soulless, at best.

He rolled over on his cot and felt an unexpected tenderness for Cedric, despite what he had done.

All through the night, the pitiable screaming went on.

Fourteen

She was never certain if she dreamed or not. Sometimes, the face that leaned over her, full of concern, was that of Trasa. Sometimes, it was her mother. Others, it was the Morrigan herself. It seemed unlikely that any of it could be real, but she could not sort it out.

Time passed. She did not know how much, but she was certain that it passed, because she felt herself becoming stronger. She also woke to cool hands helping her sit up, and a cup pressed against her mouth. This happened more than once, and each time she drank the bitter liquid offered, she slept until it was time to drink it down again.

She woke once in the night, and did not know where she was. A fire burned in a stone hearth, and she saw through the wobbly glass in the window beside her bed an ink-black sky full of stars. But she did not remember having a bed next to a window in a stone cottage. She did not remember traveling to one.

Her head swam, throbbing with exhaustion and pain, yet still feverishly alert and fighting against the confusion the drugged concoction wrought. She meant to call out for water, and to ask where she was, but when she spoke, she cried *his* name and something twisted sharp in her chest.

Trasa was at her side in a moment, urging her to lie back down. "Rest. You are not healed."

"Where am I?" she asked, and yet the words muddled on the way out, and she really asked, "Where is Cedric?"

"Safe," Trasa said, but her face blanched. "He wishes for you to rest."

Why would she not tell her? And then, with clarity that stung far more than the knife blade had, she remembered. He had done this to her. He had stabbed her, had held her down and slashed at her with a dagger, torn flesh from her arms with the blade as she tried to protect herself.

She opened her mouth to be sick— What a strange thing, to be sick…. Could a Faery do such a thing?

What came out instead was a feral scream. She hugged her knees and rocked to comfort herself, but no comfort would come.

Trasa smoothed her tangled hair at her back, hummed a comforting mother's tune to her as she wailed. How strange, that one who followed a warmaker Goddess, a death Goddess, should attempt consolation in such a time of pain.

"I do not know why," Trasa murmured, and only

then did Cerridwen realize that what she had been sobbing, over and over, was "Why?"

When the tears subsided, and she lay back on her bed, not moving, not really seeing the small cottage before her, Cerridwen asked in a whisper, "Where am I?"

"You are in my home," Trasa told her, straightening from the pot that hung over the hearth. "Rustic by the standards of modern Human society, but Our Lady calls us to lead a simpler life, to stay in touch with the spirit of the land that is drowned out by televisions and radios and computers."

"I have seen a television." It seemed important, somehow, to let the Human know that she was not ignorant to her culture. "There was one in a pub on the Strip, in the Underground." She remembered how it had looked like a window into another world, or a painting that moved, hung as it was on the wall. "How long have I been here?"

"Fourteen days." The Human ladled out some stew from the pot and brought it to Cerridwen's bedside. "Eat."

The sight and scent of food suddenly reminding her of her need for nourishment, she snatched the bowl and fished hot chunks of vegetables from the steaming broth, not caring that it scorched her fingers and burned her tongue.

"Easy—easy!" Trasa took the bowl back, and pressed an implement into her hand. "Use a spoon!"

Cerridwen pushed a tangle of hair away from her face. "Sorry," she said sheepishly. Her stomach lurched at her next thought, but she could not wait any longer. "What happened to Cedric? Have you seen him?"

"I have. I brought him water this morning," she stated, hard, matter-of-factly. "He admitted to what he did to you, and the Court believes you dead."

"Why would they believe that?" Cerridwen sputtered around a mouthful of stew.

Trasa did not answer immediately, pretending instead to be more concerned with the frayed hem of her sleeve. "Because it is safer for you, if she thinks so."

"Why?" And then, mocking, she realized. "Danae was behind this somehow? But that is impossible. Cedric—"

Cedric had wielded the knife. She looked down at the rough black robe she wore, held up her arms and let the sleeves fall back. Bandages swathed her forearms. Cedric had done this to her, the morning after he had met with Danae in private.

"No." She shook her head and pushed the bowl away, suddenly no longer hungry. "No, that is not possible."

Trasa did not argue. It was not enough. Cerridwen wanted her to apologize for thinking such a thing, to laugh away the suggestion. Her silence was as harsh an accusation of Cedric as her words had been.

"It is just not possible," Cerridwen repeated firmly. She looked out the window. She saw no trees, just an endless expanse of night. "Where are we, now? In relation to the Court?"

Trasa gazed out the window as well. "Outside the

forest. Far enough that my Sisters and I could hide here to escape the Enforcers. Close enough that I can still serve at Danae's side."

"You will continue to serve her? You said that you were loyal to me." If the Human truly believed that Danae had tried to kill her, what kind of loyalty was that? Was she even safe here, in the cottage?

"We are loyal to Our Lady," Trasa corrected, no sign of regret on her features. "But we do still remain allies of yours. If we stay close to Danae, we will be on hand when all is revealed and the Court sees her for what she truly is."

"And what is she?" Cerridwen needed to hear her slandered, even though it was a pathetic revenge, at best.

"A coward," Trasa said simply. "She wanted you dead, but did not possess the courage to do the deed herself. She sent someone in her place."

They fell silent then, and Cerridwen's wounds throbbed, as if to remind her of the agony her heart should still feel. "I thought Cedric found me. In the woods."

"No." Trasa went to the hearth and stirred the embers. "No, that was Amergin. He found you within hours of your disappearance, and good thing, too. You would have died had he not."

"Thank you," she said, miserably picking the bowl back up. She would eat, whether she was hungry or not. Not to would be ingratitude. "For all of your kindness."

Trasa nodded. "Do not thank me just yet, though.

You are not healed, and you cannot have given thought to what you will do next."

Not only had she not given thought to what she would do next, she hadn't thought that it was something *to* think about. Now that the Human had brought it up, it seemed obvious that she could not stay here in the cottage forever. And she had no money, no possessions, no connections. Where would she go?

Perhaps it would have been better to die in the forest.

"You cannot lose hope, Your Majesty," Trasa told her, kneeling beside the bed. "You have more allies than you know. It will simply be a matter of calling them together, and striking at the right time. You will be Queene, and greatly admired, if you plan your next steps carefully."

Cerridwen did not have the courage to tell the Human that she was no longer interested in being a Queene, that none of that mattered now. She might survive for centuries, but she would never live. She would merely exist.

The brew Trasa fed her later, before she banked the fire and went to her own pallet, was not as strong as it had been before, and Cerridwen lay awake, staring through the blue-dark night. She had grown so used to Cedric's presence beside her, it was unsettling to sleep without him there. She balled up the blankets and tucked herself next to them. It was foolish, she scolded herself, to miss him, after what he had done—even more foolish to pretend he was there with her. All it did was delay the inevitable, that one day the reality of his absence would strike her a crippling blow. He would never lie beside her again, never tell her that he loved her as he had the night before that horrible morning.

As he had whispered while trying to kill her.

Her stomach turned at that, and she punched at the blankets wildly, unwinding them. Instead of comforting herself with phantoms, Cerridwen chose to spend the sleepless night alone.

Cedric woke, unsure when he had fallen asleep. The raw ache in his throat reminded him at once of the night before, the horrible sight of those feathers in Danae's palms. He closed his eyes and willed his heart to stop beating, but the immortal will of his body to go on living could not be broken.

The crow came to bring him water. As always, she looked on him with disgust. Today, though, instead of staying silent as she pressed the dipper to his mouth, she said, "You have a guest to see you."

He gulped greedily, far more eager to get the liquid down so he could speak than to slake his thirst. He choked on the last bit of it, fought through it before she could leave. "Who?"

"A friend," she said tersely. Striding to the flap that separated the space from the Throne Room beyond, she said, "I hope what you did to her was worth it, in the end."

It was the first time anyone, apart from Danae, had mentioned Cerridwen's murder to him, and her words shocked him. He was not surprised that she would condemn him—he condemned himself, so why should she not, as well—but it surprised him that Cerridwen had been embraced by anyone in the Court during the very short time since her arrival.

"You don't have much time," the crow whispered to whoever waited in the other room. "Danae will return before the noon meal. Leave the way you came."

Cedric struggled to sit up straighter against the post he was tied to, the muscles of his back and his folded wings protesting with the motion. When he saw who had come to him, he stopped breathing.

Amergin stood at the doorway, looking at him with a strange mixture of pity and loathing. Danae's words floated back to him on a cruel wave of hope. *You cannot tell anyone, Human or Fae.*

The man who stood before him was not wholly Human, but neither was he Fae. He was something apart, elevated to the level of Demigod by the faith of a people who had immortalized him.

He was Cedric's last hope, if any remained, and the man knelt before him now with a concerned expression on his sharp features.

"I am under a spell," Cedric blurted, and hoped that Amergin would not dismiss it as a foolish defense.

"I can see that," the Human said simply, looking at a spot over Cedric's shoulder. "Anyone who would bother to look at you would be able to tell that."

"Corpse Water," Cedric said, unable to hold back, now that he could speak the words. "She poisoned me with Corpse Water and ordered me to kill Cerridwen." He stopped, his chest squeezing tight, as though he had just uncovered a hidden well of screams. "I did not want to. I fought it, I tried to warn her, but I could not tell her. I could not utter a word of it to anyone Human or Fae."

"And I am neither." Amergin rocked back on his heels. "I should go, before anyone knows I was here, then."

"Do not leave me!" Cedric could not let him go, not without… "Cerridwen… Danae said, that is… They brought back feathers."

Amergin looked away. That one gesture told Cedric all he needed to know.

"She was alone. She fled to the forest, and she died there." He nodded his head, as though he could force himself to accept it. "I killed her."

"Do not think of that now," Amergin said faintly. "I cannot stand another night of your wailing. You must be strong if we are to repay Danae for this."

"You know the truth," Cedric insisted. "You can tell them, and Danae can be—"

"Your revenge will not come today, friend." Amergin moved to the back of the room, lifted the cloth wall. "I will do what I can, but for now, you must keep this meeting secret."

"I will do what I can," Cedric vowed as the Human slipped under the curtain.

His revenge would not come that day, but waiting another would not be impossible. Cerridwen was gone. If nothing else kept him alive, it would be his hunger for vengeance. No matter how long he was forced to wait.

* * *

The long hours that Trasa was away serving with the other Sisters were unbearably boring now that Cerridwen was conscious of them. The long, black robes that Trasa had lent her covered her wings, so she felt safe enough wandering on the grounds of the cottage.

The building stood halfway down a gentle slope. The grass appeared exceptionally greener against the sunless white sky, and dark lines of stone fence dissected the hill into neat squares. For as far as Cerridwen could see, there were no other Human dwellings, only the vague imprint of a Human road at the bottom of the hill suggested that mortals had ever lived there, aside from the presence of the little cottage. The road made a ghostly impression with chunks of broken black paving, grown over by sickly yellow grass. On the other side of it, another stone fence, and beyond that, the forest.

Cerridwen had watched from the window as Trasa made her way down the hill that morning, toward the V-shaped break in the stone. She had passed through it confidently and strode straight into the trees, though no path showed that any foot traffic went that way at all.

Sitting on the warped bench outside the door, Cerridwen contemplated the forest and listened to the wind teasing around her ears. Cedric had told her before to listen to it, to listen to the land, that it would tell her something. Now, though, she was not interested in hearing anything it might say.

If she used her other sight, she could find her way

back to the camp. When she got there, things would
be as they should. The guards would laze around the
fire, the little servant girl would be busy puttering
away at something. Cedric would be inside the tent,
and when she came into the clearing and the guards
called out upon spotting her, he would emerge and
run to her, catch her up in his arms and demand to
know where she had been. He had been so worried.
If anything would have happened to her, he could not
have borne it. He loved her, and she should never go
missing for so long again.

There would be another feast, to celebrate the
return of the Queene, and she would preside over it
and accept the tributes of the Court, songs and
masques in her honor. She would sit on the throne
and gaze adoringly at her mate, and all who saw
them would say how very fitting it was that they
were so well matched.

From where she sat, there was no reason to believe
that it would not be possible, and yet she knew how
foolish that delusion was. Trasa tended to Cedric
every day that he was held prisoner by Danae. He did
not wait at the camp for her; he sat in abject misery
tied to a pole in the middle of Danae's tent. The
Monster Queene had dared to imprison him even
after they had plotted together, all the better to cover
her own nefarious deeds.

Cerridwen pushed back the sleeves of her robe and
stared down at the bandages. Slowly, she picked at
the tape that held the gauze in place. Should she look,
or leave her wounds to heal, never confronting them

until they had faded away? The end of the bandage was free before she could make her decision, and having come this far, she unwound the gauze.

Faeries healed quickly, but there had been no one to heal her properly. What another Fae could have done with their energy in mere moments, her body struggled to mend on its own over days. It seemed more horrible, somehow, than when they had been fresh. Her blood had clotted in uneven furrows down the length of the exposed cut, and Cerridwen ran her finger across the hard, shiny surface. The scab was itchy and tight, and when she bent her arm experimentally, fissures formed in the dried blood and fresh liquid oozed out.

Her arm aching anew, she returned the gauze and tucked the end under itself to keep it in place. She tried, just to see if she could, to blame Cedric for the pain he had caused her, to hate him…but she could not. That hardly seemed fair, that she should not be able to relish the discomfort she knew he suffered now.

Despite what he had done, she loved him. That was the sickening thing. She had defied and betrayed her mother to escape her betrothal to him, and it had been for nothing, because she loved him. She turned her gaze back to the forest. This time, instead of entertaining the delusion of returning to the campsite, her imagination went further, across the sea, to the Underground. She could walk into her mother's Throne Room, beg forgiveness, and they would embrace. Her father would beam proudly at her, and a great feast would celebrate the smart match the Queene had made between her daughter and her most trusted advisor.

A low groaning sound startled her from her destructive daydream, and she jumped with a yelp. An animal stood beside her, larger than anything Cerridwen had ever seen. She edged away from it across the bench, but it did not appear a danger to her. It merely surveyed her with dull red eyes, its long-lashed lids drooping lazily closed. Beneath its nose, pierced with a gold ring large enough that Cerridwen could fit her hand through it, had she a mind to, its jaws worked, staining the snow-white fur around its mouth green from the grass it chewed.

"You are a bull!" Cerridwen cried, delighted to have recognized the creature from her dream.

Slowly, she stood, not wishing to startle the animal. The whole of its body was snow white, and the hair that sprouted from a spiral between its massive horns was somehow lighter. With a trembling hand, she dared to touch its face, dodging out of the way of its horns as it ducked its head.

"I do not know about bulls," she told it, not caring how ridiculous she might sound speaking to an animal. "Are you a male bull, or a female one? I would not know how to tell the two apart!"

If the animal was bothered by her relentless chatter, it did not say. It bent its head and placidly ripped a chunk of grass and soil free from the ground with its teeth and chewed away.

"I do not envy you your diet." Cerridwen dropped

to her knees to watch it eat, examined the strange ends of its legs. "It's as if you have your own boots!" she squealed, tapping the hard, yellowed material. "Is that bone?"

As if the creature could answer her! She stood, laughing at herself. "You are the only company I have had all day. And you have given me the only smile I have felt in ages."

The animal raised its head sharply, made a huffing noise, its great wide nose flaring. Its tongue snaked out and lazily probed one nostril. Then it turned, the whole of its mammoth body wobbling as though it would collapse, and strolled around the corner of the cottage.

"Oh, do wait, please," Cerridwen called after it, feeling more than a little foolish. But the creature was fascinating, and she had rarely seen actual animals before, not counting the rats and bugs of the Underground. She rose and hurried after it and found it had paused at the side of the house, as if waiting for her. It turned its dim gaze to her and made another low groaning noise, then jerked its head back and turned the corner to go behind the cottage.

It was almost as if the thing wished her to follow it, but in all the stories Cerridwen had heard about animals, they had never seemed to display any sort of intelligence. Still, it was an interesting diversion.

At the back of the cottage, a tangle of thorny ivy crawled up the stone. The beast stood well away from it, and Cerridwen slipped between the plant and the animal. "Is this what you wanted me to see?" She scrubbed her hand over the animal's back. "I do not think you should eat this. It does not look pleasant."

A strange shushing sound caught her ear. It was the wind, yet not the wind, and it grew stronger as it approached, and gained a growling undertone, punctuated by squeaks. "What is that?" she asked the bull, though she had the sense to know that it could not tell her.

She crept to the corner of the cottage, intending to peek around it, and the bull made a high, panicked sound. The beast stepped sideways, giving her no choice but to flatten herself against the prickly ivy.

"I only want to see," she protested, pushing on the animal's hide, but the creature would not budge. She twisted in the small space and rose up on her toes to peer over the windowsill. Through the glass, she could see the light of the open door. Beyond that, the shape of a Human machine bouncing its way down the long-forgotten road.

Without knowing why it did so, Cerridwen's heart pounded. The machine, similar to something she'd seen in a Darkworld pit once, stopped beside the breach in the stone fence and grew quieter. Humans exited it, dressed in clothes that made them almost invisible against the trees, hefting Human weapons similar to the ones the Elves had used in the battle underground, climbed out of the vehicle and made their way through the gap. They examined the ground and one of them lifted something from it to his mouth.

Something wet dripped down Cerridwen's arm, and she realized she gripped the thorn-dense ivy tightly in her fingers. She gasped, then covered her mouth. Could they have heard her?

The Humans went back to their machine, where all but one of them climbed inside. This one, a man, came up the hill, marching purposefully toward the house.

Cerridwen's entire body trembled. She knew that she should duck down from the window, but she could not move. Someone whimpered, and it took a moment to realize that it was her.

The bull made an impatient sound, and she turned to hush it, only to see its huge body come crashing toward her. It slammed her against the wall, and she fell, the wind crushed from her lungs, head swimming with starlight. The animal ran, far more gracefully than she would have expected from such an enormous beast, bellowing, and the Human shouted.

Cerridwen struggled to keep her wits about her, but her thoughts swam, as did the ground beneath her feet. She slumped down, and in the last moment before she lost consciousness, she heard the sound of the Human car-machine roaring to life, then growing fainter in the distance.

Fifteen

The campsite was dark and abandoned, even by the guards who had stayed there. Amergin kicked aside a bundle of flowers that had been left at the mouth of the clearing. Danae had done that, to pay tribute to the fallen Queene. Her great sorrow had been expressed by a bunch of wildflowers left behind, and a simple prayer urging the Court to move forward "with their conscience." So long as their conscience would lead them to elevate her back to her former status, Amergin had no doubt.

He did not know why he had come here. There would be no evidence, nothing tangible to hold against Danae. She was too clever to leave behind any traces, and this was not the true scene of the crime, anyway.

He must have come looking for inspiration, he reasoned, for he did not accept that he ever did anything without a specific meaning behind it. Even if that purpose was unknown to him, it would reveal itself in time.

He went up the steps, trained his flashlight on the wood beneath his feet. Splashes of her blood lingered there, brown and copper-smelling. So, the Queene was mortal, at least in part. He had thought that another of Danae's slanderous rumors.

The floor creaked inside the tent, and he whipped his light up. "Who goes there?"

Another creak, but no answer. The clearing was silent and still, the eerie kind of silence that contained a person who did not want to be found out. Amergin threw the tent flap back and swung the beam of light around inside.

Crouched on the floor, behind a trunk, was Mothú, that ridiculous spy. She shielded her eyes from the unnatural light, and Amergin clicked it off.

"What are you doing there?" He strode across the floor, caught her by the wrist. She cried out, like a wounded animal, as if the motion hurt her.

"There is so much pain here!" she sobbed, fists clenched, knuckles white as she clapped her hands to the sides of her head.

He dropped her, the desperation and pain in her clinging to his skin.

She continued to babble, lying motionless on the floor. "I only did what my Queene asked of me. I only did it because she asked. I told her what I knew, I did my duty. There is so much pain."

Amergin gazed down at her, not certain how to proceed. He had known only a few Empaths in his considerable existence, but he had not envied them for their rarity. It was a blessing from the Gods that more of them did not exist. "What did you do for your Queene?"

Mothú looked up, a haze of confusion over her eyes. "Did you feel it when he killed her? You can still feel it here. All around. All there is...pain."

"I will take that pain away," Amergin promised. "You only have to tell me what you did for Queene Danae."

"What, a spell?" Mothú laughed and clapped her hands together, her eyes filling with tears. "You know a spell that will take the pain away?"

"Yes, a spell." Gods forgive him. "But you must tell me what you did."

Mothú laughed again, tears spilling down her face. "He loved her. He loved her so much. Danae is brilliant. The plan is brilliant."

"What is the plan, Mothú?" He dropped to his knees before her, tried to look her in the eye, but she would not hold still. She swung her head from side to side, agitated, a hand pressed to her mouth.

"She knew it would kill him." She looked him in the eye then, a terrifying clarity coming over her. "I told her that they loved each other. And they didn't know. They thought they were pretending, but...I told her, and she used it against him. She knew it would kill him. She knew it would kill me, when I did it."

"What did she do?" He knew, though he had to hear the confirmation himself. The filthy spy had told Danae all she had needed to know to form a cruel plan.

"Corpse Water." Mothú laughed again. "Do you think she knew? Do you think Her Majesty knew that it would hurt me, too? When he did it? Do you think she knew what would happen?"

No doubt she had, and that added another depth to Danae's cruelty. She knew the Empath would feel Cerridwen's pain, and Cedric's, and that it would drive her mad. All the better to cover her tracks, for who would believe a Faery gone crazy?

"No," he lied smoothly. "I do not think she intended you any harm."

Mothú smiled gratefully, closed her eyes. "She is a good Queene. She is kind."

Amergin rose to his feet. "No. I am kind, though."

"Are you going to do the spell now?" Mothú asked, as hopeful as a child.

He did not answer her, did not offer any further platitudes, before he thrust his dagger through her neck.

The sound of raised voices woke Cedric. It was not the ranting he had become so used to hearing, the screaming that ensued of late whenever Danae didn't get something she wanted.

She had not always acted that way, the crow had mumbled to him when she brought his last dinner. Just since the Undergrounders had come. Cedric had found that hard to believe, but he had not argued. The woman was the only company he ever got, and she had only grudgingly begun to speak to him.

No, the voice that shrieked hysterically now was not Danae's.

"He knows I have done something, and now Mothú has gone, as well." Danae's voice hiccuped in panic. "Find him. Find both of them. I'll have their eyes put out. I'll roast their tongues on a spit!"

The tent flap pushed back, and Danae stormed into the room, the sleeves of her nightgown slashing black arcs in the air before her face. "There is no end to the torment I am to endure, of that I am more than certain."

"Your plans are coming unraveled." Cedric could not help but relish this small victory over her. "Soon, everyone will know what you did. To me, and to Cerridwen."

Her name cut him like glass, like the blade that he had used to kill her. He pushed the pain down, not to ignore it, but to keep himself focused on his task: humiliating Danae, forcing her to crack so badly that all of her secrets spilled from her at the slightest pressure.

She laughed. "No one will know! They ask me, over and over, why haven't I put you to death yet? Why have I not given Cerridwen the justice she deserves?" Danae stopped, breathing hard. "I will. I will give her the justice they think she needs."

When Cerridwen had wanted to die, when she had said the words, Cedric had thought he would never be able to imagine that longing, that desperation. But now, knowing almost certainly what Danae would say, his heart finally returned to him, let him feel something other than loathing and self-hatred. *Say it,* he urged her silently. *Say it, and end this.*

"You will be put to death," she said simply, folding her arms. She looked for some reaction, some fear.

She did not expect the laughter he gave her. "Do it now. I welcome it."

Her face flamed red, her antennae buzzed audibly. "I will give you no such quiet mercy! You will be executed publicly—so that I might weep anew at the loss of our precious Queene, and decry the evil that you have done. So that you can listen to your crime recounted, and I can watch it break your heart in hearing it."

"Danae, I relive those moments with every breath." He forced himself to sound bored, to rob her of her pleasure in her cruelty. "Nothing you can do now, short of forcing me to live forever, will be more of a punishment."

With a cry of fury, Danae stormed from the room, to immediately put her plans for his execution into motion, he had no doubt.

But he could no longer contain his joy, and he laughed, squeezed his eyes shut tight against the tears that filled them. There was nothing to dread, anymore. No fears of an eternity held prisoner to Danae's whims. The ax would fall, and nothingness would await him. A nothingness in which he would no longer be tormented by the memory of Cerridwen's screams.

It could not come soon enough.

Clutching the cold cloth to her throbbing head, Cerridwen tried for the third time to tell the story of what had happened to her that afternoon. "And when the Human came up the hill, the bull became scared and ran. It knocked me into the wall, and I fell."

Trasa nodded, a kind face on her disbelief. "I understood that part. But there are no bulls around here, Your Majesty. The Court raises their animals in clearings in the woods. And there hasn't been a Human farm around here for…hundreds of years, at least."

"Maybe it was a wild bull," Cerridwen insisted stubbornly. "It was here! It was all white, and had—"

"Red eyes, I remember." Trasa patted her knee compassionately, as if assuring a child that no monsters lurked in the dark. "In the morning, I will look again, but I saw no tracks, no dung. Are you sure that you were not simply feverish again? Perhaps you should take the healing brew…."

Cerridwen turned her face to the hearth. She had refused the bitter tea that morning, and again at night-fall when Trasa had returned to find her lying behind the cottage. She could bear the pain easier than she could bear being senseless.

"I will not press you," Trasa said, quiet but firm. "Can I get you something to eat?"

"No." Cerridwen dropped the cloth and tried to rake her hand through her hair, but found it too matted. "Perhaps I am going crazy."

"I do not think the Fae suffer from insanity," Trasa told her with a smile. "Though it would certainly explain the actions of some."

That was too close to the subject they had not spoken of since Cerridwen had woken the first time, and she took a shaking breath.

"I'm sorry. I don't know why I said that." Trasa

stood and went to the bed, straightened the covers needlessly.

Cerridwen was grateful for the space between them. She was not used to being so close to Humans, with their uncanny ability to say the wrong things, and the too-right things, and their strange concept of forgiveness. She leaned her chin on her hands and gazed into the flames.

Trasa suddenly darted to the window.

"What is it?" Cerridwen stood, pressed her hands together in front of her mouth. She hoped it was the bull, back again, feared it might be the Humans again.

"Someone is coming," Trasa said, waving an urgent hand at her. "Cover your wings, quickly! And your—" She gestured frantically at her forehead.

Cerridwen pulled down her hair to cover her antennae, and folded her wings tight to her back, flipping the back of her robes down.

Whoever had approached rapped urgently on the door. It did not seem likely that the Humans, with their brute weapons, would not have simply used force to enter.

"It is Amergin, son of Míl! I must see the Queene."

Cerridwen's spine straightened from the mere mention of her title, though she knew she must look ridiculous and very un-Queene-like in her plain robes and bandages, with her hair matted into ropes around her head.

Trasa hurried to open the door, unhooking the small iron latch that would never keep anyone truly determined out. The strange mystic who had helped her out of the tunnel when she first arrived those endless days ago entered, fairly trembling in his urgency.

"It is a cold night," he said, by way of greeting, before making a quick bow. "Your Majesty."

Cerridwen nodded to him. He had found her, and brought her here. She thought she should thank him, then wondered if Queenes thanked anyone. Trying to remember if she had ever heard her mother thank anyone, she missed what the Human had said.

Trasa had not, and she insinuated herself angrily between Cerridwen and the Druid. "She is not yet recovered. And why should she care for his troubles? You saw yourself what he did to her!"

"What did he say?" Cerridwen shook her head. "Amergin, what did you say?"

"Cedric needs our help." He pushed past Trasa and dropped to one knee before Cerridwen. Like a knight in a storybook, she thought, and she almost snickered at how ridiculous that imagery was, considering her own state and the strange clothes he wore.

What he said next, though, killed all the humor in her. "Danae put him under a spell. That is why he did what he did to you."

The tears were so sudden that she could not guard against them. They rolled down her face in twin rivulets, and she thought it undignified to brush them away. "I do not understand."

"What spell?" Trasa demanded. "What magic could Danae have that would be so great as to make a Faery kill his mate?"

"Corpse Water," Amergin answered without hesitation. "She poisoned him with Corpse Water, and sent him to do her bidding."

"She did it at the feast," Cerridwen realized, a stone of unease settling in her gut. "What is Corpse Water?"

"Water used to wash the dead," Trasa supplied slowly. "It is very powerful."

"Plainly, it made Cedric her puppet. Whatever she told him to do, he was forced into." Amergin paused. "He did not want to harm you. He is in agony. He believes that you are dead."

"You have seen him?" Cerridwen's heart pounded, but she could not let herself believe, not yet. "And you did not tell him I survived?"

Amergin's compassionate gaze lowered. "I feared he would reveal it to Danae, through no fault of his own. I feared the Empaths might recognize new, hopeful emotions in him." He looked up again. "He loves you. So much more than I would have expected a Faery capable of."

Cedric had not wanted to hurt her. Memories fell into place as though they had been held back before, simply because she had not been able to make sense of them. He had tried to give her time to protect herself. He had tried to let her get away, since he was incapable of stopping himself. He had done what he could.

"Your Majesty?" Amergin's gentle voice brought her out of the horrors of the past. "We must act quickly. Danae had a spy in your camp, a servant girl. She was under the effects of Corpse Water, as well, and she will undoubtedly reveal to Danae that I am aware of her plot."

"But she does not know that I live." Cerridwen dabbed at her eyes with her sleeve. "I am in no danger."

"Cedric will be," Amergin said softly.

Something fierce clenched in her heart. She tried to imagine being forced to harm him, wanting to warn him, and being completely powerless. The result was that she wished, more than anything, to put Danae through that pain. Vengeance was not an elegant concept, but she did not care for elegance now. What enveloped her was primal fury, a wish for an appropriate, unending torment for Danae to endure.

"I have to go to him, then." There was a calm about her that she did not feel, and that struck her as unnatural.

Amergin and Trasa exchanged glances, and Cerridwen braced herself for what would come next. They would speak to her slowly, as though she were a child, and look at each other, worried, when she argued with them. She had played this game far too many times to have patience with it.

"I beg Your Majesty's pardon, but…we have no proof to offer the Court that she has done anything to force Cedric's hand." Amergin gave her a long, sympathetic look, giving her time to work out the problem on her own.

Gods, was there some instruction that she had missed growing up in which she would have learned to treat younger beings as though they were simpletons? "Is my word not good enough? If I say I trust Cedric, will not the rest of them?"

Trasa shook her head. "I am sorry, but the mood

in the village is not sympathetic toward Cedric. You might return and claim the throne, but they have seen Danae publicly mourn you, and Cedric imprisoned for your murder. You will have a difficult time convincing them of Danae's guilt after the grand spectacle she has put on in your absence."

"Is there nothing you can do?" Cerridwen asked Amergin. "You are ancient. The Humans worshipped you as a God, though you are not one."

"That is true, although Your Majesty embarrasses me by mentioning it." But he did not look embarrassed. He appeared pleased that she would speak of him so. "I have lost much of that esteem. Danae has painted me as an ineffectual jester in her Court."

"That will end when I hold the throne." Cerridwen chewed on her thumbnail, eyes staring at, but not seeing, the floor in front of her. "There must be some way we can trick her into revealing what she has done, then." Her gaze shot up, found Trasa's. "You could! If we had some more Corpse Water, you could poison her! Then, we could make her admit everything."

"It's not a bad idea," Amergin said slowly. "You do have access to Danae—"

"I cannot do something so low and cowardly." Trasa's face contorted in shock and outrage. "It would be a slight against Our Lady to use trickery, rather than strength."

"Strength will not work in this case," Amergin argued. "There must be some exceptions to your Goddess's commandments, else she is no better than the One God."

"She is nothing at all like the One God!" Trasa snapped. "Beloved Morrigan wishes for us to call upon courage at such a time, not fall to the same level of deception to which Danae has stooped."

"But if you were caught," Cerridwen began slowly, praying silently that she would choose the right words, "you would be punished. Severely. Put to death, if I am not overestimating Danae's temper. Would the Morrigan believe that such an action was cowardly, if you undertook it knowing the full consequences?"

Trasa considered for a long moment. "I feel you are manipulating me to your own ends. I don't like it."

"You don't have to like it," Amergin said cheerfully. "But you have to admit, she has a very good point."

Cerridwen chose to focus on swaying Trasa, rather than reprimanding Amergin. "Please. If you do this for no other reason, do it because I am in need, and no one else can help me. I know that you have already done much to help me, at great danger to yourself. My respect for you will not fade if you do not undertake this task. But you are, truly, the only person in this room who stands a chance of saving Cedric and restoring the rightful Queene to the throne."

Trasa squeezed her lids shut tight, deepening the wrinkles at the corners of her eyes. Her shorn head sagged on her neck, and she sighed. "Let me pray on this, and seek the guidance of the Morrigan."

"We haven't much time," Amergin protested, but Cerridwen warned him into silence with a glare.

"Do what you need, in order to decide with your

conscience's guidance." Though she was as impatient as Amergin to know the answer, Cerridwen recognized the danger in pushing.

Trasa looked up then, tears shining in her wise eyes. "I will go walk, and think on this. Please know that I do not take this decision lightly."

"I know," Cerridwen assured her, and watched with a heavy heart as she left.

"You could have ordered her to do your bidding, Your Majesty," Amergin said, softly breaking the silence that followed Trasa's departure.

With a weariness that plagued her bones, Cerridwen shook her head. "No. No, I could not have."

For the first time, no mist shrouded the clearing in Cerridwen's dream. Between the tall crowns of the trees, the stars shone down from the blue-velvet sky; they showered over her like crystal raindrops. She captured one, and it glittered in her palm in the shape of the three-pointed symbol she had seen in her dreams before.

Out of the darkness lumbered the same blinding-white bull that had met her in the cottage yard, but this time, on its back perched the Warrior Goddess. Her three faces gazed serenely as she rocked and swayed with the bull's movements.

"I know this animal," Cerridwen said, her voice unintentionally loud in the quiet of the forest. "What does it mean?"

"Have you heard tales of the Connacht Queene, who started a war by coveting such an animal?" The

Morrigan hopped down from the bull's back and caught it by the ring at its nose to lead it.

The tapestry from the Great Hall flashed through Cerridwen's mind. "That was a red bull. This one is white."

The Goddess's triplicate mouths bent in wry smiles. "The symbol remains the same. This animal is strength, and power. His white hide is for purity. He was fashioned to send a message to your enemies—you are stronger than them, and more worthy. This will not be lost on the Faery Court you seek to claim."

"I could do without the Faery Court," she said with a sigh. "I want my mate, and to see justice done for him, and that is all."

The Morrigan cocked her head. "You wish for revenge. We do not approve."

"Then you will not let your follower do what I have asked of her?" Cerridwen felt her disappointment rise as a phantom promising harsher despair when she awoke.

"My expectations of her are different. She will do this thing that you ask. But you must not act toward Danae as you have acted toward your enemies in the past. You have ended their lives without honor."

"What should I do, then?" Cerridwen knew, in a sort of far-off way, that she should not speak to a Goddess so plainly. "Am I to fight her? I will lose. I have never fought anyone before, and she is a warrior."

"A true warrior knows when it is best to fight, and when it is best to give order to a situation and leave the fighting to others." The Morrigan took Cerridwen's hand in her own and pressed her palm around the golden ring in the bull's snout. "Take him. He is a gift."

Cerridwen stared down at her fingers wrapping the gold, looked up into the bull's red eyes, which seemed more intelligent in her dream than they had during her waking hours. "What am I supposed to do with—"

She jolted awake to rough hands shaking her. Trasa gripped her shoulders, pulled her to sit up.

"I thought the Morrigan said it was all right to help me," Cerridwen managed through the fog of new wakefulness. The light in the cottage was too bright for early morning. Trasa should have left hours ago.

"I did help you," Trasa said quickly, grabbing a pair of boots from beside the bed and stooping to force Cerridwen's feet into them. "I went into the Palace this morning, early, and found Danae's Corpse Water. I put it in her breakfast. But we must act quickly. I could not afford to arouse her suspicion by commanding her, already, before we were placed to act."

"Why?" She rubbed her eyes, thinking vaguely that she should be more excited at this development, that she should spring into action. Her exhausted limbs would not oblige her. "Does it wear off?"

"Because she is going to have Cedric put to death tonight!" Trasa's knuckles were turning white where she clenched her fists around the laces of the boots.

Cerridwen's heart stopped, then started again with a fearful lurch. Cedric, put to death? As a possibility it was one thing, to know a date was set and her mate's life was now an hourglass draining away was quite another. Death—she could not let that happen to him. Nor could she let herself dissolve into hysterics, as she so desperately longed to do. "Find Amergin, tell him what has happened. I will dress and we will leave immediately." Noting the Human's flushed cheeks and the grim set of her mouth, Cerridwen asked, "We can reach him in time, can we not?"

"We might," Trasa said, a note of hysterical uncertainty. "Your Majesty should fly."

Cerridwen tested her injured wings, tried in vain to open them. "No. That will not be possible." She swallowed down a panicked sob. "Go. Find Amergin. We will do what we can."

Only when the holy woman had gone did Cerridwen allow herself a moment of fear. Then, the moment passed, hardening into a promise that beat in her chest.

She must save Cedric. Against all odds, she must save him.

Sixteen

꧁꧂

She dressed herself in the white gown that Danae herself had given her, the one that Cedric had torn apart in his passion and stained with her blood under the witch's spell. She did not leave it in tatters as it was, though. She ripped the bodice free from the skirt, used the sleeves to knot it about her neck and tied the gaping front closed. She wrapped the ruined skirt around her waist and knotted it, approving of the mud that stained it, and the browning slashes of her blood that remained there.

It was somehow a more fitting ensemble for her purpose, as it displayed Danae's cruelty with every crease and tear like a badge. She wore the pendant of the Morrigan's symbol like a shield.

She pushed the door open just as Amergin and Trasa returned, their expressions grim with determination. They stopped and gaped at the sight of her.

"Your Majesty might also remove the bandages,"

Amergin offered as he came closer. "It will show them, undeniably, the hardship that you have endured."

She nodded and unwound the gauze from her arms. The scabs beneath crackled on her withered, damp skin. "Let us go, then, before it is too late."

They let her lead them, marching down the hill toward the gap in the wall. They had nearly made it when a noise behind them, the droning bellow of an animal, stopped them.

"By the Gods," Amergin said with a laugh. "Look at that!"

The white bull loped down the hill, as though it would bowl them over. It came to a halt before them, lowing impatiently.

"I saw this creature in my dreams," Trasa said, eyes aglow with wonder.

"As did I." Cerridwen approached it confidently and gripped the ring in its snout. It followed her as she turned back toward the forest. "I saw it yesterday, as well, though no one believed me."

She clucked to the animal as she lead it over the gap in the fence, and looked back, with no small amount of satisfaction, at her two companions, who stared, openmouthed, after her.

Regarding the last war between the Humans and the Fae, Mabb had often remarked at how bloodthirsty the enemy mortals were, how very primitive and foul their desire for destruction was.

As Cedric listened to the cheering of the Faeries gathered outside the Palace, the ones calling for his blood and eagerly anticipating the sight of it being spilled, he regretted not arguing with her then. The Fae, Humans, all living beings, contained a seed of cruel destruction within them.

The night had fallen, and the old crow had not brought him water or food. He would go to his death on an empty stomach, which seemed fitting, going from one emptiness to another. Danae had not come to him to gloat, either. He assumed she saved that for the moment he laid his head on the block. It would add the dramatic touch she craved.

The flap in the fabric wall moved back, and a guard entered. One of their former Underworld guards, he realized with a shock, dressed in the rough uniform of Danae's soldiers. "It is time, Cedric."

"I never thought to see you change your allegiance so quickly." He did not condemn him for it. How could he, now?

The guard shrugged. "I never thought to see you executed for treason against our Queene. But here we stand."

"Here we stand," Cedric echoed, struggling to his feet, hands still bound behind him.

The guard came forward and cut the ropes, helped Cedric get his footing.

"This is embarrassing," he said, to himself, though the guard could undoubtedly hear. "I will not have the dignity of walking unassisted to my own death."

His feet came out from beneath him, pushed by the ankle of the guard who stood over him, fists clenched. He struggled to keep his hard expression, but it faltered, assailed by unmistakable sadness. "Why should you have dignity?" the guard asked through tightly clenched teeth. "Did she die with dignity, alone in the forest?"

"You cared for her." Cedric's heart clenched in a grief he had thought long since burned out.

The guard gripped him by the arm, pulled him to his feet roughly. "No. I did not know her. She was not a Queene. She was a kind Faery. That is a rarity, I have come to find."

Cedric agreed, but he did not say so. It was not what the guard wished to hear. He let the guard have the moment for himself, to assuage his own grief. The pain of loss made them kindred, though the guard would not believe it, and that comforted Cedric as he was led out of the tent, into the angry throng in the clearing.

The scaffold had been erected over the central cooking pit. The fire had been buried, but the heat of it wafted up through the cracks between the boards. Cedric had listened to them building all through the day. Each hammer strike had been a blessing, bringing him closer and closer still to the end of existence. When the ax fell, he would be free from the pain of what he had done, free of the prison of Danae's spell.

The witch herself waited at the top of the scaffold steps, beside the burly Human who wielded the delicate silver ax that would sever him.

The pitying look on Danae's face was not meant for him, but for the crowd that pressed forward as he mounted the steps. She played her role so convincingly, he could not fault them for falling under her sway.

Danae said nothing to him, but turned and walked to the front of the scaffold, standing just slightly left of the block, so that she would not block the view. "As you know," she began, as Cedric was made to kneel on the straw behind the oak block, "I have struggled with myself over the decision to see this traitor put to death. It is not an easy thing, to take a life. I recognize how precious it is, and how very tragic the consequences of a death in these times are, when we are not certain of an Afterworld. But our Queene, may she rest easy in the Summerland now, believed in vengeance. She put the traitors Bauchan and Flidais to death, as she had every right to. I do not make a judgment now on whether that was wrong or right. I merely do what I believe she would have wanted, were she here to consult on this decision."

Cedric shook his head. Each time he thought he'd seen the very limit of Danae's treachery, she had set the bar surprisingly higher.

She paused, turned to him, her annoyance flickering briefly over her face before she could compose a hurt expression. "Even now, you mock her? Does your cruelty know no bounds?"

The crowd cried out with its disapproval, and it took a long moment for Danae to calm them again. While she did, guards looped rope around Cedric's wrists and tethered him by the arms to iron rings affixed to the floor.

"The sentence I have passed gives me no pleasure. As the mate of the Queene, the sacred line of our Faery rulers passes from him to his next mate, and then to their children. But he has so tainted that bloodline that I fear it might never recover. And so, Cedric, mate to Queene Cerridwen, I sentence you to death. Your head will be struck from your body, and both parts burned, and the ashes scattered to the wind. Have you anything to say, before the sentence is carried out?"

She expected him to beg, or to try to denounce her, to struggle against the spell and ultimately fail in despair. He almost laughed at her. She had no notion of what he felt, how it pained him every moment that passed without Cerridwen.

Instead of speaking, he merely shook his head again and held her gaze.

Fury built up in her eyes, and he felt a stab of satisfaction that she was the one struggling between what she wished to do and what she was able to. Though there was no spell on her, she was not free to act as she wished. She was not free to strike him and rage aloud.

"Executioner," she called out, moving past him with a haughty flick of her skirts. She had worn black, he noticed, the same gown that she had used to make her pretend mourning over Cerridwen seem genuine.

The guards pressed him forward, until his chin fitted over the groove in the block. He closed his eyes, saw Cerridwen's face in his memory, the wonder in it as she looked out over the sea and the wind lashed her porcelain face with her copper hair.

"When you are ready," the executioner said, awfully solicitous of the condemned, in Cedric's opinion.

"I am ready now," he told him, joy welling in his chest as he remembered the feel of Cerridwen's soft curves against him, her eyes fluttering beneath their lids as she slept.

The executioner's boots crushed the straw on the scaffold floor, and the ax scraped on wood when he lifted it.

In Cedric's mind, he saw the beautiful white curve of his mate's neck, the sweat-damp hair at her temple as he had leaned over—

"Stop!"

The familiar voice jolted him from his imaginings, and for a moment he thought that the deed had already been done, that the blade had fallen and he had not noticed its strike. He opened his eyes, struggled to lift his head, as the awed whispers of the crowd rose to a frenzy of shouting voices.

Cerridwen, alive and whole, rode into the clearing on the back of an enormous white bull. The light from the torches in the trees gilded her copper hair, matted against her head where it had been pinned up for the feast, the curls that had cascaded down her back then twisted to tangled ropes. A crow led her. The same that had brought him his supper all those days. Amergin followed behind, dressed in ridiculous Human clothes, but somehow still possessing an air of dignity.

But Cerridwen. It was not possible. He pulled against the ropes that held him, no longer content to die there. "Let me up," he called out. "Let me up!"

"Release him," Cerridwen shouted, gesturing to the guards. When they did not move, Amergin raced forward, but was held back.

Danae came back to stand at the front of the scaffold. "Your Majesty," she called out, sounding as though she would choke on every word. "You are alive. Thank the Gods!"

"I am alive, yes." Cerridwen's cold eyes fixed on Danae as though she could turn the harpy to ice. Was it possible that she knew what had occurred? The breath seized in Cedric's lungs at the mere hope of it. "I am alive," she repeated. "So you do not have any reason to put my mate to death."

Danae swallowed audibly, spread her hands and then twisted them together again, wringing her sleeve between them. "Your Majesty, I only thought to avenge you, the way I believed that you wished—"

"You thought to kill me, to kill my mate, and take the crown back for yourself!" Cerridwen shouted.

Silence fell over the clearing, as though all of the murmurs and whispers of the crowd had been wiped away.

"Your Majesty—" Danae began again, but Cerridwen interrupted her with a shout that echoed to the treetops.

"Silence!

"Release my mate," she ordered, and the guards finally moved to do her bidding. The moment his ropes were cut, they hauled Cedric to his feet, and he thanked the Gods that he did not have the strength to run to her. He was still under the spell of the Corpse Water, still compelled to end her life.

Cerridwen was alive. Though she was there, right there, he could scarcely believe it. The gory wounds on her fair arms mocked him, and his pain at causing them flared to new life. He lunged at Danae—that, he could not help—and Faeries and Humans alike gasped. The guards held him, and he sagged back, body feeble from weeks of captivity and immobility.

"Tell her," Cerridwen calmly instructed the crow. "It is you who must order her to reveal her secrets, yes? I think now would be an excellent time."

"What are you talking about?" Danae, no longer able to conceal her fury, turned her fiery gaze to her handmaiden. "Trasa, you will tell me the meaning of this, immediately!"

"I will do no such thing." The woman straightened, arms folded in the wide sleeves of her black robe. "Danae, we of the Order have long looked down on your deceit and underhanded trickery. We have served you, because in the past you were a great warrior. Your greed and your villainy has grown, like a fetid canker, all of these years. You gave this Faery Corpse Water, and forced him to make an attempt on the Queene's life, didn't you?"

Danae laughed, and shook her head, but when she spoke, all that came out was, "Yes." Her eyes widened, her laughter died. She cleared her throat. "I did not mean… Yes. Yes, I did."

"Tell them, then," Trasa commanded. "Tell them your plan to kill the Queene."

Though she struggled to hold back her words, they broke free, cascading from her lips like water over a damn. "I poisoned Cedric with Corpse Water. At the feast. I instructed him to take the Queene back to her camp. To make love to her. To tell her that he loved her. And to kill her before first light."

Cedric closed his eyes. He had lived the moment once, and he could not stand to endure it again.

"Why did you do this?" Trasa asked, in the voice of a parent scolding a child, pulling out the answer that was already plain, but that needed to spoken aloud by the guilty party.

"Because I hated her." Danae's shoulders sagged in defeat. "She killed Bauchan. I loved him, and she killed him. She ruined my Queenedom here. She ruined…" Her voice broke and died into a whisper. "She ruined everything."

Cerridwen climbed down from the animal's back and left him standing there, placidly chewing what little green he could find on the trampled ground. As she came forward, Cedric saw that she wore the same dress she had the morning of her disappearance. She did not look at him as she passed, but he saw more clearly the damage he had done her.

Cerridwen stood in front of Danae, emotionless and still, contemplating her for a long, silent moment. Then her face contorted and her hand came up, landing with a resounding crack against Danae's cheek.

"I woke to find my mate kneeling over me in my

bed, a dagger in his hands!" she screamed, her face turning red with the exertion of rage. "I flew into the forest, bleeding and terrified, and I lay in the rain and prayed for death! I would have died…had Amergin not found me." She slapped Danae again, a wordless cry accompanying the action. "And this makes you happy, does it? Answer me!"

"Answer her," Trasa echoed, and Danae was forced to nod.

"Kill her!" someone shouted in the crowd, and a ripple of approval followed. They would tear Danae apart, Cedric realized, and he felt no horror at the thought.

"I will not kill her!" Cerridwen called over the crowd. "I will not! I would be no better than she is, if I did. Only a coward seeks to remove their enemies in such a way. I do not fear her. What can she do to further harm me? Nothing. I am Queene. She is nothing but a viper. I will send her away, banish her from her kind. Let her see then if her tricks can help her survive on her own."

"Before she goes," Cedric said quickly, "she must remove her spell. Else I will still be obligated to kill you."

Cerridwen flinched, and he ached to take her into his arms and comfort her. He could not, he knew; her trust would be long in coming, if he ever gained it again.

"Remove your spell," Cerridwen told Danae.

The stubborn witch did not act until Trasa repeated the command.

"From this day forth, Danae is forbidden from

contact with anyone in this encampment. If a member of this colony is caught supplying her with food or comforts, they will be branded as a traitor and banished, as well," Cerridwen pronounced, appearing so much like her mother that it took Cedric's breath away. "You will go now, and take with you only the clothes you stand up in."

Danae looked out to the assembly, her chin quivering. "I have kept you safe all of these centuries," she cried. "I have kept the Enforcers out, and welcomed you Humans into our world. I have built the very colony that you live in! How can you turn me out?"

"Danae," Trasa called. "Do not speak."

Her mouth clamped firmly shut, and tears of defeat rolled from her eyes. She made her way down the scaffold steps, and no one hindered her progress as she walked through the clearing, toward the path that led away from the encampment.

"Guards, see that she goes," Cerridwen said quietly, and the two holding Cedric released him to do her bidding. He swayed on his feet and fell to the floor.

In an instant, Cerridwen was at his side, her beautiful face lined with concern, her white hands moving over his hair, his back, his arms. "He needs a healer," she told the executioner. "Could you please bring one, and help him into the Palace?"

The man who had been only seconds away from ending his life now lifted Cedric to his feet and helped him make his way down from the scaffold. The crowd cheered, and Cerridwen shouted over them, "Let Danae's banishment be a lesson to all who have witnessed it today. I am your Queene. My throne in ensured by the will of the Gods. My life is protected by their good graces. Any who seek to destroy me will fail. And any who seek to destroy you will be met with my wrath."

They cheered louder. Cedric turned his head, wished he could see her in her moment of triumph, but he glimpsed only the curve of her back, and her arm raised, hand clenched to a fist over her head as she stood in the adulation of her Court.

Cerridwen left the scaffold without further remark. She did not have an ounce of eloquence left in her tired body. The heady mix of emotions pounding through her veins had nearly robbed her of the few words she had managed. Now, she wished only for solitude, and silence.

Trasa met her at the bottom of the steps, and Amergin, as well. They both offered their congratulations and embraced her enthusiastically, but she could only stand stiff in their arms. "I want every trace of Danae removed from this colony. Start with the Palace. I want all of it, everything she owned, out of my sight."

"Yes, of course, Your Majesty," Trasa said with a bow, her worry plain on her face. "Will you require anything else at present?"

"I want to be alone," she replied, knowing how impossible that would be, now. She was Queene. There would never be a moment alone.

Still, she went up the steps, into the Palace, in the vain hope of solitude. The room behind the Throne

Room was a flurry of activity, the healers tending to Cedric. She went into the room to her left, a small sitting space with stools and a low table set with fruit and wine, probably put there by Danae in anticipation of an execution celebration. Cerridwen sat and miserably picked over the apples and grapes but ate nothing.

She did not wish to see Cedric. The healers could do their work, and make him strong again, and then he could return to Bauchan's camp, or go farther, if he wished. Perhaps to another settlement, somewhere far from her. The idea was at once painful and enticing. If he stayed, she would have to face him, sooner or later. She might see him at festivals and celebrations. He might expect to stay on as her advisor, and she would see him every day. That would only prolong her hurt, but when she thought of him leaving, of never seeing him again, she wondered which would cause her more pain.

She would not force him to stay. Not now that she knew his declaration of love to be false. Somehow, it had been less depressing when the proof of his lie had been his act of attempted murder. She might have been able to force herself to hate him, over time. Now, she knew that he had not told her he loved her to be cruel. He had not told her because he truly loved her, either. He had told her because he had no other choice, and no emotion, negative or positive, had molded his words at all.

She kicked the bowl of fruit, sent it clattering from the table in a move so sudden that she surprised herself.

How had Danae known that this was the way to strike at her heart most effectively? Had she been able to see something that Cerridwen herself had not, some lack of warmth or tenderness that her affection-starved brain hid from her so to continue her delusions? How could she have been so foolish as to not have seen it herself?

How could she have believed that impassioned declaration?

Because she had wanted it, more than she had ever wanted anything. She wanted him, and she wanted him to feel the same, to think of no one else but her, to have the passion for her that he had felt for the Human Gypsy he mourned. She wanted him to feel for her what Fenrick had pretended, wanted for herself what her mother had felt for Malachi. An immortal life without love was not something she thought she could bear, and she could not be Queene of this Court alone.

"Your Majesty?" Trasa pulled back the fabric and stepped into the room, glancing quickly away from the food strewn across the floor. "I think you should submit to the healers, as well. You have not fully recovered, and you will need your strength."

"Yes, fine, send them in." They could try to heal her, but nothing, short of the power of the Gods and Goddesses themselves, would make her whole again.

Seventeen

〜⤳⦿⤶〜

Cedric slept through the evening, past the start of supper, and Cerridwen was glad for it. She called Trasa and Amergin to sup with her, and they ate in relative silence.

"This is strange," Cerridwen said, for what had to have been the third time since they had all sat down. "Being here. I suppose I knew I would be Queene one day, but yet not so soon."

"Yes, Your Majesty," Trasa said with a nod.

"We need to think about the Humans," Amergin said suddenly. "The ones you saw at the cottage. They were Enforcers, there is no doubt. Why they are drawn to this place, when we have such powerful magic shielding us, is a concern."

"There is little Cerridwen can do about this right now," Trasa said, almost scolding. "She has only just healed, and this camp has been greatly disrupted. We must simply hope that they do not come any closer than the edge of the woods."

Cerridwen slipped the sleeve of her gown back to examine her arms. The healers had done what they could, but too much time had passed, and lumpy, pink scars, tight and shiny, marked her flesh in each place that Cedric's knife had fallen. "They will come closer. They will probably come in greater number, too, if they realize that the white bull wasn't Earthly in origin…" she said absently. She looked up at Trasa. "You should not return to your cottage. They might follow your trail. You could lead them directly here."

"My cottage is my home—" Trasa protested, but stopped herself. "No, Your Majesty is correct. For Danae, I would not abide such a request, but for you, I will stay here. Some of the Sisters live in the colony, and I can stay with them."

"You could take Bauchan's tent," Amergin said, biting off a bit of bread. He spoke around it. "No one's using it now."

"Cedric will need somewhere to stay," Cerridwen said, a little faster and harsher than she had intended.

"I do not see why," a voice said from the doorway. Cerridwen looked up reluctantly to meet Cedric's eyes.

"May we be alone?" he asked Trasa and Amergin, and they both stood, nodding, and took their plates with them when they left.

Cedric sat on the stool Trasa had vacated, at Cerridwen's left. He did not speak at first, and he did not touch her. He gazed at her with an intensity that made her fidget, and she would not meet his eyes.

"Why," he asked slowly, "why would I not stay here, with you?"

She did not want to have this conversation. She did not wish to show him how he had hurt her, and that there was no way she could pretend he had not. There was nothing she could say to disguise how she felt for him, not after she had admitted to it that night. Still, he would not accept silence from her, she knew him too well to expect that. "Because you do not love me, and I will not force you to stay."

He reached for her hand, and she fought to control its trembling. "You would not have to force me to stay. And I do love you, Cerridwen. I was under a spell—that was the only reason I harmed you. You cannot believe that any part of that was me."

"I do not." Gods, how she could not stand it if he thought she held him accountable for that attack. "I know that you would never have... I could not believe it, even as you wielded the dagger against me. Even as I lay on the forest floor, it did not seem real to me. I tried to accept it as reality, and every time, I could not bring myself to hate you.... You were under a spell. That, I know all too well. That same spell bade you to tell me that you...love me." She stumbled over the words, feeling foolish that she had to utter them.

"No." Cedric squeezed her hand. "No, I did not say those things because of the spell. Or I did. But the spell did not make me feel them. I said what I felt in my heart, truly."

She pulled her hand back.

With a curse, Cedric stood, and, though she did not wish to, she shrank from his sudden movement.

His face paled in horror. "Do you still believe that I would harm you? I love you, Cerridwen. I went to the block today happy, glad to know that my life would end and I would no longer have to bear the grief and guilt I felt over your death."

"Stop!" She could not hear it, because she could not believe it was true. There had been so many stories read to her as a child, the valiant prince breaking the evil spell out of true love for his princess. It was foolish, she knew, but her heart broke at the thought that whatever Cedric had felt for her, it had not been enough to stop the knife from cutting into her. "If you love me, why did you do it? Why did you…hold me down and…why could you not stop?"

"I wanted to!" He raked his fingers through his hair in frustration. "I fought so hard to warn you. Holding myself back until you woke was… Gods, I have never felt such pain! I took no pleasure in what I did to you! How could you even think that of me?"

She stared at the tabletop, unable to think of the words to forgive him, certain she would not be able to say them if she could.

A guttural noise of disgust broke from his throat and he stalked toward the opening in the tent wall. Without knowing why, Cerridwen sprang to her feet and ran for him, his name tearing from her lips on a desperate cry. He turned and caught her in her flight, gripped her shoulders and hauled her up to smash his lips against hers. The tears that fell onto her cheeks were not her own.

"I have wanted to touch you—" he gasped against her mouth "—since I saw you come into the clearing. I thought you were dead. She told me you were—"

"I know," she whispered, fitting her palm against the hard curve of his jaw. "I thought that you had wanted me dead."

"Never." He kissed her again, with less grateful urgency than before. The need in him now was not simply to touch her, but something closer to the desperate passion he had displayed the night before their horrible parting.

She pressed herself against him, arched as his mouth slid down to the hollow between her collarbones. An ache rose up in her, pulsed between her legs, and she wound them around his waist as he dragged her skirts up and laid her on the end of the long table.

Trasa and Amergin, not to mention other members of the Morrigan's strange Sisterhood, remained in the Palace, and a flush heated her skin at the thought that they would certainly know what was transpiring in the dining room. "Someone will hear," she whispered against his ear, and then she could not resist biting it.

"I do not care," he growled, pulling his robes open. He hissed as she traced her tongue over the Guild Mark at his neck, paused as if trying to regain self-control, despite his remark.

It occurred to her that she did not care, either. The fear of someone condemning her behavior was the only motivation she could think of for caring what they thought of her, a trait drummed into her from her time in her mother's Palace. After all that had happened here in the Upworld, she could no longer pretend that the opinions of others mattered to her.

All that mattered to her, in that moment, was that Cedric was safe and healed, and that she was alive, and that, despite the tremendous hardships they had faced, no force existed that could drive them apart.

She lifted her hips, eager to feel him again, ignoring the pain in her still-tender wings as her weight settled back against them. As before, the excitement of touching him was all her body had needed to make itself ready for him, and when the wide, firm tip of him pressed against her opening, he slid in easily. Sheathed in her completely, he rested his forehead against hers, hot breath brushing over her face.

"I love you," he whispered. "Do not ever doubt that again."

There were no words that could convey the answer she wished to give him, so she held his face between her hands and kissed him, body rigid with the tension of not moving, though her every instinct demanded it.

With a rough groan, he tore his mouth from hers and gripped her hips, pulling her hard against him, so quickly that it forced a shocked moan from her throat. His hands slid to the curve of her buttocks, to her thighs, underneath her knees, where he urged her wordlessly to wrap her legs about him again. She complied readily, grinding against him, and with a growl deep in his throat, he pounded into her, over and over, fingers digging into the flesh of her thighs.

The table beneath her rocked and creaked; for a

hysterical moment, she wondered if it would fall. But the thought fled on the wave of energy that flooded her, forcing her into the other sight. The usual green color of her energy had been replaced by something bright white, something not moving in bubbles or sparks but blazing flame through each part of her, most specifically to the place where she and Cedric were joined. The light in her pulsed with her heat, with his heartbeat, each ripple growing in intensity until it was so bright that she could not look at it anymore. She opened her eyes to the sight of the dining room as her body jerked and her mouth opened to release a cry that hung suspended on the very edge she teetered over: herself. She did not need the other sight to know the moment she went over and the flames within consumed her. She shuddered, gripped his arms as anchors in fear of being swept away, and shouted, finding her voice again in the moment of pleasure so intense that it both grounded her and unhinged her further.

Cedric drove deeper into her, and then went still with a cry of his own. He bent and laid his head against her breast, his skin separated from hers by the soft fabric of her gown.

"One day," she began, in a voice so calm that she found it comical, "I would like to do this in a more comfortable manner. Not against a tent post, or a table. And perhaps not quite so violently."

He kissed her, then withdrew from her with a slight grimace and carefully put his robes back to order. "I did not tear your clothes, this time. That is progress."

She rolled to her side and spotted her trencher, still sitting abandoned at the head of the table. "I did not finish my dinner."

"I did not get any." He cheerfully offered her his hand. "This was a fair trade."

She gripped the front of his robes, stopping him as he tried to turn away. "I must know," she said, clinging to him so desperately that she was almost embarrassed. "You told me, once before, but I must hear it again. If she had not put that spell on you…if she had not told you to do it, would you have told me that you loved me?"

His arms closed around her, and she pressed her face to his chest rather than look into his eyes. She could not bear it if his words did not match what she saw there. "Perhaps not that night, if things had gone differently," he admitted, "but your tears, not her command, moved me to tell you." He hooked his fingers under her chin, gently forced her to look up at him. "I would have told you, eventually. I could not have kept it secret for much longer," he said, voice dying to a whisper before he pressed his mouth to hers.

It was not the romantic declaration of a Prince in a Story, but that mattered little to her heart.

They lay in what had once been Danae's bedroom, though it had been stripped bare of everything but the bed and the oil lamps that lit it. Cedric had—foolishly, in hindsight—asked Cerridwen why she would dispose of so many fine things. She had flown into a rage then, demanding why she should keep them when they reminded her of the traitor who had harmed them. Cedric wisely dropped the subject.

"What are you doing?" he asked, rousing himself from the half-sleep he had succumbed to.

Cerridwen lay in the crook of his arm, all her warm softness pressed against him, one arm braced against his chest as she leaned over him, tracing the edges of his Guild Mark with her fingertips. "This is so ugly," she said, in the same tone that she might have used to describe a child as adorable. "I remember Mother always displaying her Guild Mark like a banner. It looked better on her."

"Ugly?" He pushed himself up onto his elbows. "How so?"

She sat up, as well, stroking her hand down his neck where the mark covered his skin in black swirls. "I do not care for it. I do not think I will require my Assassins to wear it."

"All of your Assassins already have it," he reminded her, sinking back down on the pillows.

"There will be more." She snuggled against him again, resting her head on his shoulder. "And I will not ask them to wear it."

"Your Majesty does not understand the purpose of the mark, I think," he teased, and at once knew that he should not have. She went stiff beside him, the air of content they had shared evaporating into tension once again.

"Do not call me that," she said, pleading tingeing her words. "Not you."

"I will not do it again, in private company," he promised, kissing the top of her head. "Would you like to know then what the mark is for?"

She nodded, relaxing again. "It has been a long while since I have had a bedtime story."

"Do not do *that*," he warned her with a chuckle. "I do not need any reminders of your youth. The mark was given to me when I became an Assassin. Not when I had completed my training, and not after some long trial to prove my worth. It was given to me the very moment I pledged to serve as Assassin for my Queene."

"Mabb?" Cerridwen asked, idly lacing her fingers with his, as though putting a possessive barrier between him and the ghosts of the past.

"No, not Mabb. Her mother." He smoothed a few curls of her hair against her bare shoulder. "I was not in love with Mabb, you know. I admired her."

"You were lovers," Cerridwen insisted. "Everyone at Court knew it."

He shrugged. "We were. But I did not feel for her what I feel for you." After a silent moment, he continued with his original purpose. "The Guild Mark displays to everyone who sees it that I have committed my life to eradicating the enemies of the Queene. After I became the Guild Master, it reminded me of the lives that I commanded, and my responsibility to them, as well as to the Queene."

"But you are no longer an Assassin," Cerridwen said, rolling to her side to face him. "Do you still wish to have this mark on you, if that is no longer a part of your life?"

"I will always be an Assassin. That training never leaves you." He closed his eyes, feeling the lure of sleep again. "And you need more than six in your Guild."

"I am still unconvinced," she said, mocking a haughty tone. "But for now, I will bow to your experience."

His lips twitched into a smile that he was almost too tired to see through to the end. "Thank you, that is very kind."

The warm heaviness of sleep had sunk into his bones, the familiar feeling of drifting into deep blackness washed over him. He had thought Cerridwen asleep, but then she spoke, almost hesitantly. "There were Enforcers in the woods, near Trasa's cabin."

At once, sleep fled, eluding his tired body as his mind snapped to frantic attention. "What?"

"I should not have said anything." She sat up and wound the bedclothes around her body, as though she would leave.

She seemed almost guilty, and Cedric could not fathom why she would blame herself. "Why did you not tell me?"

"You were with the healers, and I thought it best if you were allowed to fully recover...." She shook her head. "I did not trust you enough, yet."

"Have I ever done anything that would make you not trust me with this?" he asked, then quickly amended that statement. "Anything while not under a spell?"

"I did not know if you would stay." She would not meet his gaze. "I did not want to tell you and make you feel obligated to stay."

"I would have been obligated to stay, anyway. I swore an oath to your mother that I would keep you safe. If nothing else existed between us to keep me here, I would have stayed, knowing this."

"Exactly." Her shoulders sagged. "It would not have been fair. And I did not want…"

He sat up, reached for her, but she held herself away from him. "What did you not want?"

"I did not want to spoil this night." A tear rolled down her cheek when she faced him. "I have the most awful premonition, Cedric. I do not believe our time here will last any longer than my time lasted underground. I feel as though there will never be permanence. I will never have a home again. And for tonight, I wanted to ignore all of that, and ignore the Enforcers. I think that they are what will drive me from this place. And if I go, what will happen to the Fae here? What of the ones who followed us from the Underground? Who will lead them when I am…"

Her silence, and the heartbreak in her eyes, sent a chill of foreboding up his spine. "You have foreseen something?"

"No, not this. Not yet." She wiped at her eyes with the back of her hand and laughed through her tears. "I am probably imagining terrors that are not there."

"It is understandable, after all that you have been through," he soothed, pulling her back to lie down. "You are tired. We will sort out the problem of the Humans in the morning."

"You are right," she said, but it was clear that her fear was not dispelled by simply ignoring the problem.

The dread that gnawed at him all night proved that he could not put it from his mind, either.

The dawn brought the sun, and actual sunlight, into the clearing, rather than the misty gray that had plagued the forest since the Underworlders had arrived.

Cedric had not slept. The revelations of the night before were not solely to blame. The few times he had managed to drift off, he had woken with a start, terrified to look at his hands, sure that he would find a knife there. He could not rest easy until the sun had come up, and Cerridwen had opened her eyes to greet him with a sleepy smile.

He had taken her again, while her body was still warm and limp with sleep, thankful with every breath that the spell was truly gone, and the danger had passed. Though he would have preferred to stay in bed all day, limbs tangled with hers, it would have been irresponsible, no, plainly idiotic, to do so when Enforcers prowled the forest around them.

After taking their breakfast alone in their room, they faced the daunting task of rebuilding the governing body of the Court. It was not an easy task. Amergin and Trasa met with them and were kind enough not to mention what had taken place on the dining table they all sat around.

"Danae never had a traditional Council," Amergin told them. "She started off with one, but each member fell away as they disagreed with her on one point or another…and she kicked them out."

"That sounds like Danae," Trasa said, her face

pinched with annoyance. "If I did not know you, Your Majesty, I would say that all Faeries were the same. Selfish, cruel, thinking only to advance themselves, no matter the cost to anyone else."

"And you would be right, for the most part," Cedric agreed. "But this is something we hope to change. In the Underground, things were not much better, but at least there was a cohesive goal. We were united in our hatred of the Darklings below and the Humans above."

"We wished, and still wish, to take the Earth back for the Fae," Cerridwen clarified. "It would be unfair to expect you to aid us without knowing that, to help you in your decision."

Cedric took a deep breath, not certain whether he should be proud of Cerridwen for her honesty, or dismayed by it. He had seen the way the people of the colony, Danae included, treated the women he had come to think of as crows. Cerridwen had told him of their devotion to the Morrigan, and the nickname had only seemed more apt. They were revered, almost as the representatives of the triple Goddess on Earth, and he did not wish to lose their support, especially if they could sway the colony's Humans to follow them, as well.

But Cerridwen had a point. If they were to work toward the long-held goal of their race, dominion over the Earth in the absence of an Astral home, it would not be fair to expect the Humans to aid them in their own extinction.

Trasa regarded her Queene with a placid expression. "Is this what you will work to achieve, Your Majesty? The destruction of my people?"

"There is no way to peacefully share the Earth with Humans," Cedric said, as respectfully as he could manage.

"There is no way to share it with those Humans who seek to destroy us," Cerridwen corrected him. Any hint of the loving, unsure mate, who had been so eager to please him in private, had vanished in the presence of her subjects. It was as it should be, he supposed, but he could not help the protest from his wounded pride. It had been different with Mabb; he had not cared for her, not as he loved Cerridwen, and so her casual dismissals of his opinions and words had not stung quite as much.

Cerridwen rose from her seat, bracing her palms on the table in front of her. "If we are enemies with the Humans, why do they remain here? Danae treated them as slaves, but what kept them here?"

"A desire to be among magical creatures," Amergin supplied. "Many of them do not care that they are little more than slaves, so long as they are enslaved to a magical creature. The Enforcers have, in their strict forbiddance of any magic, made it a much more tempting plum."

Cerridwen shook her head. "You are right, and wrong at the same time. It is not merely their desire to be near magic, but their desire to be away from the Humans who do not believe as they do. We have no quarrel with these Humans who walk among us, nor any other Human who worships the Old Gods. They lost the Astral Plane, as well, when the Veil rent. We are immortal—" her gaze flickered over Trasa, as if to say she were excluded, of course "—and so we do not truly have to fear death. Unless we are killed in accident, or by assassination, we go on. Humans become ill, they reach the ends of their normal lives and then they die. Where do they go then? To nothingness?

"I cannot condemn an entire species to that grim fate. So, I will no longer strive for a world free from Humans. We will protect ourselves, and the Humans who are loyal to us. We will kill the Enforcers, if we must. But I will not become involved in an all-out war against the Humans." She took a breath. "Not when Human blood also runs in my veins."

"My Queene!" Trasa exclaimed, her eyes filling with tears that seemed to surprise her as they surprised everyone else.

"This is true?" Amergin looked from Cerridwen to Cedric, and Cedric nodded in Cerridwen's direction. It was for her to confirm it.

"My mother was half-Human. My father was a mortal, but not Human, not fully." She stumbled over the words, confusion on her features. "He was a Darkling. But I do not know…"

"It is not important," Cedric said quickly. "As far as your parentage, you must remember that Garret, brother of Mabb, was your mother's mate, Your Majesty."

She winced. "I should not have said that."

"Your secret will remain safe with us," Amergin assured her, and Trasa hurried to agree.

"There will be those who disagree with your choice to break from the old ways," Cedric cautioned. "How will Your Majesty confront those who dissent?"

"I will tolerate no dissent," she said firmly. "If they disagree, then they mean to take up arms against members of this Court, Human or Fae, and they will be branded traitors."

"And banished?" Cedric pushed, cautious not to move her to anger. He did not wish to insult her, but to enlighten her to the challenges she would face. He was not sure if he supported her idea, himself. The Earth had been a paradise before the Humans had grown to such a number to cover it all, sending the Fae into hiding and, finally, to the Astral permanently. He would gladly return to the Astral, if that were an option, and he was not fond of the idea of an immortal life in the company of constantly dying mortals.

Cerridwen nodded. "I have learned when to fight, and when to leave well enough alone. I will not ask them to follow me on pain of death."

"Then they can band together and rise up against you," he warned. "I fear Your Majesty has not thought this through."

"As always, I appreciate your guidance, but in this matter I will stand firm." A smile quirked the corners of her mouth. "Of course, you could always choose to leave, with the banished, if the idea is so distasteful."

She was a confident ruler. That was one problem that Cedric had never thought he would encounter with her.

"If Your Majesty does plan to keep the Humans free, what then?" Amergin asked. "The Humans believe that, one day, the Astral will return, and they will be allowed a place there for following the Old Gods. Will you promise them this?"

"I cannot, and I will not promise them something that I cannot be certain of giving them." She paused. "I do not know much about the differences between the Old Gods, and the One God, and I do not know of the Astral. I was born here on Earth. Beneath it, actually."

"The circumstances of your birth are no excuse for continued ignorance," the wizard stated. From anyone else it might have been insulting. "The Astral was a world that ran parallel to this one. It occupied the same space, though it was not constrained by the space of Earth. At certain times of the year, the in-between times, the two realms overlapped and became one. Everyone kept to their own business, though, and did not meddle. Humans guarded the secrets of magic fiercely. It was only after they began to see magic as an endeavor of commerce that the Veil was damaged beyond repair."

"It was not just magic users," Trasa interrupted. "The followers of the One God were not free from blame. They abandoned their leaders, the men who could talk to God, and sought to communicate directly with a being who, by the admittance of its own followers, had only spoken directly to a handful of righteous men. They prayed and demanded ridiculous favors from the One God regardless of their ability to provide for themselves. That was frivolous magic, in itself."

Cerridwen rubbed her forehead with her hand,

squeezing her eyes shut. "And these…breaks in protocol created this trouble we find ourselves in today?"

"I am afraid so, Your Majesty." Cedric could not help his amusement at her reaction, the weary condemnation of Human foolishness. "The Veil had become so thin, and so many pulled magic from the other side into this world, that it tore away and spilled everything out."

"No one has been able to enter the Astral since," Amergin told her. "It is simply gone."

"It was not just the fault of the Humans," Trasa spoke up, her anger plain on her features, which could conceal nothing. "Your kind have flitted between worlds for centuries." She turned to Cerridwen. "It was not only Humans desiring Faeries. Some Fae were content to dally with Humans, as well."

"I will think over all of this. But my decision stands. I will announce it to my subjects tomorrow. Put up notice to gather in the clearing at the noon hour."

"It will be done, Your Majesty," Trasa said with a bow of her head.

"Good. Now, leave me. I need time to think." They all stood, but she put her hand out to touch Cedric's arm. "You, stay a moment," she said. "There is something I must ask you."

He sat back down, studied her while the other two made their bows and exited. Dark circles ringed her eyes, as though she had not slept. That, he knew, was not the case, as he had watched over her through the long night. But she had not slept well, tossing fitfully and occasionally whimpering, as though some evil dream plagued her. "What is the matter, Your Majesty?"

"We are in private now," she reminded him.

"Cerridwen," he began again, taking her hands in his. "What troubles you?"

She pulled her hands back and folded them in her lap. "You will think me strange, I am sure, for saying this. But...I can no longer hide the truth about my father."

Breath filled his lungs before he could still its harsh sound, and he leaned back, hands braced on the tabletop. "Your claim to the throne—"

"Runs through my mother," she interrupted. "My 'official' father, Garret, was never King. He was the Queene's mate. My mother was Queene because she was his mate. The circumstances of my birth would not change that."

"It might give your subjects cause to protest," he warned.

"They followed a field commander with no blood claim to the throne, and called her Queene. I doubt Court protocol will matter all that much in the wake of her death." She paused. "Besides, my father was not Human. He had wings, but he was a mortal. He could not have been Human. What was he?"

"An Angel. A Death Angel, he would say." He struggled for a way to explain the creatures, even though he did not really understand them himself. "They are messengers of the One God of the Humans. I think. I am not sure. But they belong to him, and follow his will. Malachi told me of his past, but honestly, I did not want to hear. It was easier for me if I thought him like us."

"It is easy for me, too," she admitted. "I cannot imagine that I am…less Fae than mortal. What does that mean?"

"If you have but one drop of Fae blood, you are Fae." He did not know where the ferocity in his tone came from, or why it was so important to make her understand. Perhaps because he did not want to think of her as less than completely Fae. It seemed absurd, after his willingness to abandon the Lightworld and his entire race for Dika.

But then, looking back, that willingness now seemed absurd. He had not lusted after Dika, he realized, but for a return to the Upworld through the Gypsy.

He took Cerridwen's hands again, and this time she did not resist him. "Do what you must," he said, though he could not help his hope that she would change her mind. "You rule these Faeries now, and the Humans. Your parentage does not matter."

She nodded, but did not meet his eyes. "You may go now."

He did as she asked, but looked back before he ducked out of the flap, into the room beyond. She sat motionless, her gaze trained on the tabletop in front of her, but she did not truly see it, he could tell from the faraway look in her eyes.

She was a confident ruler, and that he was proud of.

She was not as secure in herself, and that tore at his heart.

Eighteen

~~~~~~∽◦◦◦∽~~~~~~

Cerridwen did not emerge from the dining room as the noon meal passed, and did not accept food at supper. Only when Cedric had entered and informed her of the hour had she gone to her bed, and she had refused the bread and wine he had urged her to take. The thought of what lay ahead of her had consumed her, and she had not wished to cloud her mind with Earthly things.

No, she had planned it, in the time she sat, staring at the rough grain of the table but seeing nothing in particular. She wanted to face her subjects made of nothing but herself, her Fae and mortal blood, her scarred body and her belief that what she would tell them was right.

It was a heady thing, to carry responsibility for so many lives.

It would have been too easy to dismiss Humans as lesser beings. No matter the time she had spent among them on the Strip and in the Darkworld, she had been told over and over in her youth that Humans were not the same as Fae, not as important or developed. But Cerridwen had never seen Humans as petty and cruel as Faeries, and she could no longer believe that all she had been told by Governess was true.

The night had brought her no dream visits, no guidance, and she had been disappointed at that. Perhaps it was too much to ask, to be guided in everything she did. She would have to assume some responsibility for her own choices.

As the noon hour approached, the activity outside the thin walls increased. Voices buzzed, curious Humans wandered around the perimeter of the tent. Inside, all was quiet, though no less frenetic.

Cedric paced their bedroom, stopping now and again to face her, as she sat, still and composed, on the edge of the bed. He'd look as though he would speak, but then would shake his head and go back to pacing.

He was nervous because he did not agree wholly with what she would say today, that was plain, but also because he wished her to do well in her first public address. His nerves made her nervous. She wished he would stop.

"Have you practiced what you will say?" he finally asked, shrugging his shoulders. "If you have, I have not heard it."

She made an "Mmm" of consideration. "That is because I have not."

"Your mother practiced all of her speeches," he said. "Well, not her first."

"Did that go well?" She raised an eyebrow.

He hesitated. "Yes. It did."

"Then stop worrying."

At the appointed time, she exited the tent. The crowd in the clearing broke into a chorus of cheers, and that was enough to wipe away any lingering doubts she might have had. She looked down at her gown, a bloodred one that a Human seamstress had just put the finishing touches on. It was not like Danae's dresses, or those from medieval tapestries. The slender cut of the bodice fell to full, graceful skirts, but there were no sleeves, leaving her scars exposed for all to see. Better they see them, Trasa had advised, than let them think she was ashamed of them. The dress tied at the neck, and her hair, still tangled into ropes that would never be unwound, was bunched at her nape and wound with a long, black ribbon. Let them see her for what she was, she thought. Let them see that she could be a warrior, as Danae had, *and* a Queene, without compromising that.

She walked out to the edge of the steps and smiled at all who stood below, beamed up at those who watched from their treetop homes. Their voices grew louder, and for an instant she could believe that they truly loved her.

That was dangerous. She raised her hands to silence them, and as their enthusiasm evened out, she began to speak. "You see I am whole. Not the creature who stood before you two days ago."

The tone of the murmurs in the crowd became uncomfortable. They did not want to confront the fact that anything unsavory had happened, not when faced with this new beginning. She had not wanted it, either. "Forgive my bluntness, but it must be said. I am a stranger here. It would be easy for me to remain elusive, to not be honest with you, and let you form your opinions based on rumor and propaganda. It would be easy, for now. I would never be able to live up to the expectations you might form of me. Or, perhaps I would, and that would be a great tragedy."

She took a deep breath, braced herself for the first irrevocable disclosure she would make. "I cannot stand before you, then, and say that I was not deeply and profoundly affected by the attack against my person, made by my mate, under the direction of your former leader. I hold none of you accountable. But if any of you feel I was too…soft in punishing her, I warn you that you will not like me as a Queene. I do not wish to reign with a hand of death, or fear. I value life. All life, mortal and immortal. Immortal creatures, I find, are too careless with both. I care for mortal life, because mortal blood flows in my veins, as well as Faery. My mother, Queene Ayla, protected me from the Underground Court by circulating a lie, a lie I told when I came to this camp, myself. That my father was Garret, Royal Heir and brother to Queene Mabb. He was not. While my mother was mated to Garret, she conceived me with a mortal, a former messenger of the One God. And she, herself, was half-Human. She was still Queene; do not think I will brook, for one instant, insults to the validity of my position. But I will not stand before you and claim to be Fae, not fully.

"I tell you this because I do not wish to begin our friendship in dishonesty. I say friendship, because I do not see myself capable of being your ruler in any other way. I can and will certainly rule, and do so with your best interests at heart. But I cannot rule over a group bent by threats. Except in this one thing I will ask now. The Humans who live in this camp have done so blind to the true goal of the Fae on Earth. For centuries, since the split in the Veil, we have washed our hands of the Astral, certain that if we could not access it, it must no longer exist. We set our sights on claiming the Earth for our own, when it is not ours to claim. The Humans are not inferior, nor are they invaders. We share their home, and yet we treat them as slaves. From this day forward, there will be change."

A few angry voices rose, but she ignored them. "The Humans in our camp will no longer be our servants. They may stay. We have no quarrel with them. But every Fae here will roll up their sleeves and help with the daily work of the camp. You will get your own water, your own food, tend your own gardens and stoke your own fires. If you do not, you will compensate those Humans who do it for you. Not with promises of magic or the privilege of being near you. You will compensate them with a fair trade of services or material goods. You will help the Humans have their own lives, in this way."

Outrage. It was what she expected. She did not look back to Cedric for reassurance. He did not agree with her, in the first place, and she did not need that agreement to do what was right. Still, knowing that he stood behind her was comforting.

"We are no longer at war with the Humans," she declared, to even more cries of anger. "Enforcers have been spotted in these woods. We will deal with them as our enemies, certainly, for they wish us harm. But any Human who leaves us in peace, who does not seek to harm us, will not be deemed a threat to us. This includes the...*demented* goal of taking the Earth for ourselves. Do we not have a life here that is sustainable *without* exterminating an entire race?"

Now, a voice of agreement shouted from the crowd, and it emboldened her.

"Just because the Astral is not open to us, does not mean that it is not there. It means that we have not found the way in again. That is not the fault of the Humans, and we will no longer make war against them.

"I know that some of you are thinking me mad. But I say that you are mad, if you believe you are fighting, and winning, this Earth. If you wish to stay in this forest, away from all the Humans who defeated you before, then stay here, but do not pretend it is a great victory. Instead, turn your attention toward re-gaining *our* home. Saving those Fae who are still scattered to the winds, beneath other cities, living the horrible existence that I have risen up from.

"You may do this, by staying here, and abiding by these laws that I have set before you today. Or you may leave. I care not what you do once you are beyond the borders of these woods. But if you stay, and you seek to undermine me, you will be charged with treason, and banished as I banished Danae."

"Our choice, then, is banishment, or banishment?" a male Faery called from the front of the crowd. Encouragement rose from those near him, and Cerridwen let them have their moment of victory.

"Your choices are to stay, and be a part of this wondrous new life, in which Human and Faery work together, and to be present when we find our way back to the other side of the Veil, or to leave here, and settle for this Earth for the rest of your days. The choice is yours. I hope you do not make it lightly."

She turned and did not meet Cedric's eyes as she strode back into the tent. Behind her, the angry voices dwarfed the few claps and cheers her speech received.

She went into the sitting room and found her robe, also new, from the seamstress, lying over a chair. She fumbled with the ties of the dress, then heard Cedric's footsteps, felt his warm hands brush her skin as he untied the knot for her.

"You spoke well," he said, pushing the strips of fabric over her shoulders. As she slipped the gown off, he seated himself cross-legged on the floor. "How many do you think will leave?"

"From the sound outside?" she asked with a dismayed laugh. She let the gown whisper into a pool of red at her feet and took up the white linen robe, wrapping it around herself like armor. "All of them."

"It will not be that bad," Cedric told her, not encouraging but stating what he truly felt. If he had lied to her to keep her calm, she would have been able to tell it in an instant. He continued, "Half, I would say, of the Faeries. Less than a quarter of the Humans."

"The Humans? Why would they leave at all?" She rustled her wings to ease the fabric down that had become hung up on them.

"I think there will be some less scrupulous Faeries who will entice the Humans to remain in their bondage and leave with them." He considered a moment. "And I think there are some Humans in this camp who are Elf-struck."

"Ugh, I hate that term," she said with a shudder. "I should outlaw it."

Cedric laughed and motioned to her to sit with him. She knelt beside him and leaned into his arms. "Do you really believe I did well?"

"You are your mother's daughter, that is no doubt," he whispered against her ear.

It had taken twenty years, innumerable tragedies and a journey by sea to make her see it for the compliment that it was.

In the days that passed, Cedric's estimate had proven so accurate that even he was surprised at it. Slightly more than half of the Fae had left, none without first airing their grievances loudly in the central clearing, so that all could hear. Cerridwen had let this go on for three nights before asking that the practice cease.

"I hate silencing them," she had grumbled when Amergin suggested it. But she had seen the point behind it, easily enough. If they were allowed to carry on for as long as they wished, eventually they might win over those who had resolved to stay of their own accord.

It was the Humans who left that made Cerridwen's heart ache. They viewed her with more hatred than did the Fae, because they were being uprooted from the only home they had known, the only life they wanted. They resented her for their freedom, and she could not fathom why.

One fear that had plagued her, silly though it was, was that the Humans would continue to shoulder the chores of the camp, to the point that there was nothing for their Fae counterparts to do. Sure enough, as the Humans left, the operations of the colony stuttered and nearly ground to a halt, until Faeries began to shoulder more of the load.

Cerridwen, included. Though Cedric had balked at the idea of a Queene doing menial chores, Cerridwen had begun spending her days tending to the animals in the livestock yards. She took particular pleasure in tending her white bull, which received more attention and comforts than the rest of the animals.

She had managed, despite his grumbling, to enlist Cedric's help in the gardens, working alongside the other Fae to create false sunlight and encourage the plants to grow.

In the evening, they took their supper with Trasa and Amergin, and occasionally they invited a Human laborer to eat with them. All of their meals were cooked by the Humans who had served them before, but now the meat and vegetables were provided by the Queene and her household, rather than harvested by the Humans who also worked to cook them. The portions made were large enough to share with those same Human servants, and Cerridwen had granted them the huge, round room at the center of the tent for sleeping quarters, as well. Cedric had vowed never to set foot in that room again, and Cerridwen had not wished to see it, either, knowing that he had been tortured there for so long.

The nights were what Cerridwen looked forward to most of all. She cherished the little time she had alone with Cedric. Even though their bones were weary and their bodies ached by the time they retired to bed, they did not forsake intimate relations in favor of sleep. It was very nice, Cerridwen had learned, to let go of that dizzying passion, to go slower, to discover what pleased him and, in turn, show him what pleased her. More exciting than physical pleasure, though, was the time spent after, lying in his arms. He told her stories of his past, of what life was like on the Astral Plane, of the fun Faeries had in the days when they did not worry about scratching out an existence, when all was provided for. He told her things about her mother, and things about her father, which she treasured above all.

If they were not too tired, they would walk in the forest after dinner, and he would show her some new trick of the other sight, a new magic that, simple though it might be, felt as though it bound her closer to her Fae heritage. Occasionally, he taught her something from his days as an Assassin, and she fancied herself a promising fighter, once she learned to best him in combat.

She suspected he let her win, a few times.

The days passed, and the camp returned to, if not normal, a more compact version of normal, that everyone had begun to grow accustomed to. Weeks went by, and the weather grew warmer. They celebrated Midsummer with a feast and dancing, and Cerridwen delighted when the Humans performed a masque in her honor, portraying her as the Goddess, belly ripe with child. That was, until she saw the light in Cedric's eyes, the longing for what he had lost, and what he clearly hoped to have again.

But those tensions aside, life as Queene was more than she could ever have hoped for. Even the daily activities of planning rations and monitoring the situation with the Enforcers, which could be mind-numbingly boring, seemed far easier than she had expected.

It was at such a meeting that Cedric brought up her most hated subject of all.

"I think we need a stronger military presence in the camp," he warned, sounding as tired of repeating himself as she was of hearing him.

Amergin tapped his fingers on the tabletop, and Trasa groaned audibly.

"I do not wish to discuss this again," Cerridwen said in a light voice, reaching for the parchment that reported the latest yield of summer berries.

"Whether you wish to discuss it or not, I would not be doing my duty by this colony if I were to let such an obvious hole in our defenses go un…." He balled that hand that lay flat on the table into a fist, a telltale sign of his frustration. He loathed misspeaking, or speaking badly.

She hid a smile behind her hand as she tapped her lips as if in thought. "The Assassins have increased their number, have they not? And the training is coming along well? Let them handle things. If the Enforcers were to intrude into the forest—"

"Does Your Majesty believe that our Assassins outnumber the Enforcers? That is, I beg your pardon for my frankness, laughable."

"I do not see how it would be to our benefit to pull laborers away from the livestock, and the gardens, and the woodcutting and weapons-making in order to form a militia." She shook her head. "I am sorry, but I do not wish for us to be a war-minded people. You were in the Underground, as I was. You were in the battle against the Elves and Waterhorses, as I was—"

"Yes! You were in one battle!" he shouted, standing. "One single battle, and you have discounted any notion of protection because of it."

"I did not see the great protection that battle resulted in! Rather, I remember you running with me, through the woods, away from our home." Her voice wavered slightly. She was not being fair to him. The war against the Elves was her fault. But she would not admit that now.

"Your Majesty, I ask only for the means necessary to protect our lives here. I have come to care about this place. It is my home, as the Underground once was, the Astral before that. There are families here. Would you have me leave these families at risk?" As he spoke the words, his meaning was clear. He wanted the colony safe, for their family. Her heart lurched, but he continued. "Let me take those who have a skill in and an inclination toward fighting. That is all I ask. They will train, in addition to the duties they already perform, and no resources will be lost."

She waved her hand, beaten into submission by his words and her lack of desire to argue the point any further. "Fine. Do what you must."

"I will. I will go now, and spread the word that I am looking for skilled warriors." He stood and gave her a springy bow, as though he were a fresh, new thing, not ancient as he was.

Trasa watched him go, then leaned forward and hissed, "You have not told him yet?"

"Berries," she said, shuffling the sheets of parchment with a pointed glare. "And what we are to do to preserve them."

"Wine," Amergin said at once, then, with less enthusiasm, "Or, jam."

Trasa sat back and listened to the discussion, but Cerridwen could not meet her piercing gaze.

The trouble was, Cerridwen reflected a few weeks later, having escaped to the gardens to do the hard work of pulling up carrots, that she did not see a family in her future.

She frowned as she tugged on a particularly stubborn root. No, that was not it at all. She saw a family, Cedric and herself, and that was all the family she was interested in having.

There was so much more to life than simply bearing children. At least, she thought there must be. With her twenty-first birthday months away, she was not sure yet of what exactly there was to life. Cedric was impatient, because he had made the choice to become a father long ago. So long ago that his children were grown, and spread to the corners of the world. But they were immortal, and there would be plenty of time. Now seemed a poor moment in the history of their species to start adding to it.

Trasa believed it was unfair to believe such, and Cerridwen found no reason to argue that it was not, to feel this way and keep it from Cedric. She simply did not wish to cause him pain. Not after all the heartbreak they had already endured, certainly not after they had settled into their comfortable routine. Perhaps she would someday wish for a family. But that day would not be in a year, perhaps not in ten, or fifteen.

A noise in the trees caught her attention. The flight lines, long ropes that indicated clear paths through the trees—she would not make the others learn from her airborne mistake—shuddered, and the sound of foliage rustling grew louder and louder. The Humans working near her did not notice it. Humans, she had come to learn, did not observe things as quickly as the Fae did. The Faeries tending the rows of cabbage noticed, and they looked skyward.

The Assassins flew into the clearing and dropped

down, landing in a ring around her, their weapons drawn. *Gods, they have come to murder me,* she thought, remembering how her mother had feared a coup in the years of her reign. But one of them, the Pixie, shouted, "Secure the Queene," and the group began rushing her toward the path that would lead to her Palace.

Cedric had been working in a neighboring garden, too far away to have seen what took place. He ran toward them now, discarding his sleeveless tunic and reaching for the dagger in his belt as he raced toward the Assassins.

"No, no!" she shouted, pushing her way past them, to put herself between her rampaging mate and her Assassins. "They have not come to harm me."

With a sheepish look, he sheathed his weapon. "I apologize, brothers," he said. The tight set of his jaw pushed his veins against the tattooed skin of his Guild Mark.

"Enforcers. They have camped out on the rise behind the forest," Fionnait said, breathless from her flight.

"You have left the woods?" Cerridwen looked to Cedric for confirmation. "When did this happen?"

"Scouts, from the militia," he clarified, and, as if summoned, a Human ran into the clearing, his large, dark eyes casting everywhere until he spotted them.

"Charles? The piper?" Cerridwen asked, wrinkling her nose. "Really, Cedric, how can musicians be a help to us?"

As he drew nearer, Charles slowed. "They spotted me," he gasped. In the V-ed neck of his tunic, his skin dripped with sweat. "I tried to lose them, but they know we're here. The spells are not holding. If I did not know better, I would say they're using magic to counter our own."

"They will advance," Fionnait warned. "Your Majesty, we must go."

"Go where?" She laughed, because it was better than bursting into tears. "We cannot outrun them. Not with the Humans and their children."

"We leave them behind," Prickle spat. "You need to worry about our skins, now."

"Enough!" Cedric shouted, and his voice disturbed the birds who slept in the trees. They flew upward with a tremendous chatter, and he cursed. Then, he took her hands and held them tightly in his own. "I did not wish to tell you of this, until there was an emergency. We all thought it would be best, not to tell you."

"Oh, you know how I dearly love secrets," she hissed, snatching her hands back. "Tell me what is going on!"

"Tunnels, Your Majesty," Fionnait said, her voice flat, emotionless. "Amergin told us about them."

"Tunnels?" Cerridwen looked to Cedric, understanding coming to her the moment she saw his downcast face. "No. No. Absolutely not."

She marched away from them, pulled the woven satchel she wore over her head, spilling the carrots she had harvested to the ground.

"Cerridwen, please, listen to reason!" Cedric called after her. He ran to catch up with her furious pace, but she would not slow for him.

"If reason means fleeing underground, letting them force us underground, then—by the Gods—I will not listen to reason!"

The rest of the Assassins scurried after them, as though attack would spring from the trees. She turned, addressed Charles directly. "How many did you see?"

"Enforcers? But a handful," Charles said. "Perhaps twenty-five. But they are armed with tanks and guns."

"What is a tank?" she snapped, secretly glad to have a Human there to explain such things.

"A machine that rolls, and shoots enormous projectiles. It can cover the ground quickly, and uneven ground poses no challenge. There are three, and their guns—"

"I know what guns are." She stomped up the path a few more paces, then faced them again. "I do not fear their guns, or their tanks. Not as much as I fear going under the ground again. When we were forced under by the Humans, it took a hundred years to become barely civilized. I will not allow such a thing to happen to us again."

"Faeries have come with them," Fionnait warned. "The same Faeries that left here. And Danae leads them."

Cerridwen turned to Cedric, saw the conflict in his eyes. He did not wish to go underground again, either. And he did not wish to lose to Danae.

"Colm," she ordered, "fly ahead of us. Tell Trasa to gather her Sisters, and prepare my armor. We will go to war."

Nineteen

The crows surrounded her, chanting, waving their burning incense, but Cerridwen had already connected with their Goddess, already felt her presence.

It had happened when Trasa had helped her fit her new leather armor over her head and secure the buckles at her sides. That bulkiness, the feeling of security that it brought with it, had sparked something within her that she had not felt in a very long while, since the moment she had ridden the white bull into the clearing and denounced Danae. It was a combination of fury and confidence, and that, she knew, was fueled by the Morrigan herself.

"Bring the mirror," she ordered in a flat, emotionless voice. The calm she comported herself with on the outside was a barrier, holding back the war spirit in her that would spill out onto the battlefield.

The reflection in the looking glass startled her. She had dressed in a long white tunic and loose linen pants, over which her leather carapace and bracers had been buckled. The Sisters had shaved her hair—it would not have fit under her helmet—and the short, spiked stubs rendered her almost masculine in appearance. She worried for a moment that Cedric might not like it, then scolded herself. There were more important things now than her vanity.

He stepped through the flap into the bedroom, looked her up and down. He had already donned his armor, and his shining hair was plaited into a long braid down his back. His wings, far more fragile than hers, were strapped down beneath his tunic. "You are a warrior," he said, and though he tried to sound proud, he looked terrified.

"I have the Morrigan to guide me," she said, ducking her head so that Trasa could slip the copper shield pendant over her head.

"Thank you," Cerridwen addressed the rest of the Sisters. "I will not forget your kindness when we return victorious."

"You speak as though we will remain behind, like weak women," Trasa scoffed. She opened her robe and shrugged it from her shoulders, revealing a body encased head to toe in black leather, buffed to a shine and inset with gleaming metal plates over the shoulders, breast, abdomen and legs. "The highest form of worship to Our Lady is combat." She pulled a sword from her back and touched the flat of the blade to her forehead before bowing. As Cerridwen watched in amazement, the rest of the Sisters followed suit, revealing themselves to be similarly garbed and armed.

"You have our blades, if you will accept our help," Trasa said, head still bowed.

"Of…of course I will have them," Cerridwen stammered. Then, she laughed. "What a secret to keep from me!"

"We are a secretive order, Your Majesty. We do not wish to repeat the follies of the past." She gave Cedric a hard look. She had not forgotten that he had laid the blame for their current state solely on the Humans.

He gave them a respectful bow, now. "I am humbled by the presence of so many fierce warriors."

"Could you excuse us a moment?" Cerridwen asked the Sisters, and they filed out, leaving their robes behind like shed skins.

When Cerridwen finally stood alone with Cedric, she could think of nothing to say. Finally, she said, "You were right. We needed a militia."

He nodded tersely. "I know we did." He pointed to her head. "All of your hair is gone."

"Yes. They cut it, so I could wear a helmet." She touched the couple remaining strands self-consciously. "It looks ugly now."

"No, it…" He faltered. "It will grow back."

They stared at each other for a long moment, and then, as if a line holding them apart had snapped suddenly, they rushed to each other. The armor held them apart, frustratingly so, when all she wished was to feel his arms around her and hear the rumble of his voice in his chest as he spoke.

"I do not want you to go," he said between frantic kisses, holding her face between his hands.

She pressed her cheek against his, wound her arms round his neck as best as she could reach. "I cannot send my subjects to die while I hide here. I could not live with myself."

"And I will not live if you are killed." He held her back from him. "You remember the battle against the Elves? This will be worse! More death, more destruction! Why not flee to the caverns and be done with it?"

"Because I cannot." She looked into his eyes and saw the cowardly hope in him die, harden to something that matched the drive in her. "And you cannot, either."

"I would, if it meant…" But he stopped himself, unable to finish those words. "Cerridwen, if something happens today, I want—"

"No." She shook her head. "I do not wish to exchange these sentiments. I know what you feel for me, as you know what I feel for you. That would not change at the moment of death, so I do not wish to dwell on it."

He crushed her to him again, buried his face against the top of her head. "Do not try to be heroic. Lead your army, but then, let them lead. You do not have the training for battle, and…" He stammered the last part, as though afraid to speak it. "I—I do not trust this Goddess to deliver you safely."

She stepped back, her chest constricting like a vise. Until he voiced his doubts, she had not realized how much faith she had put into the Morrigan. Though she did not wish to part now in anger, his lack of faith disappointed her.

If he noticed the change in her, he did not reveal

it with his actions. He tugged on leather gloves that had been tucked into his belt, and inclined his head toward the outside wall. "We should go. It will be better to meet them on open ground, rather than fight them in the forest."

In the clearing, the militia had assembled. Behind them, the worried faces of the rest of the colony pierced Cerridwen with their eyes. They wanted her to say something, to tell them that all would be all right.

She could not. But she could give them this: "The Enforcers have come. Humans, like many of you, but different in that they do not believe this world large enough to share. They come to force us underground, to send us scurrying, like vermin, into holes and tunnels and caverns, forsaking our way of life for hardship.

"I say, let them come. Let them see that, though we may be peaceful, we are fierce. That Fae will not accept a lesser existence, that our Human friends will not be punished for choosing a life different from what the Enforcers will allow them.

"I ask all who are able to take up arms today and follow us, to stand up to our enemies, and to the traitors who once lived among you as kin, but who would now shed your blood. If we fail today, we lose much. But if we do not try, we will lose more."

Please, she prayed, *please let them follow me.* "Who is with me?"

Faeries, men and women came forward, and they were welcomed by the militia with victorious cries. Cedric leaned close to her ear and whispered, "They are not trained. They do not have weapons."

"They will improvise," she hissed back. "They are not simpletons."

He moved past her, down the steps, and took the reins of a huge, black horse. "Will you ride her, Your Majesty?" he offered, patting the animal's neck.

She shook her head. "No." A smile spread across her face, an overwhelming feeling of right flowed through her limbs. "No, I have something else in mind."

They heard the sounds of the Human battle machines before they exited the forest—the low, grinding growl of them as they gained speed and ground. When Cerridwen emerged from the trees, on the back of the white bull, she took her first glimpse of the Enforcers.

She wanted to run.

The tanks that Charles had spoken of, the source of the terrifying noise, were larger than anything she had ever seen. They lumbered over the hilly field like giant, metal roaches, one long, slender rod extending from them like a questing antenna, feeling its way over the battleground. Human vehicles like the ones she had seen previously came with them, but they halted at the top of the largest rise, and the Enforcers spilled out, their guns drawn. Behind them, the Traitorous Fae.

How primitive her own forces must look, she realized, scanning the line that stretched to either side of her. Ten were seated on horses: Cedric, Trasa and a handful of her crows, Fionnait and Colm. They looked straight ahead, their faces grim. Behind them, the soldiers who had walked to the battle, some armed with weapons, others with torches and farm implements. But fifty of them, altogether.

"All is not lost," Cedric said quietly next to her, and when she looked at his face, she saw he truly believed it. That gave her strength. "Do you wish for me to lead them, Your Majesty?"

No, she did not. She wished for him to turn back, to hide himself somewhere safe. But when she opened her mouth to say so, the words would not come out. At least, her voice knew better than to shame her in this moment, if her heart did not. "Yes. Gods be with you as you go."

He nodded, then, pulling the reins tight, he lifted his hand and shouted the charge.

The militia flowed onto the field, like water through a broken dam, and she watched them go. Those on horseback were the first to reach the line, behind them, the Fae that had chosen to fly. The Humans and Fae on foot came next, though a few hung back, knelt on the ground to ready their bows and arrows.

Beneath her the bull shifted restlessly. Cerridwen patted its neck absently, her eyes trained on the figure that rode at the head of it all, his sword raised high. One of the huge machines belched a smoking charge, the deafening report coinciding with an explosion of dirt and debris from the ground. The cloud of settling dirt obscured her view. When it cleared, she did not see Cedric.

The Enforcers used their weapons mercilessly,

cutting down the Fae who flew above them in explosions of blood and screams. But as they concentrated on the creatures above, the handmaidens of the Morrigan rode fearlessly into their ranks, slashing with their swords. Faeries on opposing sides struck out at one another in the sky, while the tanks fired more echoing shots, blasting clusters of bodies into the air. They went up whole, but seemed to come apart as they rained down. Cerridwen's stomach lurched.

She could still not see Cedric.

Her hands tightened on the bull's neck. It took an agitated step forward. She felt for the sword at her back. Cedric had taught her how to use it, in theory. She had never had a chance to test her prowess against someone who was not going easy, in fear of damaging them. She had no place in battle, would last no longer than a few seconds, at best.

But she could not see him.

A horse ran, screeching in panic, back toward the forest. She could not tell them apart enough to know if it was his. Battles in stories always seemed to go on for hours, but it appeared to Cerridwen that they were losing quickly. She must do something. To save Cedric. To see him dead. Either way, to have her answer. To die on the battlefield with her army, who she had led there, to their deaths. Still, she could not move, could not force herself into the nightmare of blood and fire that unfolded before her eyes.

The bull made the decision for her. It bellowed and broke into a run. She clung to it, eyes squeezed shut, then, not wishing to appear cowardly, not wishing to *be* cowardly, she opened her eyes and sat up as best as she could without being thrown from the animal's back.

Bodies littered the ground, seemingly more of them than had come to fight. Perhaps, she thought, growing sick at the thought, they were in more pieces than when they had arrived. She squinted through the smoke and dirt, desperate for any sign of Cedric.

She saw him, his pale hair stained with blood— his own, gauging from the huge gash that split his forehead. His sword crossed with another Faery's, but he turned his head, distracted by her sudden appearance on the field, and in that moment the Faery sank his blade into Cedric's side. He cursed and gripped the blade with gloved hands, pushing it from his body with enough force to send the Faery who wielded it flying back. With a shout of fury, Cedric charged and sliced his own blade down, and the Faery fell, cleanly halved, to the trampled grass.

Cedric ran toward her, calling her name. Cerridwen looked frantically around her for the danger he tried to warn her of. At the top of the rise, one of the tanks fired; the crack of it reached her ears just as the ground opened in front of her and the bull reared back.

She clung to the creature with her legs, arms windmilling for purchase in the air above her head. Chunks of rock and debris blasted her face, and she felt skin come away. The hot, wet taste of blood flooded her mouth, and she gagged. Then, she was falling, away from the animal. She hit the ground, disoriented, and saw only the contorted form of the bull's enormous back as it crushed down upon her.

* * *

Cerridwen opened her eyes to find herself standing in a field. Alone. Panic seized her. Something had happened, something she could not remember, though she tried. She opened her mouth to call for help, and realized that she did not know who she would call to.

The ghost of some strong emotion plagued her. She had been searching for something, she was sure of it. She had set out from somewhere, somehow, to find something. Every moment that she did not recall what that was, her heart thundered louder in her ears. She heard her name on the wind, a desperate cry, but no one had spoken.

"Cerridwen."

The voice that had uttered her name aloud was calm and familiar. She turned, tears in her eyes. "Mother?"

Her mother stood before her, her long, flame-red hair still, despite the wind. A long, white gown draped her slender limbs. She looked different, somehow younger, than she had appeared on Earth.

On Earth. That struck her as strange, but she did not know why.

She went to her mother and collapsed gratefully in her arms. It had been so long. Why had she stayed away?

The realization struck her as her mother stroked her hair and murmured comforting words. She looked up. "I am dead."

"Yes," her mother told her. "You have come home."

"My father..." She remembered those last moments, her mother leaning over his body, her eyes shrouded in tears. That was why she had looked so old in that last moment. Her grief.

Another hand fell on her back, large and warm and sure, and she looked up into Malachi's face. He was younger, for certain. No mortal lines of age marred his face, no scars from battle. The joy in his expression filled Cerridwen's own heart, almost to bursting, and tears flowed down her face. "You are here. How?"

"Do not worry about the how, or the why," another voice said, and she turned, never leaving the warm circle of her parents' embrace, to see the Morrigan, the triple Goddess, walking toward her, across the field. Instead of one person, they were three: a girl, a woman and a crone, their hands linked as they came toward her.

"You did well," the crone said, lifting her wobbling chin with pride. "Better than we could have hoped for."

"What did I do?" She fought to push her mind through the haze that clouded it.

"You brought your subjects to a new understanding. You learned what was worth fighting for, and taught them, in turn."

A flash of blood and fire swept across her vision, and she staggered, kept upright by her mother's strong arms.

"This will pass," she whispered into Cerridwen's ear, as another anguished cry floated over their heads. "It is disorienting, if you have never been here before."

"The Astral?" Cerridwen stared at the ground beneath her feet. "I knew it was somewhere. It could not have just…gone."

"It did not," the Goddess said from the young woman's mouth. "It was here. They just needed someone to lead them to it."

"To lead them to death?" Something seemed wrong with that. "But I did not mean to."

"Not to death. To hope. Those that will die will come home. Those that do not will know that they can return." The young girl aspect lifted her face to the sky as Cerridwen's name tore through the gray clouds.

She knew that voice. She knew it, but she could not… "I was not finished."

The girl gazed at her, unblinking. "You achieved your purpose. You are a great hero. They will never forget your name."

Cerridwen groaned, doubled in pain. It made no sense. If she was dead, how could she…

"You are dying," Malachi told her gently, lowering her to the ground. "You have not completely crossed over the divide. This will pass."

She did not want it to pass. There was something she wanted on the other side, something she had not finished. She sat up, clutched at his arm. "This cannot be. I have…something I was searching for."

Her mother and Malachi looked to each other with pained glances, as though there was something they wanted to say to her, but could not. She turned to the Morrigan. "There is something I was doing…. I have to go back."

"Why do you need to go back?" the crone asked, cocking her head to the side in a birdlike gesture. "You could stay here, be with your mother and father. This place is your heritage. Your home and your birthright. Why would you want to leave it?"

"Because..." She looked around the field. It was unscathed, as though no one had set foot on it before. As she watched it, though, it wavered, revealed smoke and bodies, fire and pain.

And she remembered.

She climbed to her feet, and stood before the Morrigan. But this time, it was the triplicate Goddess with three faces, dressed for war. She regarded her with cold respect, a glint of humor in her eyes.

"I must go back," Cerridwen argued. She turned to her mother and father. "I will return. I swear, I will return one day. But there are too many. They are in caves and underground cities like the ones we endured. This battle was only the beginning." She faced the Morrigan again. "You must let me go back."

"Your Earthly form was destroyed," the Goddess said. "You cannot return to it."

"I will return in the body of a gnat, if I must!" she shouted. "I will not let my kin die slowly underground! Not when they can return to their home!"

As if she did not care, as though the trials she had seen Cerridwen through meant nothing to her, the Morrigan shook her head. "Only a God can grant them access."

"Then send one with me!" Cerridwen looked helplessly around her for inspiration. "Make me a priestess of your order…grant me the power. Or let me tell one of them what to do. I cannot live here, happily, while the rest of them are…locked out. Tell me what to do!"

"Become a Goddess," the Morrigan said simply, spreading her hands.

"You mock me," Cerridwen whispered.

The Goddess narrowed her eyes. "Do you challenge me?"

There was no reply that she could give. She cast her eyes down.

"There is a reason you are here. There is a reason that you are one of my chosen," the Morrigan continued. "You will return to them. But you will not return as a Faery. You will not return as a mortal. You will go to them, as their Goddess."

Cerridwen stared. "Why?"

The Morrigan did not answer. Ayla and Malachi said nothing.

"Why?" she asked again, the frantic pain racking her once more. "I have done nothing to deserve this. I betrayed my mother. I caused the downfall of the Lightworld. My father is dead because of me, and I killed out of vengeance."

"You recognized what others did not," the Morrigan said evenly. "You did not despair because the Astral was missing, you sought to find it. You did not care only for your race, but for the mortals, as well. And you convinced others to believe."

"You fulfilled the prophecy," her mother said gently. "Years before your birth, I learned of it. I thought I might be the one, but I never truly understood it. Neither did Mabb, who thought the same. In you, the Lightworld and the Darkworld are mingled. You are Fae, and you are mortal."

"Your mother is Fae, your father a messenger of the One God," the Morrigan told her. "All that is left is the spark of the Divine, and you can unite them all. That is the gift I give to you now, Cerridwen. If you will accept it."

She nodded mutely, unsure if what happened was a dream, the last fevered fantasies of her dying brain.

"Then go now. And do not squander this gift." The Morrigan reached out and touched Cerridwen's forehead. "Go, now."

She fell back to the ground, back into the constricting confines of her crushed body. The light sucked away at the edges, and she struggled to open her eyes. Cedric knelt above her. He tried to heal her, to send his energy into her. The grief, the heartache, she had seen too much of it.

She closed her eyes, and breathed her last.

Twenty

─❦─

Her eyes opened, just before the end. Cedric pushed, with all his might, all the energy that he could muster. He was too badly injured, as was she.

He would live. She would not. He would be alone again.

Her eyes slid closed. "No!" he pleaded, shook her by the shoulders. "No, no!"

He barely gave a thought to the battle around him as he stared down at her lifeless body, other than to hope they killed him, and quickly, before the disbelief wore off and gave way to the pain he would feel. He could not bear to feel it over her.

The sounds of battle slowed, then ceased, as he stared at her closed eyes. He willed them to open, willed her to come back to life, though he knew it would be impossible. When he had lifted her in his arms, she had been heavy and liquid, a bag of blood and ruined bones.

He did not know why she had come onto the field. He did not care why. He only wished he could take the moment back, spot her before the blast had killed her.

A hand touched his shoulder, the touch light, radiating healing warmth. He brushed it aside. "I do not want healing. Go back to the battle."

The hand stayed. He looked up.

She stood over him. For a moment he did not recognize her. She glowed, a faint halo of light around her skin. Her white gown looked dim by comparison. Her copper hair fell in long waves that spilled over her shoulders. She had no wings, no antennae. For a horrified moment, he thought she might be Human.

He turned back to the body he held in his arms, watched it shrivel and flake away into autumn leaves and black feathers. When he looked back to her, he asked, "Is this real?"

"It is real." She looked out to the battle that had paused all around them. Faeries and Humans on both sides stared, openmouthed, unable to continue fighting against one another. "I have seen the Astral. And I can take you back there!"

A few Faeries tossed their weapons aside and began shambling toward her, as she continued, "It is not open only to the Fae. Any Human, any of you who wish to, may go. You do not need to pledge an oath to me. You do not need to die. You do not need to fight anymore! Come if you will. Go, if you must."

Humans, including a few Enforcers, drifted down the slope of the field.

She looked down at the bull, where it lay in the

black pool of its life blood. A wrinkle of pain formed between her eyes as she stared down at it. She knelt, so close Cedric could touch her, if he dared, but he did not, and touched her fingertips to the blood. A spark of light from her fingertips illuminated the surface, painted it a reflective gray. Water. She turned the blood to water, into a deep pool that reflected the sky. The bull shifted, and sank below the surface. The Fae that had come to the edge stepped back.

"This is the way," she told them. "Through here, you will find your Astral home. Once you have gone, you cannot return. Not yet. The Veil is not strong enough."

"What about our families?" one Human asked. Another shouted, "My brother is dead! What about him?"

"The dead have already gone before you. And this is not your only chance. If you choose to stay here, you may return to the Astral at another time." She looked up to the line of tanks and Human vehicles. "You may come, at any time. All it takes is a soul willing to believe that we can share this physical Earth with the planes that overlap it. If you can find it in your heart to abandon any wishes for vengeance and destruction, you can come to me, and I will lead you home."

It was Cerridwen, but it was not her. The voice she spoke with sounded like her, but the confidence, the faith...it was as if she were someone else entirely.

He had still lost her.

The Fae filed into the pool, one after another. They sank below the water with expressions of gratitude, weariness, joy. The Humans, though, touched the water with awe. They gripped Cerridwen's hands and thanked her.

The Human Enforcers who still lined the hill seemed paralyzed in the face of real magic. But it would not last. Hesitantly, Cedric touched the hem of her garment, and she looked down. "Is it safe to be here, with them?" he asked, motioning to the hilltop.

She raised her eyes to them, sadness overwhelming her expression. "No. It is not. But perhaps they will grant us the boon of more time. But I do not see…" She scanned the horizon, then called out, "Danae! Danae, show yourself."

The door of one of the Human vehicles opened, and the familiar form of the traitor stepped out.

Cedric reached for his sword, and Cerridwen put her hand on his shoulder. "Stay your hand. We will not fight her."

The clouds overhead had darkened with the dying of the day, and Danae's orange dress stood out against the hill like a fire against the green. She grew closer, eyes hard as she took in the sight of Cerridwen. When she was close enough to be heard, she called, "Shall I come nearer, so that you can kill me?"

"If I wanted you dead," Cerridwen said, her voice echoing through the field, "I could do it from here."

Danae stepped to the edge of the pool. "Is this a trick?"

"This is a gift," Cerridwen told her. "More than you deserve. Take it, and do not show your face to me, ever."

Danae hesitated. "Why do you not kill me?"

"Because I know when to fight," Cerridwen said.

Humbled, Danae lowered her head and dipped one foot into the water. She stopped, looked up with a gasp. "I only wanted what was best for them! I only wanted—"

"You wanted glory," Cerridwen said coolly. "That is why you stand in your place, and I in mine."

With a breath that sounded like a sob, Danae sank below the surface of the water. The rest of the Humans that stood around them, those who would not go in, lifted their weapons, prepared to continue the fight.

"No!" Cerridwen ordered. "If you wish to live, return to your homes. Show the others that we have no quarrel with them." Reluctantly, they tossed down their weapons, turned their backs to the Faeries, climbed into their vehicles and drove away.

Cedric watched them go, and watched the Fae turn, as well. "They gave up," he said, laughing in disbelief. "They gave up."

"They will return," Cerridwen said, her eyes, gray as the sky, following their retreat. "When the shock has worn off, when they realize what they have done, they will return."

He stood on numb legs. The feeling of her dead body still haunted his arms. He longed to reach for her. He did not. She gazed at him, the glow around her dimming.

"You do not have to stay. You can go. I saw my mother, and Malachi. They were whole, on the Astral Plane." She looked down. "It was beautiful there."

"It looks the same as this place." He shrugged. "Without the corpses and the death."

Cerridwen's eyes met his. It should have been a shock to him, to gaze into the eyes of a Goddess, but looking at her had always had that effect on him. "Go. The Astral is your true home. I cannot ask you to stay."

He took a shuddering breath. "You do not need to ask. I will never leave your side."

They embraced, and she fell as easily into his arms as she had when she had not been divine. It was the same Cerridwen, the same that he had loved. He kissed her, touched her, to remind himself that this was real.

"There is so much left to do," she said, stepping back. "So many more to save, Fae and Human."

"You will not do it alone." He laced his fingers with hers. "And you cannot do it all tonight. Come home," he urged her. "Come home with me."

She nodded and looked to the sky. "I am home," she said, turning to the forest and squeezing his hand. "Wherever I go, I am home."

* * * * *

ACKNOWLEDGMENTS

Factors that directly contributed to me being behind on this book: Facebook, Livejournal (especially sf_drama), and my infant daughter who is probably not mentioned in my bio because I never thought to update it.

Factor that directly contributed to me actually finishing the book on time: my husband, Mr. Jen, who quit his job so I could keep on writing, despite all of the teasing he got about being a housewife. I love you, Mr. Jen, and I'm sorry our friends were so cruel to you.

MIRA®

A brand-new trilogy from
the bestselling author of
the Blood Ties series

SAVE $1.00

JENNIFER ARMINTROUT

THE LIGHTWORLD/DARKWORLD TRILOGY

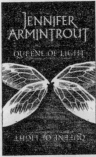

October 2009

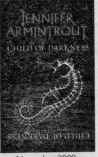

November 2009

VEIL OF SHADOWS

December 2009

SAVE $1.00 on the purchase price of one
book in Jennifer Armintrout's
Lightworld/Darkworld trilogy.

Offer valid from September 29, 2009, to December 31, 2009. Redeemable at participating
retail outlets. Limit one coupon per purchase. Valid in the U.S.A. and Canada only.

52608807

5 65373 00076 2 (8100)0 11626

REQUEST YOUR FREE BOOKS!

2 FREE NOVELS
FROM THE ROMANCE/SUSPENSE
COLLECTION PLUS 2 FREE GIFTS!

YES! Please send me 2 FREE novels from the Romance/Suspense Collection and my 2 FREE gifts (gifts are worth about $10). After receiving them, if I don't wish to receive any more books, I can return the shipping statement marked "cancel." If I don't cancel, I will receive 4 brand-new novels every month and be billed just $5.74 per book in the U.S. or $6.24 per book in Canada. That's a savings of at least 28% off the cover price. It's quite a bargain! Shipping and handling is just 50¢ per book.* I understand that accepting the 2 free books and gifts places me under no obligation to buy anything. I can always return a shipment and cancel at any time. Even if I never buy another book from the Reader Service, the two free books and gifts are mine to keep forever.

185 MDN EYNQ 385 MDN EYN2

Name	(PLEASE PRINT)

Address	Apt. #

City	State/Prov.	Zip/Postal Code

Signature (if under 18, a parent or guardian must sign)

Mail to **The Reader Service:**
IN U.S.A.: P.O. Box 1867, Buffalo, NY 14240-1867
IN CANADA: P.O. Box 609, Fort Erie, Ontario L2A 5X3

Not valid to current subscribers of the Romance Collection,
the Suspense Collection or the Romance/Suspense Collection.

Want to try two free books from another line?
Call 1-800-873-8635 or visit www.morefreebooks.com.

* Terms and prices subject to change without notice. Prices do not include applicable taxes. Sales tax applicable in N.Y. Canadian residents will be charged applicable provincial taxes and GST. Offer not valid in Quebec. This offer is limited to one order per household. All orders subject to approval. Credit or debit balances in a customer's account(s) may be offset by any other outstanding balance owed by or to the customer. Please allow 4 to 6 weeks for delivery. Offer available while quantities last.

Your Privacy: Harlequin is committed to protecting your privacy. Our Privacy Policy is available online at www.eHarlequin.com or upon request from the Reader Service. From time to time we make our lists of customers available to reputable third parties who may have a product or service of interest to you. If you would prefer we not share your name and address, please check here. ☐

BOB09